The Kings of Charleston

KAT H. CLAYTON

First Edition: June 2012

Cover Design: Streetlight Graphics

ISBN-13: 978-0-9857442-0-5

Dedication

For my husband, Michael Tyler, and Mom and Dad.

Acknowledgments

THERE ARE NOT ENOUGH PAGES in this book for me to truly express my gratitude to those who have helped me get to this point, but I will try to express my thanks the best that I can to the following:

First and foremost my parents, who always encouraged me to write and told me to go for my dreams. I must thank my high school English teacher, Ms. Chafin, who loved the short story that became *The Kings of Charleston*. She believed in the story and for that reason she gave me the motivation to bring it to life. My first reader and dear friend, Karey who helped me immensely when my story was still a (very) rough draft. To Alicia and my mother-in-law, Kaye, who were also both supportive first readers. To my father-in-law, Mike, who has always been in the cheering section for my writing debut. My editors, Marlene Adelstein and Anna Genoese, I don't know how I got so lucky to work with such great and insightful women. The people at Streetlight Graphics, who helped put it all together and for creating the absolutely amazing cover of my dreams. And thank you to my husband, Michael Tyler, who's brightened my life in so many ways.

Chapter 1

THE SMELL OF FRESH HAY filled my nose as I walked into the dark barn. I stood still in the darkness for a moment before turning on the overhead lights. I flipped the switch and the bright halogen lights illuminated the rows of stalls on either side of the barn's long hallway. A couple of horse heads appeared from behind their stall doors, curious as to who had just walked in. A smile formed across my face. It had been such a long day, and all I wanted to do was take a midnight ride on the back of my favorite thoroughbred.

I walked toward the back of the barn, several horses neighing as I passed by. "Hey, guys," I said, stopping to pat one of the horse's foreheads. "How's it going, Little Ghost?" I whispered, as I put my face against the white colt's cheek.

As I came to another stall, I placed my hand on the wreath of red roses that was slung across the stall door. The roses were still fresh and soft under my touch. "How does it feel to be a celebrity, Casper?" It always felt weird to say his name since it was my name, too.

Casper the Friendly Ghost was just the latest Kentucky Derby winner for my parents' prestigious farm, Ghost Hill Farms, and who better, I guess they figured, to name their only daughter after than a line of horses? Casper blew air out of his nostrils and bobbed his graceful head.

"So you liked all the attention, huh? I know you liked the winner's circle more than I did." I put my hand on his forehead and rubbed his dark coat.

It was tradition for me to appear with my dad in the winner's circle. I felt awkward in front of the cameras and hated seeing my photo appear in the newspapers and on the news channels. Not to mention, I couldn't see straight for at least a couple hours afterward.

I gave Casper a final pat and walked to the farthest stall, where Wendy waited patiently for me. Her big brown eyes were trained on me. Wendy was my favorite. When she looked at me, it was as if she understood me better than any person could. After a long day at school or a fight with my mother, I would run to the barn as fast as I could and curl up in Wendy's stall. Wendy would almost always lie down near me and I would stroke her beautiful chestnut coat. And when the day had been beyond unbearable, Wendy and I would hit the trails.

"Ready for a run?" I asked her, kissing her black muzzle.

The wind whipped through my loose hair as I guided Wendy over the narrow path near the farm's border fence. The moonlight was bright, casting a shadow of us barreling through the dark green grass. The air was cold and my ears and nose were numb, but I didn't care. My heart was racing and all I could feel was freedom. I buried my face into her long brown mane and pushed her as fast as she would go. Everything disappeared and all I could hear was the pounding of her hooves and my own fast beating heart.

After several minutes of going full speed, I slowed Wendy to a trot, gave her thick neck a pat, and turned her toward the barn. Once we were back, I pulled her saddle off and gave her a quick brushing before putting her in her stall. I returned the saddle to its place in the center room of the barn, switched off the lights, and closed the heavy doors.

I sat down on the damp grass, leaning against the barn wall, and stared at the back of my parents' massive house, which was just far away enough for me to not be seen. The giant patio and pool area were lit up with lanterns brought in especially for their victory party. The clinking of champagne glasses and muffled laughter infiltrated the night air. I hated the parties and my parents' snobby friends, with their Botoxed lips and Cartier diamonds. I had snuck away to the barn as soon as possible, which hadn't taken too long, since my mother was too busy impressing the reporter from *The Lexington Herald* to notice me walk out the back door.

I loved the horses, but the lifestyle was something I could do without. I couldn't care less about trendy Louis Vuitton purses or Louboutin heels. If it weren't for my mother's insistence, I wouldn't own a dress or a stupid pantsuit. What seventeen-year-old wears a pantsuit anyway? I preferred to live in worn jeans and a T-shirt. The dressiest I cared to be was my riding gear for a show jumping competition.

I looked down at the grass and plucked a couple of blades, twisting them between my fingers. It had been almost a year since my accident at the Adequan Select World Championship. I was lucky to walk away with only a broken arm, but I didn't want to think about that now. I shook my head, trying to shake the thought out of my head, and looked back at the house.

I had to find a way to sneak back in and up to my bedroom without Mother seeing me. I had never had a curfew, so I couldn't be in trouble for being out so late, but I could definitely get grounded for walking into the party in dirty jeans and a sweaty T-shirt.

A couple of camera flashes went off at the far

end of the patio. I was sure my mother was posing for pictures to be featured in the paper tomorrow. That meant she was distracted. I got up and walked slowly down the sloping hill, toward several large oak trees near the white split-rail fence that separated the pool from the rest of the farmland. After pausing to look again, I sprinted to the side door and opened it as fast as I could.

I could instantly smell garlic and pepper as I walked into the kitchen. A couple of waiters stopped and looked at me curiously, but most of the kitchen staff didn't pay me any attention. My mother always hired the same company for her parties and they were pretty used to me sneaking in through the kitchen and up the servants' stairs. A waiter walked by with a tray of melon wrapped in prosciutto. I plucked one from the tray.

"Thanks," I said with a smile and whirled around to the stairs.

I ran up the steps, down the hall and into the safety of my room. I pulled off my muddy jeans and T-shirt and threw them at the laundry basket in the corner, barely missing the basket. I ran into the bathroom and turned on the hot water. I pulled off my underwear and bra and tossed them on top of the long marble countertop, where they landed on the gold faucet.

I stepped into the warm water and sighed in relief as I laid my head back against the Jacuzzi tub. I searched for the stereo remote along the tub ledge, picked it up in my soapy fingers, and turned on my iPod. Adele's jazzy voice filled the air as I closed my eyes and relaxed for a while, soaking up the warmth from the bubbly water.

The air had been frigid this weekend, and being out today at the Derby had been unbearable. Especially since I was required to wear a skirt suit and a flimsy hat that refused to stay on my head. I couldn't remember a Derby day in the past being so cold. Usually it was warm and pretty by the beginning of May, but not today. At least it had been exciting to watch Casper run around the track in record time, leaving all the other horses in the dust. I had cheered so loudly that my throat was sore.

I grabbed the fancy, hot pink bottle of shampoo my aunt had brought me from New York, and scrubbed my hair until it tingled and smelled like white ginger. I shut my eyes, took a deep breath and bobbed my head under the lukewarm water. When I popped back up to the surface, a thick swath of black hair was entangled around my neck. A slight chill settled on my shoulders, sending goose bumps up my arms. I grabbed a towel from the nearby rack and pulled it tightly across my body.

As I stepped out of the tub onto the glassy marble floor, my foot slid halfway across the marble. I grabbed the tub with both hands to keep from tripping the rest of the way out of the tub and landing face-first on the solid surface. What had my parents been thinking? I knew for a fact they were more concerned with the prestige found in having floors covered in ornate marble than the fact that it's as slippery as an ice rink. Who needs a floor that requires ice skating skills to walk on? I did have some fluffy blue bath mats, but my mother confiscated them. They didn't "match" and "they look like something a little kid would have" according to her.

I just liked them because it meant fewer bruises and head traumas.

After a few excruciating tip-toe steps, I reached the back of the bathroom door where my white bathrobe hung. I slipped it on and instantly felt some warmth under my skin. I walked across my room and into my large walk-in closet, put on my favorite plaid pajama pants and Lexington Prep T-shirt, and collapsed on my bed. As I fell backward onto the fluffy, king-size mattress there was a loud knock on the door. Before I had time to move, the door was flung wide open, and thudded dramatically against the wall. Without looking up, I knew my mother was there. I let out a groan as I propped myself up on my elbows.

"Why do you even bother knocking?" I asked.

I looked at my mother's demure figure standing in the doorway. Her red lips were pursed and her bony white arms were crossed against her chest. She still had on her little black dress and string of pearls.

"You didn't answer," she quipped, and before I had a chance to argue, she spoke again. "What are you doing in bed already?" One delicate eyebrow flew up and creased her perfect forehead. She moved fluidly toward me, uncrossing her arms and laying one hand on the foot of the bed.

I looked over at the alarm clock on my nightstand. It read three a.m. in bright red digital numbers. "I'm tired and I have a ton of homework due Monday that I need to work on tomorrow," I replied, scowling at her.

She laughed, throwing back her graceful chin. "Honey, your family's thoroughbred just won the Kentucky Derby, don't you think you can forget about that for a little while? I'm sure I can talk to your teachers. They'll understand."

"I don't want any special privileges. I want to turn everything in on time like everyone else," I said, half whispering the second part.

She shook her head at me. "Schoolwork can wait. We have something important to talk to you about, and there are some very important people who were expecting to see you tonight. I had to tell them I didn't know where you were. How silly do you think that made me look?" she said, her deep red lips curling into a frown.

Mother's face was always a study in expressive emotions. Every word, every movement, carried a sense of dramatic weight. She could have been a mime in another life.

"What do you need to talk to me about?" I sat up in the bed, my interest piqued.

"Something important, so come back downstairs so your father and I can talk to you," she said, grabbing my forearm.

This was just another one of her ploys to get me downstairs to talk to her annoying friends. They didn't have anything important to talk to me about, except for showing me off and making sure I made a good impression to all the "important people."

"Sorry, but I'm tired and I have a headache," I said, pulling my arm from her grasp and throwing a pillow over my head.

She huffed loudly. "Fine, if you're going to behave like a toddler, I'll leave you to your pouting." She turned off the overhead light and slammed my bedroom door shut, causing the picture frames on the walls to shake. I didn't even flinch. Instead, I let out a sigh of relief and uncovered my head.

I crawled under the covers and reached over to turn off my horse figurine lamp. The room became engulfed in a comforting sea of black.

~ * * * ~

The buzz of my alarm clock jolted me from my pleasant dreams. I turned over and searched for the snooze button. Piercing rays of sunlight streamed in through the double French doors and infiltrated my bed. *Ugh.* I had forgotten to close the curtains the night before.

I stepped onto the cool floor and jogged over to the French doors in an effort to close them, but my eyes had already adjusted to the warm, peach-colored light. I looked out onto the rolling hills of our farm. One of our colts pranced across the field, kicking his hooves up like a practiced soldier. I smiled to myself and a warm, fuzzy feeling filled my chest. There was no peace and happiness I could find like flying through the woods on the back of a beautiful thoroughbred. No expectations, no rules to follow.

I refocused my attention to the dreary day that had already been planned for me. I decided after breakfast, church, the luncheon party, and the CNN interview, I would spend some time reading in the comfort of Wendy's stall. I needed to read four chapters of Jane Austen's *Pride and Prejudice* for English class before Monday, and I couldn't think of a better place to do it. That thought alone would get me through the rest of the day.

I walked toward my closet in search of something to wear. Without stepping outside, I knew the air was still icy, so I looked for a warm skirt or pantsuit. I found a skirt suit in an emerald tone, with black lace trim around the collar and cuffs. I knew the color would bring out my eyes and pretty up my ghostly-pale skin. Funny and ironic that my family owned "Ghost" Hill Farms and had named me Casper. I was ecstatic that vampires were the cool thing right now so I didn't have to waste time on self-tanner. No matter how much time I spent outside, I only burned before returning to my pasty shade of white.

I pulled the skirt and the black shell off the hanger and threw them on. Ugh, I had forgotten the pantyhose before putting the skirt on. I pulled out a drawer in my closet and searched for a pair of black hose. I couldn't wait to go to college, where I could wear sweat shirts and jeans every day. No more prim and proper suits that were *so not* what I wanted to wear. They weren't trendy, comfortable, or anything that my friends at school had to wear on a regular basis.

After finally getting the suit on—and the ugly black pumps—I went back into the bathroom and applied a little makeup. I pulled out a pair of diamond stud earrings and a simple necklace, and rushed downstairs for breakfast.

As I walked into the formal dining room, I instantly realized something was off. The aura in the room felt too calm and peaceful. Normally, Mother would be staring at her reflection in the large gold mirror behind the dining table, fixing her hair, makeup, or clothes, all the while fussing about the maid's inability to pick up after a party. Dad should be lounging at the table with the paper in one hand and a coffee mug in the other.

He had a cup of coffee in his hand, but neither *The Lexington Herald Leader* nor *The Wall Street Journal* appeared on the long mahogany table. They were both sitting quietly, looking up at me with timid-smiles. A sense of panic crept into my empty stomach. Mother tapped her French-manicured nails on the table, and then signaled for me to sit beside her. I did her bidding without any protest. I sat down at the table and took a deep breath.

"Honey, I've got some good news," Dad said

with a big smile. His face was finely tanned from the hours spent out on the farm. His black hair was slicked back in a way that always made me think of a mobster.

"What?" I said in a clipped tone, crossing my arms over my suit jacket. This wasn't going to be good news at all.

"We're moving to Charleston," he said matter-of-factly.

No discussion? Simply a stated fact. I was blown away. So Mother hadn't been lying last night. This was big news and I regretted not getting up from bed to talk to them. Several emotions were all competing in my head.

"Charleston? *West Virginia?*" Bewilderment won the mental fight.

Dad gave a hearty laugh. "No, honey, Charleston, South Carolina." He looked over at Mother, shaking his head at my inability to telepathically understand what he had meant in the first place. As if I shouldn't have even considered West Virginia, even though it's *way* closer than South Carolina.

Without warning, hot tears stung my eyes and threatened to cascade down my burning red cheeks. I looked up at the crystal chandelier dangling above the dining room table and bit my bottom lip. I refused to let a single tear fall. I hated crying in front of anyone, especially my parents.

"I'm not going." I closed my eyes and shook my head.

"It's not up for discussion," said Dad, his

voice deep and commanding.

I took a deep breath and opened my eyes. I stared at his cat-green eyes, which I had inherited. They were flat and without their normal sparkle. I wasn't used to him being so firm with me. He had always been my ally when my mother and I had one of our famous fights.

"But what about the horses? And it's going to be my senior year!" I got up from the table and stood behind the chair I had been sitting in.

I looked over at my mother. She sat with her bony arms crossed over her chest, looking down at the table. Normally, by now Mother would have said something, but she was quiet and refused to look at me. She wasn't completely on board with this idea either.

"The farm manager will handle things here. Since the Derby is over, we don't have too much to worry about until the Preakness. And you'll make new friends."

I felt the tears coming on again. Yeah, I knew I could make new friends at school, but I had no desire to try to fit in somewhere new my last year of high school. I didn't want to be the kid who everyone barely remembered after graduation, and the thought of facing a new school without the horses to run home to was unbearable.

"No." I clenched my hands around the back of the dining room chair.

"We're moving and we'll move right after school lets out." He took a gulp of coffee, sat the mug on the table, and snapped his fingers for the maid to come in and take the empty cup.

"That's only a week away!" I shouted. How could they have made a decision like that so fast? Or had they been planning it behind my back for awhile? That thought sent my temper through the roof. I let go of the back of the chair and backed away from my parents.

"Yes, I know. We'll leave that weekend. No need to pack, really, just a few things. The movers will pack what we need, and we'll buy the rest."

I searched desperately for the words to challenge this lunatic idea. "If we're keeping the farm, then why do we need to move?" I was beginning to get desperate to change his mind. Stabbed in the back by my own parents! I was so angry that the tears were starting to blur my vision.

"I got a call a couple of weeks ago from a friend offering a business deal that I couldn't afford to pass up in this economy. You have to understand this is in our family's best interest. I'm doing this for you," he said with vindication. He was trying to make me feel guilty, because I was being ungrateful in his mind.

Please—all for me. He always used, "You're the future of this family and it's all for you," to justify any thing he did. I wasn't buying it today.

"Then I'll stay here until I finish school and then I'll go to the University of Kentucky. There won't be any need for me to move to Charleston. I'll stay here . . . at the farm," I said as my final offer.

"That's not an option. We want you with us

during your last year of school before you go to Harvard."

I instantly bristled at his demands for me to not only come with them, but that as a Whitley I *was* attending Harvard. Sure, I had the grades and the scores to get into Harvard, but I had no desire to go to that pretentious school. I wanted to go to the University of Kentucky, where I could stay close to the farm.

I wanted to eventually take over the family's thoroughbred legacy. I had no desire to take over any of my dad's other ventures. Our family owned several factories in Lexington, Louisville, and Cincinnati. We also owned a publishing company, a movie production company, and a stake in a fashion house. But none of that interested me. I didn't want an empire to run. Money always changed people into zombies who were only looking to feed their greed.

I looked over at Mother, who was still suspiciously quiet. Her lips were pursed and she fiddled with her pearl earrings. When I stared at her, she intentionally avoided eye contact.

"What do you think, Mother?"

She finally looked at me. "I think it's a great idea," she said quietly, her lips pursed. I was convinced she was telling the truth.

"Fine, I guess there isn't much I can do about it, but don't expect me to be happy. And, by the way, I'm not going to Harvard," I said, turning my back on them and marching out of the room before he had time to respond.

I stomped up the stairs, charged into my

room, and slammed the door behind me. I flung myself onto the bed, not caring if I messed up my makeup or hair. If they were lucky, I'd show up for their stupid press conference. I was seriously thinking of riding Wendy across the rolling fields into a picture perfect horizon and never coming back.

Chapter

2

A WEEK LATER, I FOUND myself on a private jet bound for Charleston. I had resolved not to talk to either of my parents during the trip. I had barely spoken to them the entire week. I had spent every free moment I had in the barn with the horses, or out on the trails, riding Wendy. My eyes were puffy from the constant tears. I had given up on caring whether my parents saw me cry or not. I hoped if I cried hard enough in front of them, I could change their minds. It hadn't worked.

I stuffed earphones into my ears, turned up the volume, and listened to "Hometown Glory" by Adele and "Fix You" Coldplay on my iPod over and over again, because they fit my current mood. I peered out the small window of the plane and watched the bluegrass fields disappear under the wispy clouds. I was leaving my life behind. Slowly, the landscape changed into deep green mountains—and, as we approached Charleston, it shifted again into watery marshland.

After landing at the airport, we got into a sleek black limo and headed for our new home. I gazed out at the scenery, but noticed little about it.

"Is everyone excited?" Dad asked cheerfully. I turned and scowled in his direction. His smile instantly disappeared, but he continued his chatter. I returned my gaze to the window.

"Our house is right across from White Point Gardens and we can even see the harbor. Won't that be a change, Casper?" he prodded, his words filled with hope. I couldn't have cared less about the harbor and White Point Gardens. It was probably a stupid park full of dog walkers anyway.

I liked the beach. Every year, we spent a week in the Hamptons with Grandmother Livingston, and two weeks with Grandma and Grandpa Whitley in Florida, but it just wasn't going to be the same. No more white Christmases, no more weekends in the barn with Wendy or Little Ghost. My eyes filled with tears again. I wiped them away with the sleeve of my shirt and continued to stare out the window.

"I think it'll be great," Mother said in a subdued voice. I looked over at her and, for the first time since Dad had announced we were moving, there was a small smile on her red lips.

She was dressed more casually than usual and her hair was up in a neat bun. She had on a pair of dark denim jeans, a white tank top, and a black blazer with a multitude of Chanel necklaces draping the front of her ensemble. She looked softer, less formal, which was a nice change from her usually dressy attire. Mother's clothes indicated her current mood, kind of like a fashion mood ring. From what she was wearing, I could tell she wasn't feeling her best. It was just one more indication that she was about as thrilled as I was about this move. I felt a tiny bit of encouragement.

After all, I wasn't the only one who was going to be starting all over. Mother had always been a social person, with lots of friends, party circles, and women's groups to fill up her time. Those circles were now all nestled in their mansions on sprawling farms hundreds of miles away. That was fine by me. I had never been much for the parties, which were always full of pampered people with fake laughs. I preferred my afternoons at the horse barn, curled up in the hay with a good book. It was a trait that my mother had been unsuccessful in breaking. I think she finally realized I preferred horses over people ninety-nine percent of the time.

Dad was getting the better end of this whole insane deal. He had gotten the offer from a longtime friend . . . supposedly. Tyson Roman had been one of Dad's college classmates, according to his ramblings on the plane. They had been members of the same fraternity and lived in the frat house for two years together. They had pulled off several memorable pranks, which he had described in painstaking detail. Tyson was now a business tycoon in Charleston, with several construction companies to his name. This was the first time I had ever heard of him, and I was pretty sure it was the first time for Mother, too.

A few minutes later, we pulled up to the curb of our new home. Once the car stopped, I put away my headphones and looked out through the darkly-tinted window. Our house was really close to the other houses on the street . . . like, I could literally reach out a window and touch the other house. Palm trees lined the sidewalk, and most of the houses had short iron fences guarding their tiny, well-manicured front lawns. It was a big letdown. I was used to not having a single neighbor within earshot.

There were three imposing porches, one on each level of the house, that ran the length of the house. The exterior was a warm honey color with black decorative shutters. Its front façade reminded me of a grand plantation home from *Gone with the Wind*. I hated to admit the house was really pretty.

"Isn't it beautiful?" Dad asked, as he hastily got out of the car. I stepped out onto the street as well, but with less enthusiasm. The air was thick and muggy with humidity. It almost took my breath away. It was just as blistering in

Kentucky this time of year, but the air didn't have the same heavy, salty quality. I could almost taste the ocean on my lips.

Mother and I walked toward the house in a daze. Neither one of us uttered a word as Dad continued to gab away about the house.

"It was built in the late seventeen-hundreds—amazing, right?" He was still cheery, but it was obvious he was looking for a reaction from someone at this point. Mother and I shared the same stubborn quality. We walked in silence, ignoring his attempts to get us talking about how "amazing" all of this was—in reality, it was nothing more than a bad dream.

We reached the front porch, which had a beautiful wood floor that glistened like it was encased in glass. The front door was ornate, with white decorative molding and windows at the top and along both sides.

It was very different from our home in Kentucky, but no less impressive. My mother had extravagant taste and Dad would do anything to please her. When she had complained that the original house had been too small, he had a contractor on hand the next day. The new house had marble floors, mahogany paneling, and gold-plated fixtures throughout its massive structure, which spread across the farm like a miniature White House.

Dad finally reached the front door and unlocked it cautiously. It creaked as he swung it open. A crystal chandelier dangled from the tall ceiling, which cast a tranquil glow across the foyer's wood floor. I looked to the right of the front door. A dark wood staircase wound up like a mahogany corkscrew to the second floor. A long hallway stretched ahead of us toward a set of frosted glass double doors. I took a few steps toward the left to a set of pocket doors. With a little effort, I pulled them apart and revealed a large formal living room.

I was shocked by all the furniture that was perfectly arranged in the room like a museum exhibit. I walked across the hall and opened another set of pocket doors next to the stair case. They squeaked from disuse, and once again I found furniture in perfect arrangements.

It looked as if someone already lived here and we were the house guests. Everywhere I looked there were ornate furniture, antique wall hangings, and luxurious velvet curtains enveloping both rooms. My mother was not into antiques. I didn't see any of these things lasting very long.

"I thought that our things were being shipped?" she asked, her jaw tight as she paced between the two adjacent rooms.

After several hurried looks back and forth, she stopped next to a round table placed in the center of the foyer. She touched the large silk flower arrangement on the table and frowned. She jerked her hand away as if she would be infected with some terrible interior designing disease. She crossed her arms over her chest and arched one perfect eyebrow, as if to say, *You better have a good explanation.*

"Some of them are, but the house came completely furnished. The things already here would match the style of the house much more than our own would. Besides, if we empty out the other house, we won't have anything to sit on when we visit."

"Fine," she responded, pursing her lips. It wasn't like my mother to give up so easily.

"So, what do you think, Casper?" he asked, avoiding any further confrontation with Mother, who had disappeared into one of the rooms.

"No!" squealed Mother. There must have been more fake flowers. I smiled for the first time since we'd left.

"Do you like it?" Dad stood next to me and nudged my shoulder. I let my guard down, feeling a little bit sorry for him for some strange reason.

"It's pretty Dad." He didn't look convinced. "Really," I repeated.

He finally smiled and took in a deep breath. "Why don't you go upstairs and pick out a bedroom? There's four on the second floor and three on the third."

I nodded and dutifully made my way up the stairs. The staircase curled up the side of the house. I could imagine all the families who had made their first trek up this very staircase and I was comforted by their lingering spirits—as long as they didn't show up in the middle of the night. Ghost hunting was not on my bucket list.

I stopped at the second floor and walked across a well-worn oriental rug on the landing. I made my way down the dark, narrow hallway, and peeked into the bedroom at the end of the hall. The walls were minty green with light pink silk drapes. I cringed and moved on. The next bedroom wasn't much better, with busy red and white wallpaper that looked like something Grandmother Livingston would pick out for a china pattern.

I walked back down the hallway and entered the bedroom closest to the stairs that continued to wind up to the third floor. It had delicate pale gold wallpaper, and drapes that were done in a soft blue. The bedding on the king-size bed was a soft blue that matched the drapes. A plasma television hung above the fireplace. The room felt like an ethereal and calming piece of sky. I instantly felt a sense of peace I hadn't felt since I found out about the move.

I dropped my backpack on the floor and walked into the attached bathroom. The floor and the walls were done in a soft cream tile, and matching blue bath mats were on the floor. They were just like the ones I had had in my bathroom. I seriously thought about hiding them under the bed to keep Mother from taking them away.

There was a large picture window over the Jacuzzi tub, which let in lots of light. I stepped into the tub with my shoes on and stared out into the very green, but disappointingly small, yard. It reminded me of a tiny English garden. There were several large oak trees dripping with Spanish moss, which looked like they were guarding the tiny yard with their skeletal limbs.

I drifted back into the bedroom, picked up my backpack, and pulled out a silver picture frame. I placed the framed picture of me with Wendy, my face nuzzled against her long mane of hair, on the white marble fireplace. My chest became tight as I stared at the photo and realized I wouldn't be able to see any of the horses any time I wanted.

I heard the front door downstairs creak open and some chatter, then the stomping of feet up the stairs. I exited the bedroom to see Mother coming toward me, her necklaces jingling against her chest.

"Come downstairs, Casper, Mr. Roman and his family are here to meet us," she said, batting her eyes at me.

Ah, I thought, *Mr. Roman must have a wife, which is the reason for my mother's sudden buzz of excitement.* It must be someone she could build social circles with and use to start her party life all over. *Great,* I was now the only loner in the family.

We descended down the spiral of stairs. She clutched my hand, giving it a squeeze as the front foyer came into view. A man and a woman were chatting with Dad. As we walked closer, I noticed another individual standing in the shadows behind them. He was tall, handsome, and my age.

As we approached, Dad waved his hand out toward me. "Tyson, this is my daughter, Casper."

"Hello," I responded, and extended my hand

to the debonair man.

He took my hand into his warm, dry grip and shook it like a well-trained politician. He would have definitely fit into the category of hot older men, along with Brad Pitt and George Clooney. I was immediately drawn to the sharp jaw line of his square face. He was very tan, which was only made more apparent by his white dress shirt. His eyes were a piercing light blue and his hair was a nice shade of dirty blonde.

"Hello, Casper," he said in a commanding voice. He had a thick Southern drawl that reminded me of Bill Compton, the vampire from *True Blood*, but a little more elegant and genteel. He let go of my hand and waved toward the woman beside him. "This is my wife, Jillian."

The elegant woman stepped forward. She was a tall, slender woman, who was a good two inches taller than me and my mother. She was wearing a linen suit that complimented her olive skin. Her face was shaped like a heart, with long black hair billowing around her elegant neck. I couldn't help but stare at her Angelina Jolie lips and violet Elizabeth Taylor eyes. She took my hand and shook it once before letting it go. She didn't say a word, but smiled, revealing her perfect white teeth.

Finally, the boy standing off to the side came up to me and I let out a heavy breath. He had definitely inherited his parents' glamorous, beautiful genes.

"Hey, I'm Cal," he said in a husky Southern accent.

I couldn't stop staring at his blue eyes that sparkled like a crystallized ocean. Cal exuded charm and confidence as if it were seeping out of every gorgeous pore. His skin was pale, but in a glowing, attractive way that only made his extremely blue eyes stand out even more. His face was square and hard like his father's, but he had wavy black hair like his mother. I felt my heart skip a beat.

"Hi," I finally stuttered out.

"You're very pretty. Prettier than the pictures I've seen." He stuck out his hand for me to shake it. I felt my pulse start to beat wildly as I put my hand in his. After I let go of his hand, I didn't know what else to do, so I walked back to my parents without another word. I was embarrassed that he had left me so star-struck. It wasn't that there hadn't been hot guys at Lexington Prep—there had been plenty—but there was just something different about Cal. I couldn't describe what I was thinking or feeling.

"Now that we've been introduced, I would like to invite your family over to our house for dinner," Tyson said, smiling like a used-car salesman, and I snapped back into reality. *Oh fun,* a dinner party already. I could tell Charleston wasn't going to be much different from Lexington, at least for my parents. But maybe this one *would* be more interesting with Cal.

"That would be lovely," Mother piped in from behind.

I felt the need to roll my eyes, but as I

snapped my head back to the Romans, I caught Cal's unrelenting gaze. He looked at me and instantly turned his gaze to the side. I looked away, too, but every time I met his stare, I felt a spark ignite in my chest.

"We'll have the driver pick you up at seven?" Tyson offered.

"Yes, that would be fine. Thank you," said Dad, as he moved toward the front door and opened it for them. One by one, the Romans went out the door, smiling and waving as they left.

"See you later, Casper," called Cal, as he slipped out the front door and into the humid-evening air.

"Well, they seem wonderful," Mother said, as she went to look at herself in the hallway mirror. She pushed back the few tendrils of hair that had fallen from her bun and patted her lips.

"I thought you would like them," Dad responded, shutting the front door and walking to the center of the foyer.

"They were different," I blurted out.

Mother snapped her head toward me, "What do you mean?" Her manicured eyebrows flew up, elongating her round face.

"I don't know, maybe a little too perfect?" I returned, not affected by Mother's glare. She frowned and then touched her hand to her cheek, which was what she always did when she was thinking something over.

"No, of course not, Casper, they're great people," I heard Dad chime in, as he began treading up the staircase.

He looked at me with the same glare I had gotten from Mother. His look terrified me, unlike Mother's, because he rarely made that face at me, although it was starting to become more common. Dad and I had always been close. When I was a kid, he was always going out to the barn with me to brush the horses, or take a ride on the trails. He had been my closest human confidant—until about a year ago. That's when he started spending more time working at the office, managing all the businesses. He started missing dinners, and stopped going out to the barn with me. He just didn't seem like the same person anymore.

After he disappeared up the stairs, I turned and headed through the double doors at the end of the hallway. I pushed through another swinging door to find the kitchen. It looked as if it had undergone a recent renovation, with its black granite counter tops, white-washed cabinets, and stainless steel appliances. I walked around the massive island and over to the equally massive Sub-Zero refrigerator. It was more high tech than our old fridge, but I figured the past owners must've done their own cooking. One of the first things Mother had done when she found out we were moving was to hire a cook . . . over the phone.

The refrigerator had clear glass doors and I could see most of its contents. It appeared to be stocked with the essentials, including a dark green carton of orange juice. I opened the door, pulled it out, and thought about drinking straight from the carton. It couldn't really hurt. The minute Mother saw the carton it would be thrown into the trash. She didn't like highly "processed" foods, which was convenient for her, but not our kitchen staff. All juices were to be squeezed fresh daily, and if she caught anything less being done in the kitchen, they were fired on the spot. Four chefs had found this out the hard way.

I popped the top and held the carton to my mouth. It was super sweet, almost like a soda compared to the organic orange juice I was normally forced to drink. It was completely satisfying. After a few large gulps, I threw the carton in the trash, and headed up the servant staircase I had spied off the kitchen.

Once back in my new room, I started pulling garments out of my oversized suitcase the driver had brought up while we spoke to the "wonderful" Romans. What kind of last name is Roman, anyway? It sounded grand, and made me think of Caesar and the powerful empire he built. It did eventually crumble, I reminded myself. I was sure the Romans' façades would slip away, too, revealing their cracks and imperfections.

I shook my head, wondering why I was so bent on tearing them to pieces—besides the fact that they had ruined my life and took me away from the one thing I loved. They had to be hiding something.

I shook out all thoughts of the Romans and returned to picking out something to wear. I rummaged through my suitcase, pulling out some of my favorite things and hanging them in the closet. I was immediately assaulted by the smell of cedar and mothballs.

I hung up the garments and tried to find something "appropriate" to wear to the dinner at the Romans'. I pulled out a summery dress in a pretty red jewel tone. I pulled off my jeans and T-shirt and slipped it on. I went to the gold-framed full-length mirror that stood near the closet door.

I stared at my reflection, looking the dress up and down. The color warmed up my skin, which was now not only pale, but there were dark purple rings around my eyes. My hair was beginning to frizz and curl from the extreme humidity. I didn't have time to take a shower, so I just pulled it up into a ponytail. I put on some light makeup, sparkly chandelier earrings, and a pair of gold gladiator sandals. I strolled back down the stairs to wait for my parents in one of the front rooms.

As I waited, I explored the living room, which was decorated in shades of cream, gold and dark green. There was an ornate fireplace situated in the center of the far wall and flanked by two cream wing chairs. Hanging over the mantle was a painting in a gaudy gold frame. The painting itself was very soft and ethereal. It looked as if people where returning to a ship, the old-fashioned kind, like I imagined the Mayflower would've looked like. They were leaving, but a few of the people were being held back by what looked like little angels. The painter's name,

Antoine Watteau, was in the bottom right corner. I'd never heard of the painter before, but that wasn't saying much. I was not big on art history. I had studied what was necessary to get through art appreciation my sophomore year, but that had been it. By now, I had forgotten everything that I had learned in that boring class.

As I continued to analyze the painting, something caught my eye. There was some red lettering strategically placed on the cherub statue in the far right corner of the painting. I strained on my tip toes to read it. It read, "Kythera Forever." It didn't appear that the lettering was original to the painting, because the red was so vivid and bright compared to the pastel colors that made up the rest of the painting. It looked as if it had been put on at a later time.

I pushed up on my toes as far as they would go as I held myself up on the mantle to get a better look. It wasn't enough, so I pulled one of the wing chairs closer to the fireplace. As I held onto the mantle and craned my neck forward, I could definitely see that the letters had been put on later. I wondered what they meant . . .

"Casper! What are you doing?" I heard my mother exclaim from behind me. Her shrill words caused me to jump and I lost my balance. I slipped off the chair, my butt hitting the arm rest on the way down, and I landed on a nearby ottoman. I looked up at her with scorn as pain shot up my legs.

"I was looking at the painting," I said through

gritted teeth.

She shook her head. She stood in front of me and put her hand out to help me up. I begrudgingly accepted her hand as she pulled me to my feet. She looked me up and down, and her red lips fell into a frown.

"Why do you insist on wearing those ridiculous sandals?" She continued to stare at my feet, shaking her head.

"I like them, and they're comfortable." I smoothed out my skirt and looked at my shoes. Mother moved forward to push a few strands of hair away from my face.

As usual, Mother was dressed to the hilt in couture. She had on a flowing, floor-length black dress, which was cinched at the waist by a black belt. It was a one-shoulder number, with some yellow silk showing through the long slit up her right leg. She reminded me of a modern day Greek goddess. She was definitely feeling more like herself since meeting the Romans.

"They're a fashion trend I hope will disappear soon. They are so unflattering. Why don't you change into something else?" she "asked" me.

I knew this game all too well. If I refused, she would tell me that we weren't leaving until I changed into something else. I did as I was told and when I returned, my father was also standing in the hall, looking fancy in a black suit and yellow tie.

"Is this better?" I asked. I lifted my leg up, showing her the gold heels for her scrutiny. She beamed and nodded her head like a bobble doll.

"Let's get this over with," I said glumly, and marched out the front door.

Chapter

3

AS PROMISED, A LINCOLN TOWN Car was waiting in our driveway. I could only imagine what the perfect Romans called home. I was sure it would have Roman columns, scores of fountains, and statues of the Roman gods.

I didn't have much time to really think about it, because apparently they only lived a few blocks away. *How convenient,* I thought sarcastically. The car stopped in front of large iron gates. Although the house was not far from our own, the street was dramatically different. The homes were much further apart, and they all had high fences surrounding them. I heard the familiar buzz of gates being opened as the driver slowly pulled into the driveway.

As we entered, I noticed the multitude of magnolia and oak trees lining the short, circular driveway. The car came to a halt at the front of the house. It appeared as equally old as our home, with its multiple porches, white wood siding and black shutters. It was hidden behind towering palm trees and oaks that created a bright green shroud around the third floor.

The driver stopped and opened the door for us. We proceeded up to the front door, where the Romans were waiting. Tyson looked even more handsome than he had earlier in his suit. His wife was dressed in a lilac strapless dress and her ebony hair was left loose around her face.

I searched for Cal, but he wasn't standing behind his parents or anywhere on the porch. I was disappointed and hoped he would show up soon.

"Hello! I'm so glad you could join us," boomed Tyson, as he grabbed my father's hand. "And you both look gorgeous!" he shouted in my direction, revealing his beautiful white teeth. Mr. Roman definitely fell under my definition of a fake.

"Thank you," Mother quietly whispered, and I could have sworn she half-curtsied.

We were ushered into the foyer, which was cavernous, with twenty-foot frescoed ceilings and columned archways. It reminded me of a cathedral I had seen in Rome, which was pretty ironic, given their last name.

Once in the large front living room, Mr. Roman pulled Dad to the side and began talking to him in a hushed voice. With a quick nod from Dad, they disappeared into the hallway, their dress shoes clacking on the floors. Mother was busy talking to Mrs. Roman. With no one to talk to, I decided to scrutinize the paintings in the room to stifle my boredom.

The room was very lavish and decorated with antiques, much like our house. There were thick brown velvet curtains covering the massive windows, and the walls were covered with light blue patterned wallpaper.

I was surprised to find the same painting that was in our living room. I made a rapid glance at my mother and Mrs. Roman. Their heads were tilted toward each other and they giggled together about something. I turned back to the painting and strained on my heels to look at the cherubic statue in the painting a little closer. I did have to admit Mother had been right about the high heels. They made it easier to see the painting clearly. Once again, there was the red writing of "Kythera Forever" emblazoned in almost the exact same spot.

"Hello, Casper."

I stumbled a few steps back. I teetered on my heels for a moment before falling backward. Before I could hit the ground, a pair of strong hands grasped my forearms.

I turned around to see that Cal was smiling at me and suppressing a bit of laughter. He was gorgeous, I had to admit, but that wouldn't make up for the fact that he probably had intended on scaring me.

"Sorry, I didn't know you were in such deep concentration," he said, grinning, his dimples showing.

Behind him, my mother and Mrs. Roman had both risen to their feet. Mrs. Roman was trying to suppress a laugh, but Mother looked anything but happy. Her red lips were pursed and her cheeks were set ablaze with blood. I felt my own cheeks flushing. I looked at her, shrugging my shoulders. I had never been so clumsy in my life.

"No, I should have been paying more attention," I said, loud enough for Mother to hear. She instantly perked up, smiled, and continued her conversation.

I turned my attention to Cal and forced myself to smile at him. "Your painting is very interesting. We have one just like it in our house." I glanced at the painting again.

"It's a painting by Antoine Watteau called 'Embarkation to Kythera' or 'Pilgrimage to Kythera.'"

With a quick turn of my head I was staring at Cal again, curious if he knew what the red writing might mean.

"But it's not the exact same painting you have." He raised a dark eyebrow and tilted his head toward the mantle. He took a step forward and his hand grazed mine. I stood, motionless. Cal gave me a look out of the corner of his eye, sending my heart into overdrive.

In an effort to keep my cool, I studied the painting again. He was right. This painting didn't have a ship in the background, and the statue was significantly different, with flowers growing up around it.

"Huh," I breathed out.

"He did two versions of the painting. He was a French Rococo painter from the eighteenth century. These paintings were his most well-known," he said in his enticing Southern drawl. Lost in thought, I hadn't noticed Cal had gotten so close. Warmth flooded up my spine.

"Do you know that much about every painting in the house?" I inched away from him. He looked into my eyes, his piercing gaze unsettling every nerve in my body. I felt the need to look away, my pulse rising.

"You're very pretty," he said. My cheeks were now burning red-hot and I bit my bottom lip.

"I didn't mean to make you blush. I would have thought someone as pretty as you would be used to hearing that. And no, I don't know everything about all the paintings, just this one. It has particular meaning to us," he said smoothly.

"Are you serious?" was all I could say.

He smiled again, "Of course. Why would I lie about you being pretty?" He raised a dark eyebrow again.

"I don't know, it just sounds rehearsed—you've said it so many times since we met a couple of hours ago," I said with a little bite in my voice.

"You think it's something I say to every girl I meet, right?"

"Yeah," I said hesitantly.

"Well, it isn't," he said, as he turned around and headed out of the room.

"Hey, listen, I'm sorry—that didn't come out right." I rushed to catch up to him. He took a couple more steps before he turned back to face me, a sly Cheshire grin plastered on his lips.

"I know, or you wouldn't have come after me. I must really be worth talking to if I can get *the* Casper Isadora Ghost Whitley to apologize to me," he said.

I felt my mouth drop open. *What the hell?*

"I was being polite, although you don't deserve it. You're too smug for me, and you know you're charming and good look . . . ing." As I uttered the last syllable I realized what an idiot I was. He was now smiling from ear to ear.

"From the expression on your face, I don't need to say out loud what I'm thinking," he said, laughing under his breath.

He turned around and started walking out of the room, and motioned for me to follow him. I was tempted to stand in the middle of the living room all night, but I felt I had no choice but to follow his confident swagger. I had to prove that I wasn't such a clueless dork.

As we walked through a couple of rooms, something he had said earlier finally registered in my brain, and I asked, "Hey, how did you know my full name?" He didn't turn around, but kept walking toward a set of double doors that looked as if they led to the backyard.

"I've studied," he replied.

"Why?"

He didn't answer my question as he opened the door and motioned for me to walk outside. Without speaking, he walked down the brick steps, across the well-manicured lawn and toward a separate building that looked like a barn.

"Just curious, I guess." He swung open a large door and flipped a switch. Instantly, the room was lit with harsh halogen light, which illuminated a row of cars.

"Why were you curious?" I asked, as I glanced at a Porsche 911 and new Audi A8.

Suddenly, I plowed into Cal's chest. I hadn't realized he had stopped walking and had turned to face me. It took several seconds to reorient myself. In the meantime, I was pressed firmly against Cal's body. My breath quickened as I felt the muscles under his thin dress shirt tense up. I looked up at him. I could feel his heart racing against my chest.

I pushed myself away from him and stood a few awkward feet away. "Sorry—I am not usually so clumsy," I said, laughing nervously.

He hadn't moved an inch since our collision. His cheeks were flushed, and I thought for a minute that I could see his heart literally pulsing through his shirt.

"No, it's okay," he responded, brushing his hand through his wavy black hair. He coughed nervously and stepped toward the passenger door of a black Mercedes and gestured for me to get in.

"We can't just leave. Our parents are probably

waiting for us." I pointed toward the house.

"Trust me, they won't miss us. Besides, wouldn't you rather go somewhere else instead of suffering through a boring dinner with our parents?"

He had a point. I glanced back once more and got into the car. Cal jumped into the driver's seat, pushed the key in, and reversed out of the garage. With a squeal of the tires, he turned sharply into the circular driveway and spun out into the shadowy street. I couldn't see very much of the city, between the darkly-tinted windows of the Mercedes and the fact everything was flying by in a blur.

"Have you had a chance to see much of Charleston yet?" he asked, as he drove dangerously fast down the four-lane street. He whizzed past cars like they were sitting ducks. I held onto the door, thankful I'd fastened my seat belt. I could only concentrate on surviving at this point.

"Between the flight, meeting you, and getting ready for dinner . . . when did I have time?" I asked, my voice quivering as we barely missed a couple of construction workers. I looked back to see them shouting what I was sure was a couple choice curse words.

"Are you always so sarcastic?" He turned to look at me, taking his eyes off the road. I said a little prayer, promising to never skip out on my parents' boring dinners ever again.

"No, and do you always drive like a maniac?" I let out a squeal as he barreled past a semi-truck in the right lane.

"I like to drive fast, but I'll slow down if you're scared," he said, with a grin across his face.

"I can admit I'm scared. Scared we won't make it to wherever we're going in one piece." I tightened my grip on the door.

He let out a laugh. He slowed the car down to almost the speed limit, but not before a police car switched on its blue lights. The cop pulled up behind us, sirens blaring. Cal swore under his breath and pulled to the side.

I was a mess. I had never been pulled over, not even as a passenger.

Cal pushed a button and the window slid down slowly with a whoosh. I turned to look at the approaching officer. He had a flashlight in his hand that he swept across the side of the car. Once he reached the front of the car, he paused at the front wheel and stood motionless for several seconds. I leaned over the console to see what the holdup was. The officer's face had drained of all its color.

"Can I help you, Officer?" Cal said.

I hit Cal on the shoulder and mouthed, *What are you doing?* He shrugged his shoulders.

"Oh, well, I'm sorry. I didn't realize who you were," the officer said with an uneasy laugh. Why would he be sorry for pulling over a seventeen-year-old in a Mercedes?

"No problem, you new to the force?" Cal said in a conversational tone. My mouth dropped open.

"Yes, I am. I didn't get a good look at your

vehicle till now. Hope you have a good night," he said. The officer walked back to his vehicle and drove off. Cal turned on his blinker and merged back into the flow of traffic.

"What just happened?" I asked. I was shocked and confused by how the officer had treated Cal. You would have thought he was a movie star or a diplomat with immunity to the law.

"Ah, nothing, I just know the police pretty well," he responded, smiling to himself. There was obviously more to the story and it had to do with whatever the officer had seen on the front wheel of his car. What could he have seen? I was dying to find out.

"You have a lot of run-ins with the law?"

He leaned his head over to me with a playful expression on his face. I felt tiny butterflies develop in the pit of my stomach. "Me? Nah, they have run-ins with me from time to time. I have to straighten them out, you know?"

He turned the blinker on and we entered a residential neighborhood. A few minutes later, we pulled up to a restaurant at the end of a secluded street. Cal pulled the car into a parallel parking space across the street and got out of the car. I began to open my door, but he waved his finger at me. He opened the door for me and gestured for me to take his hand. After a moment's hesitation, I stepped out of the car, my hand in his strong grip.

"I figured you would be used to a Southern gentleman," he observed.

"You've got a strange definition of a

Southern gentleman."

We crossed the busy street and walked up the front steps of the restaurant.

"How's that?" he asked, still holding firmly to my hand.

"You don't know what you're saying half the time, do you?"

"No, I'm too busy looking at you," he replied with a wink. I rolled my eyes and removed my hand from his.

We reached the front of the restaurant. It was a pretty red stucco building with two spiral topiaries framing the wrought iron door. Once again, he opened the door for me. I stepped in and was instantly hit with the smell of garlic and the sound of boisterous laughter.

The room was low-lit with candles and barely-lit wrought iron chandeliers. As I looked around, there wasn't an empty table in sight. I wasn't in the mood to wait for a table, but I was Cal's captive.

Cal stepped in front of me and signaled to the maître d'. The tall, wiry man came over to us immediately, and wordlessly picked up a couple of menus. He motioned for us to follow him. The light seemed even dimmer and I didn't know how I was going to see to eat. We were seated at a back corner table, next to a couple of lovebirds all huddled together, arms draped over each other, nuzzling and whispering into each other's ears. I was beginning to feel uneasy.

The maître d' handed us both menus. "Your waiter will be right with you; enjoy."

Cal opened his menu and began carefully studying it like a textbook. Before I picked up my own menu, I continued to stare at him. So many questions were flashing through my mind that I couldn't focus on food.

"So, does the staff here know you as well as the police do? Is that how you got a table even though it's packed?" I asked, raising my eyebrows.

Cal put down his menu. "Of course—if you are anybody in this town, you know me."

I shook my head in disgust. "So you're one of those guys?"

"And how are you any different from me? Aren't you one of those girls?" Cal put his menu back up, hiding his face from view.

"What's that supposed to mean?" I grabbed my menu and started flipping through the pages, glancing at the photos of pasta.

"Well, what's 'one of those guys' supposed to mean? If you mean the kind of guy that calls ahead and gets reservations, then yes, I am one of those guys."

"Oh," I said, a little embarrassed by the assumption I had made. "But how did you know to get reservations for tonight?"

A petite waitress with curly red hair came up to our table. The conversation ceased and Cal dropped his menu. He motioned for me to go ahead and order. I'd been too busy trying to analyze him, and hadn't even looked at the menu. Now I was going to make a fool of myself again.

"I'll have the spaghetti with meatballs." I knew that had to be a safe bet at an Italian restaurant. Cal ordered and our waitress took the menus and flitted off to the kitchen.

A few seconds later, she reappeared with a bread basket and glasses of water with lemon. I was so embarrassed; all I wanted to do was hide under the table. I wasn't used to feeling that way. Most of the guys I had been out with were intimidated by me, but I was intimidated by Cal. It wasn't a great feeling. Now I was aware of how all those pathetic guys must have felt. Shame filled my thoughts.

"To answer your question from earlier, I knew you were coming to town today. I figured you might enjoy this more than the usual dinner my parents had planned. You don't strike me as the type who likes stuffy dinners." He took a sip of water and picked up a piece of bread.

"And how do you know so much about me? Because you studied me?"

Cal looked at me for a moment. "I figured not many teenagers like hanging out with their parents and their new friends. I don't."

Although I was irritated by his tone, I nodded my head in agreement. "Well, you were right. I hate dinners with my parents and their friends. They're always so boring. And so are their kids," I said, smiling for the first time that night.

"Is that so? Well what about that Roman kid? He's on every policeman's radar with his mad driving skills. That can't be too boring, can it?"

"That depends on if your definition of exciting

includes praying and hoping you survive the ride. In that case, he's definitely not boring."

Cal smiled at me as he chewed on a roll. "So— tell me about yourself."

I looked at him, my eyebrows raised in surprise. "I thought you studied me? Shouldn't you already know everything about me?" I picked the linen napkin up from the table and placed it in my lap. I always hated that question. He might as well have asked me how to solve the Middle East crisis. I might have an answer for that one.

"I did, but *Thoroughbred Daily* articles on the internet didn't tell me anything about what you like. Just your family's business, your name, where you grew up, that sort of thing."

"What did it say about me?"

The waitress returned with our food and placed the plates in front of us. I looked at the heaping bowl of spaghetti and meatballs. *Yikes,* this was going to be messy.

"You've lived all your life in Lexington, Kentucky . . . you're the heiress to the horse racing throne and your family has the most successful line of Triple Crown winners in history." He picked up his fork and looked up thoughtfully for a moment, as if wracking his brain for what other information he knew. "And you're a champion jumper, but gave it up last year when you had a bad fall."

I tensed up at the memory. It had been the last hurdle in the sequence when my horse, Hot Stuff, locked up at the rails and I went flying over his neck. I was in a coma for two days, the hospital for two weeks, and ended up with a broken arm. I hadn't been show jumping since, but I still loved to ride horses. I had been working my way back up to jumping when I got the awful news about the move.

"That's right," I said in a low voice, spinning some of the pasta on my fork, then letting it fall back onto my plate.

"I'm sorry to bring it up. I should have thought before I said anything," he said.

I continued to stare at my plate, becoming totally lost in the memory.

"I know you still enjoy riding. There was another article only a few months ago about you and a horse named . . . Wendy . . . I think," he said, as he cut into his chicken parmigiana.

My face drooped as I remembered that Wendy and the other horses were not here. I had spent so much time with them growing up that they felt like the siblings I never had.

"Yes, Wendy's my favorite. She's a beautiful chestnut mare. I used to ride her almost every day," I said, as I fiddled with the napkin in my lap. That part of my life was over—at least for a little while. I knew eventually I would get my way and go back to college in Lexington. I'm that much like my mother.

"I'm sorry you won't get to do that every day. But I'm sure you'll see Charleston isn't all that bad."

"Maybe." I paused, popping a piece of meatball into my mouth. "If not, I may just run away," I said, half joking.

"Would you really run away?" he asked, a line of worry forming across his forehead. His sincere concern shocked me, as did the fact that he had wholeheartedly believed I would run away. Then again, maybe he could pick up my subconscious thoughts.

"No, I guess not. They would know exactly where I would go and just drag me back." God only knew what crazy punishment Mother would come up with for that one. I probably would have to commit my life to the Women's Club, and volunteer for their little projects every week. My skin crawled at the thought.

"Were you involved with any sports or anything at your high school?" he asked, completely changing the subject.

"Not really; I spent most of my free time with the horses and on the farm. I didn't have time for sports, not that I would have been any good at any of them anyway." I picked up another forkful of spaghetti. "I tried running track one year, but learned I would rather let the horse do the running. It wasn't my thing," I said, with a little laugh. "Enough about me. What about you? What's your high school like? I'll be there next fall."

"St. Mary's is okay. There are lots of things to get involved with. I think you'll like it," he said.

"You like avoiding my questions, don't you? Hope you're thinking about being a politician or lawyer. You'd be good at either one."

"It's not that I'm trying to avoid your questions, I'm just kind of all over the place. My mind moves as about as fast as my car."

I laughed and took a sip of water. "Well, then I completely understand. But, seriously, do you play any sports? A part of any clubs?"

"I'm into soccer, but I won't have time to play this year." He rubbed his fingers across his glass of water.

"Why not?"

"I'll be involved with other things." He didn't elaborate.

"Got a job or something?" I took another bite of meatball and wiped my mouth with the napkin.

"Just a lot of business stuff for the family." He looked away.

"What kind of business could a teenager be involved with that would be so time-consuming?"

He stared silently at the couples around us, agitation reading all over his taut jaw.

"I guess I know what you mean. My parents expect me to be this perfect little homecoming queen, with tons of friends, go to Harvard, and follow in their footsteps, and that's just not me."

"So, you're kind of a disappointment to them," he said.

I shrugged my shoulders. "I guess you could say that."

"Then I know exactly how you feel." Cal stared at me and smiled.

After another sip of water, I pushed my plate away. "That was delicious; thank you for kidnapping me," I said, settling back into my seat.

The waitress came over promptly and took our plates away and asked if we wanted dessert. Cal looked to me and I shook my head. He asked for the check and the waitress left with our plates.

"I didn't have to try too hard to kidnap you. I thought you came pretty willingly," he said. All the stress disappeared from his face and his blue eyes sparkled in the candlelight.

"True—but, I mean, look at your competition. It was either you or our parents. Which would you have chosen?"

"I was just better than the alternative?" he asked, a smile of amusement on his face.

"Yes."

"I have to disagree. I would have picked you over a lot of people. You're very interesting *and* you're more beautiful than any homecoming queen I've ever seen," he said with complete sincerity.

Once again, he had surprised me. My face felt warm and I could only nod in response.

The waitress returned with the check. Cal signed it and handed it to her without giving her cash or a credit card, which was odd.

Cal got up from his chair and walked toward mine. He pulled my chair out and extended his hand out to me. I accepted it and ended up face to face with him again. For what seemed like minutes, we stood there, motionless, and I was unable to look away from him. Blood began rising to the surface of my face and neck again.

Finally, he stepped ahead of me and we

walked out of the dark restaurant into the warm night air. We crossed the street and once again he opened the car door for me.

I could get used to this.

The drive home was nice and didn't involve the cops, which was a relief. Cal pulled into his driveway and stopped the car at the front door. The area was well-lit by a trio of hurricane lamps on the large front porch.

As he went to open the car door for me again, I remembered the surprise on the policeman's face and wanting to know what had caused it.

Cal opened my door and I hesitated, thinking of what I could do to have an excuse to look at his car. He leaned against the car door as he waited for me to step out. I put my hand to my ear, remembering that I had on a pair of my mother's earrings. She hadn't liked the ones I had chosen, so she had let me "borrow" a pair of her diamond drop earrings. With a quick motion, I pulled out my left earring and slipped it under the car seat.

I stepped out of the car and faced him. "That was a lot of fun—thank you again."

I pushed my hair back and brushed my hand against my ear. "Oh, no! I've lost it!" I said, pretending to be shocked it wasn't there. I had to admit, I was a *terrible* actress.

He looked at my ear and shrugged. "Are you sure you had both of them on?"

"Yes, I must have dropped it somewhere. I have to find it. I borrowed them from my mother. She'll kill me if I've lost one." That part was totally the truth.

I started looking around on the ground. "Maybe I lost it when I got out of the car here at your house. I put them on in the car on the way over."

With my head down, I walked around the driveway, making my way to the other side of the Mercedes. He was busy searching the front steps and up onto the porch, his head looking down at the ground.

I finally reached the other side of the car and bent down to look at the front wheel. I looked up over the hood to make sure he was still on the porch. He wasn't paying me any attention as he opened the front door and stepped in. The light was dim, and I had to squint to make out the fine red writing on the car. Following the curve of the wheel well was a series of letters, spelled out in cursive on the body of the car. They spelled out "Kythera." It was the same cursive lettering as on the paintings. *Weird.*

I continued my search around the car to the rear, looking up periodically at Cal so that if he turned in my direction I could return my gaze to the ground. I hadn't noticed before, but the normal lettering that should have indicated the car class and number was missing from the trunk of the car. There should have been something like E350 or S550 on the left-hand corner. In place of the normal model letters was the same type of raised lettering, but it was red instead of silver, and it was a "K" without any accompanying numbers.

"Do you think you could have left it at the restaurant?" he asked suddenly, from behind me.

"Maybe, but I want to look here before we drive all the way back. It could have fallen out in your car," I said, walking back over to the passenger side.

I bent down and pretended to search the floor board and the door before reaching between the seat and the center console. I lifted the earring up and turned to show him, a big goofy smile on my face.

"I found it! At least it wasn't at the restaurant," I said half-heartedly.

He gave me a look, as if he knew I had been lying all along. I became very self-conscious, smiling ear to ear like a clown. I sure felt like one.

"Let's go inside and see if your parents are still here," he suggested as we walked up the front porch steps.

"Why wouldn't they be here? They wouldn't leave me here." At least, not the parents I had always known—but Charleston was making them act strange.

We walked into the foyer, which was completely dark—and so was the living room. I followed Cal into the kitchen and the formal dining room, which were both empty, with no movement or sounds.

"They must have left. I'll take you home," he said. We went back out into the driveway and got into the car.

"I can't believe they actually left without me."

I crossed my arms over my chest, and slumped in the seat.

"My parents knew what I was up to, so they probably told them I would bring you home—no big deal," he said, shrugging his shoulders.

Within seconds, we were back at my new home. He pulled into the narrow driveway and stopped near the front door. Sure enough, the front porch and living room lights were glowing with pale yellow light.

We walked to the front door and I rang the doorbell. "I don't have a key to the house yet," I explained.

We stood there awkwardly, for what felt like a millennium. Finally, I decided to try the door knob, although I knew without a doubt it would be locked. It was something my mother obsessed about. She always read about crime waves hitting New York, Chicago or Los Angeles and assumed they applied to Lexington. She would have Dad check every door in the house before they went to bed. She also had him by a super expensive alarm system that went off if you breathed too loudly. Finally, Dad had had enough of the alarm going off and "accidentally" smashed the keypad. It never worked right again.

I twisted the knob and the door creaked open. I felt my mouth drop open. Where had my real parents gone and who were the crazy people pretending to be them?

"We should hang out again," Cal said, as we stepped into the foyer.

"Yeah, sure," I said, still pondering the

unlocked door.

I took a step toward the stairs—and, in one quick step, Cal moved forward, grabbed my hand, and twirled me around to face him. In one smooth motion, his lips brushed against my cheek. I felt my heart dissolve into mush.

"Good night." He squeezed my hand, released it and wordlessly walked to his car. He got in and drove away, his tires screeching as he pulled out of the drive.

I stood in the doorway, staring out at the puff of smoke he left in his wake. My body buzzed and tingled, and I had to take a minute to catch my breath. *Don't fall for him,* I reminded myself. My brain was sending signals of danger, but my heart wasn't paying any attention. The danger element just made him all that more irresistible.

Chapter

4

THE NEXT MORNING, I WOKE up and slowly turned and focused on the tiny antique clock on the night stand. My eyes flew open when I realized it was almost ten o'clock, a virtually unheard of time for me to still be in bed. I hadn't gotten up that late since I was five. I had been put on a strict schedule by my mother once I started school. *Dressed for breakfast by eight o'clock on the weekends and out the door by nine o'clock,* I recited in my head. I flung the covers off, and ran to the bathroom to take a shower and get ready for the day.

I dressed in a pair of well-worn jeans, a grey T-shirt, and my favorite sandals. I rushed down the stairs and stopped dead in my tracks in the front foyer. I looked down the long hallway, realizing I had no clue where the dining room was. I heard the clinking of silverware and my mother's high-pitched chatter. I opened the swinging door to the right of the kitchen door and saw the familiar scene of my parents at breakfast, except it was at the end of the meal.

The maid, whose name I didn't know yet, was wiping the silverware with a cloth from her apron and placing it in the monstrous antique china cabinet. Mother had found another mirror and was examining her hair and makeup. She was cheerful as she brushed back her wavy dark hair with her well-manicured hands. She was dressed in a pair of white linen pants and a red silk halter top. She looked like she was ready to sail away on a yacht. Dad was still sitting at the table, but the crumpled and well-read newspapers were thrown to the side for the maid to dispose of. On cue, the maid picked up the newspapers as she scurried back into the kitchen.

Mother turned around and noticed me standing there. She smiled wildly, her bright red lips emphasizing her glittering white teeth.

"Good morning, sleepy head. I thought I was going to have to send, Karina . . ." She paused, putting a finger to her chin. "Or is her name Katrina or Christina?" she said, talking to herself more than me. She always had a hard time remembering the staff's names. She always had a hard time remembering my teachers' names, too. "Anyhow, you must have had a wonderful evening to sleep in so late," she said, winking at me.

I stood, frozen. My mother had never winked at anyone in her life. I was flabbergasted by her. Something was completely off and I wasn't sure I liked it. She was a lot more relaxed—but unpredictable. I'd never been a fan of change.

"It was nice, but I didn't get home late. I'm just worn out from the plane ride. Where were you at last night? You weren't at the Romans' when we got back. Did you know you left the door unlocked?" I said, remembering the annoyance I had felt last night at coming home to a creaky, enormous house with the door unlocked for anybody to get in. *Not that a ghost needs an unlocked door.* I shivered at the thought.

"We left it open for you. We weren't sure what time we would get back and we knew you didn't have a key." Her voice was still nauseatingly cheerful.

"So you just left it open?"

"Yes, why not? No one is going to bother us." She shrugged her shoulders and shook her head, as if I had made a silly remark. If I thought she wouldn't yell at me for messing up her makeup, I would have put a hand to her forehead to check her temperature.

"Whatever," I said under my breath, and sat down heavily in one of the ornate chairs.

"Cal is such a nice boy—don't you think, dear?" Mother said, looking toward Dad, who was fiddling with his Blackberry. He looked up and made an "hmm" sound at her.

"Oh, yes, he's a very nice boy," he said, repeating her sentiment.

Before I could make a sarcastic remark about their feelings toward Cal, the doorbell rang. A deep, gong-like sound reverberated through the halls. I shot forward and out of the dining room. "Casper, let the butler get the door!" I heard Mother yell, but I ignored her.

I rushed to the door and flung it open. I was disappointed to see a robust man standing at the door, wearing a shirt that read "Platinum Moving Company." I was hoping for a little more *interesting* company, but I quickly admonished myself for even having the thought. I needed to forget about Cal and file his name under the *friend* category on Facebook.

"Hello, I'm Frank, from the moving company. I need Mr. Whitley to sign for the delivery," he said, his raspy voice straining.

"Oh, sure," I said, and ran back to the dining room to get Dad. He came to the door and went out to the moving truck with Frank.

"Casper, come here please!" I heard my mother's bellowing voice coming from the dining room.

I did as I was told and reappeared in the dining room. She was scrawling what I was sure was the day's schedule and wanted me to know when and where I was expected to be every minute of the day. She signaled with her hand for me to sit down. I sat down in the chair beside her, my shoulders slumping in defeat.

"We are a little behind since you slept in." She didn't look up at me, but continued to work feverishly on her list. All the playfulness from before was gone as she got down to business as usual. "Lunch today will be with a couple of women that are a part of the local Women's Club, and I would like you in attendance. At two o'clock, I need you here to help me sort out the things that you want put in your room by the moving men . . ." She paused and tapped her pen thoughtfully on the table. "After that, we have dinner at seven with another family the Romans introduced us to last night."

"What family?"

"The Watsons. We met them for drinks at the Yacht Club after dinner," she said absently, as she scrawled on her notepad.

"Who're they?" I leaned my elbows up onto the table and glanced over at her list, which was a jumbled mess of blue ink.

"Friends of the Romans. I think you'll like them. They have a daughter your age named Charlotte." She paused for a moment. "For lunch, you'll need to wear a nice dress," she said, moving on with her list. "No jeans," she added, pointing to the well-worn ones I had on. It was her least favorite pair, which gave me all the more reason to wear them.

"Lunch will be at the English Teahouse and we need to leave here by eleven-thirty. Thank goodness our cars will arrive tomorrow and I'll be able to drive myself around. Dinner will require a cocktail dress. We're having dinner at the

Watsons'," she continued, as she jotted down a few more notes.

Ugh, another dinner party and we'd only been in town for two days!

Mother went silent, lost in her own little world, and I quietly got up from the table. "I guess I better get a move on and get ready for lunch," I said, hoping she would excuse me before she found something else to add to her list.

She went back to her notepad, a serious look on her face. After a pause, she waved me away, and as quick as lightning, I was out of the room. I scampered up the stairs and back to my bedroom. I changed into a pale pink dress Grandmother Livingston had bought for me, because she said I always looked like a rag doll when she visited.

I pulled out a pair of pearl earrings and a matching strand to wind around my wrist. I put on a pair of light pink heels, which my grandmother had also purchased for me, and left my room. I went downstairs to the living room to wait for Mother. I sat on the hunter green sofa that faced the giant fireplace and the questionable painting I had examined the day before. I was clueless as to what the connection could be between Cal, his family, the word "Kythera" on the car, and the matching paintings. But I was going to make it my mission to find out.

Mother entered the room in a dark green silk dress with a matching jacket and heels. Her hair was pulled up in a graceful bun, and she had on minimal makeup. She looked like a modern day Audrey Hepburn.

"Are you ready?" she asked, pulling out a cosmetic mirror to check her lipstick.

"I'm ready as I'll ever be."

The lunch went better than expected, with only a few over-exaggerated hugs and air kisses. Everyone welcomed us genteelly to their little society. After eating tiny sandwiches and sipping tea, we left in a flurry of hugs and goodbye kisses. I sighed in relief that I had survived the event relatively unscathed.

The rest of the afternoon was devoted to unpacking, moving out furniture and replacing it with the more contemporary pieces mother preferred. I decided to keep all the furniture in my bedroom, more out of the fact I had no desire to direct the moving men than really liking it.

Six-thirty on the dot, we were in the Town Car, being chauffeured to the Watsons' home. Once again, it was a short trip. The Watsons only lived a couple of blocks from us, in the opposite direction of Cal. The car pulled up to a large, yellow brick home. It was square, without any porches, and spindly evergreen trees jutted up between the windows. It looked like a house straight out of the Italian countryside.

We got out of the car and walked up the front steps to the glass front door. Within seconds, a butler answered the door and invited us into the foyer. As we stepped in, I took in the pleasant but strong smells of butter and onions. The foyer was a warm yellow color, not much different from the outside. A petite chandelier glistened above our heads, sparkling light onto the walls and the warm brown wood floor.

Seconds later, a loud bark sounded from the winding staircase in front of us. A large, fluffy St. Bernard ran down the stairs in our direction. I looked at my mother, who hates all dogs and cats. She looked nervous, shielding the front of her dress with her hands.

"Down, Rupert!" said a deep Southern voice. I looked up to the stairs again to see an older man slowly making his way down the stairs. Rupert, the St. Bernard, came to a halt in front of me and sat down. I put out my hand and rubbed Rupert's head.

"Stop that. You'll get fur all over your black dress," Mother commanded.

The man pushed the dog aside. "Run along, Rupert, these nice people don't want your slobber all over them." The dog obeyed with a great push from the man's hand.

He was a pleasantly round man of short stature, with an equally round, cherubic face. His hair was almost white, with tufts of blonde around the temples. His eyes disappeared into the folds of his cheeks as he smiled. If he had had a flowing white beard, I would have sworn he was Santa Claus.

"Hello, friends," he said in a booming voice. His demeanor was cheery and he laughed a little after his greeting.

"Hello, Mr. Watson, nice to see you again," my

dad responded, reaching his hand out to shake the much shorter man's hand. Mr. Watson grabbed it full force and shook it vigorously, letting out another jolly laugh.

"Welcome to my home! If you will follow me into the dining room, we'll get this little party started."

The room was warm and the butter and onion smell intensified. The long dining room table was occupied by three younger women. They all stood up as we entered the room.

"You remember my wife, Kelly."

The woman extended her hand across the table to us. She was a petite woman, with bright red hair and freckles across her rosy cheeks. Her eyes were a tawny color that complemented her peaches and cream complexion. She was much younger than Mr. Santa Claus and almost looked like she could be his daughter.

The woman looked at me. "This must be Casper?" she said, directing her question to Dad. He nodded in agreement. "You are a striking young lady. I'm sorry we didn't get to meet you last night," she said in a slow Southern drawl.

"Thank you," I responded meekly.

"Casper, these are my daughters, Charlotte and Eliza. Charlotte's your age. You'll be going to school together," she said warmly.

I looked over at the two girls who had sat back down. They looked like identical twins, except one was a miniature version of the other. Eliza looked to only be about ten years old. They both had wavy strawberry blonde hair, freckles across their cheeks, and dark chocolate eyes.

"Hello, Casper, nice to meet you," said Charlotte excitedly.

"Hello, nice to meet you, too." I sat down at one of the empty seats.

Charlotte got up from her seat and pushed her little sister out of her chair so she could sit next to me. Eliza scrunched her face, annoyed at her big sister. Charlotte ignored her and sat down anyway.

Charlotte had on a tight green dress that hugged her every curve and pushed her boobs forward as she sat down. She had a voluptuous figure that most girls would kill for, including me. She reminded me of Scarlett Johansson. I felt a little depressed as I thought about my own straight hips and small chest.

"I hope you like it here," she said, staring at me as if she was scrutinizing every inch of me.

"Hope so," I said self-consciously.

She finally tore her eyes away from me long enough to pick up a glass of water and take a sip. "I'm sorry I didn't get to meet you yesterday. Your parents said you were with Cal." She lifted her blonde eyebrows and a mischievous smile formed on her full lips.

She was acting like Mother had earlier this morning. Why did everyone think there was something going on with Cal? *Seriously, people, I just met him yesterday.*

"Yes, he kind of kidnapped me," I responded, picking up the glass of water the butler had sat down in front of me.

Charlotte turned back toward me. "Well, I would let him kidnap me anytime." She picked up a piece of bread from a basket in the middle of the table and shoved it into her mouth. "He's super gorgeous," she added, the bread still in her mouth.

"He is." It was an undeniable truth. "What's his story?"

She put the roll down and looked back at me with so much energy. She was bursting with excitement at the thought of getting to gossip. I made a mental note to never tell her any deep, dark secrets.

"Cal's a great guy, a real Romeo. He makes all the girls swoon, but you've got to be a little careful around him. He's reserved. He holds a lot back; he's not the typical playboy."

Eliza tilted her head in our direction. "Are y'all talking about Cal?"

Charlotte pushed against her little sister, trying to block her from my view. Eliza pushed back. "He's really cute," she managed to get out before Charlotte pushed her toward the other end of the table. I couldn't help but smile. As an only child, I'm pretty sure I missed out on something pretty special.

"How well do you know him?" I asked, trying to get back to the topic.

"Very well, we're pretty close friends." She lifted up her glass of water—and before it touched her lips again, she abruptly put it back down. "Don't let what I just said scare you off. He's a wonderful guy. He's just a little mysterious, which seems to drive the girls completely nuts. Just know you have a lot of competition." She pointed a perfectly manicured nail toward me.

"I'm not worried about any competition, because I'm not interested in him—at least, not like that." I didn't look at Charlotte, because I was trying to convince myself to believe what I was saying.

"Sure," she said with another mischievous smile.

A maid came around the table and sat salads in front of everyone. I picked up my fork and dug in.

"We should hang out or something. Do you like to shop?" she asked, turning her head sideways like an inquisitive parrot.

"Yes, of course," I said sarcastically.

"Okay, we'll go shopping then. The mall is really great here. How about Friday?" She turned her attention back to the bread basket and picked up a wheat roll.

"Sure," I said, squeezing a little lemon into my water. I wasn't really thrilled, but I had to find something to get me out of the house. Maybe I could learn to like shopping. I took a drink of the lemony water.

"You like Cal, don't you?" Charlotte said abruptly, causing me to choke on the water I had just gulped.

"What makes you say that?" I picked up the linen napkin in my lap and dabbed at my mouth.

"I can tell. Don't worry. I'm sure he likes you,

too." She gave me another sideways glance. I was at a loss for words . . . for a moment.

"I don't like him. I mean, I do, but not like that. How could I? I just met him *yesterday*." She must not have been listening to what I said earlier, because obviously it wasn't getting through to her pretty, strawberry blonde head.

"Cal's charm works fast . . ." She paused for a second. "Like a good bottle of champagne. He doesn't waste time. If there's something he wants, he goes for it," she answered.

I was stunned. I put down my fork. "What makes you think he wants me?" I stared at her. I was more curious than offended at this point.

"Why wouldn't he?" She turned to look at me again, sweeping her eyes from the floor back up to my face. "Look at you. You're gorgeous and sweet. Why wouldn't he?" she said repetitiously, as if she were trying to drive that point home.

I began stuttering. "I . . . I'm not that sweet or gorgeous, really," I said, but the conversation abruptly stopped as another servant came in and placed more food in front of us.

I looked back at Charlotte, her attention on the cute servant guy with the blond hair and chiseled cheeks. She winked at him as he placed her food in front of her. The conversation about Cal abruptly ended.

We spent the rest of the evening chatting about girly things, like where to buy the best shoes, where to sit in the cafeteria, and who to avoid. I steered the conversation away from Cal as much as possible. Charlotte didn't bring him back up either . . . until the end of the night.

"Casper, seriously, give him a chance," she said, turning her warm chocolate eyes on me. They were almost pleading, as if she had some stake in whether I saw Cal as anything more than a friend or an annoyance.

"Charlotte, I just . . . it's not me to fall so quickly," I said, as we all stood up to say our goodbyes.

"Oh, well, then you've never been in love." She was *way* too mature to be seventeen.

She was right, though; I had never been in love. I had just dated the guys my parents had picked out for me and none of them had even given me any of the same feelings that Cal did that first night. Suddenly, I began to tingle all over when I thought about his lips on my cheek. I shook my head, trying to shake the image of Cal on my front doorstep out for good.

"He's a friend, nothing more," I said, with a measure of determination in my voice.

Charlotte looked at me, smiling mischievously, "Of course."

My parents were already leaving the table and I turned to say my goodbyes to the rest of Charlotte's family, who I hadn't spoken more than two words to the entire time. They smiled at me, and Mrs. Watson even gave me a hug. They were the poster family for Southern hospitality.

I followed my parents out of their home into the steamy night air and into the awaiting Town Car. I sighed heavily as I sat down, staring out the window as the cityscape flew by once again.

"I think Casper made a new friend tonight," I heard Dad say to Mother. I looked in his direction and, for the first time since I found out we were moving, I think I actually smiled at him.

"Yes, I think I did," I responded, and returned my gaze to the window.

The rest of the ride home was spent in silence. I had so much to think about. Charlotte was a genuinely sweet person, but she was hiding something—just like the Roman family seemed to be. Why did she have such an interest in how I felt about Cal? There was urgency to her words, as if she'd been sent to be a salesman on his behalf. They were friends, so I guess it was possible. She was a gossip, there was no doubt about that, so maybe she was reporting back to him my reactions.

I smiled to myself. Thankfully, I had said nothing that would later embarrass me. Cal was used to getting his way and dealing with bimbos who drooled at his every word. *That's not me, Cal.* He was going to have to try a lot harder than that.

Chapter

5

THE NEXT MORNING, I MARCHED down the dark hallway of the third floor and into an equally dark room at the end of the hall. I flipped the light switch and the room was immediately lit with a soft orange glow from the antique chandelier. A set of large windows were covered by heavy, burnt orange curtains, making the room very dark. A humongous ornate desk sat in the middle of the room, with a large Tiffany lamp and a computer monitor on top of it. I walked over to the desk and sat down in the chair positioned behind the desk. It was obvious that it was meant more for looks than for actual sitting.

With a huff, I pulled one of the wing chairs

near the windows up behind the desk and pushed the painful excuse for a chair to the side. I turned the computer on, waited for it to boot up, clicked on the browser icon and crossed my fingers. I'd tried the internet on my laptop, but the house must not have a wireless connection set up yet.

To my delight, seconds later the home page appeared and I stared for a minute. What should I look up first? I typed the word "Kythera" into the search engine.

Several things popped up and I clicked on the first entry. It led me to an encyclopedia page for a Greek island named Kythera, with multiple spellings, including Cythera or Kythira (in Italian called Cerigo).

Historically, it had significance to Greek mythology according to the website. Kythera was known as the island of Aphrodite, the Goddess of Love. On the left-hand side of the screen was a miniature version of the painting in our living room. I clicked on it and was met with a quote:

Kythera, an exotic place, once discovered can never be forgotten.

Interesting, but not very useful.

A split-second later, I clicked back to the main page. The rest of the information concerned demographics, and other details that I was sure were not important to my search. Another site referred to Kythera as the *other* island of Aphrodite, but I wasn't interested in that controversy.

I typed into Google the words "Kythera

painting." The first reference link took me to a page with a photo of the painting. So, I concluded the name had some significance to the Romans. But what kind of significance could it hold? Did they own the island, or did the name itself have a meaning? Those were just a few of the questions floating in my mind.

Maybe it is a favorite place for the Romans' vacations, I thought. Then again, I didn't have my favorite vacation spot on display in my house and etched on my car, nor would seeing the name of my favorite place, Buenos Aires, cause a policeman to stutter like an idiot. Besides, why wouldn't he have mentioned that detail when we were looking at the painting?

I clicked back to the search engine and started over again by putting in the words "Kythera, Charleston, South Carolina." I pressed enter and waited. I got only one hit that included all the words in my search. I clicked on the link titled "What's Kythera Hiding?" It looked like a link to an article in a local newspaper, but the page defaulted and said that it was no longer available. If I were more computer savvy I could probably find it using some amazingly cool technique, but I wasn't. It was a side effect of spending every free moment with the horses. They didn't need me to use the internet or an App. There were no other links that met my criteria.

So the information that I gleaned from my search was that Kythera referred to an island in Greece concerned with Greek mythology and with the paintings in the house. The search of the word in Charleston I was simply met with the question "What's Kythera Hiding?" So whatever or whoever Kythera referred to, they didn't want anyone to know their affiliation. Then again, how secret could it be if it was plastered all over a vehicle and the police recognized it?

Instead of coming up with any answers, my search only left me with more questions. I was beyond frustrated as I tried to put the puzzle together in my mind. Aggravated, I turned the computer off and went downstairs.

I found Mother directing one of the burly moving men into the living room with a Chinese vase in his hands. There were several other men bringing in boxes and taking out the furniture she didn't want. She looked like her hands were full and I did not want her to see me. I didn't want to be forced into helping, so I walked briskly down the hall to the kitchen.

The chef was beginning preparations for lunch by cutting up some fresh vegetables and placing them in a skillet. I had no idea how he kept from slicing a finger off, but he seemed at ease with the sharp knife in his hand. I smiled at him, returned his greeting, and walked toward the family room. No one was there, so I decided to watch some TV. I clicked through the channels until I found one of my favorite shows, *NCIS*. I sat down, happy to pass the rest of the morning away engulfed in the numerous reruns of the show that ran back to back.

After lunch, I found myself listless and bored.

There wasn't anything to do at home, and I had no idea what there was to do in this town. I had only seen small glimpses of the area and I wasn't comfortable enough to drive around. There was no way I was getting the driver to take me anywhere. It was hard enough to shake the snobby rich girl persona when I was driving a new Mercedes or Porsche, but having a driver just made the problem worse.

I wandered around the house a little longer, finally reaching the front porch. The air was a little less oppressive than it had been the day before. It was actually comfortable, with a slight breeze flowing up from the harbor. I remembered Dad mentioning a garden or park being around here. I rushed back inside looking for Dad. I was sure he was in the library or the office, working on the computer or texting on his cell phone. He was always working and today would be no exception. I tried the library first, and found him sitting on the leather loveseat with his laptop perched on his knees. He was concentrating all his energy into typing at a frantic pace.

"Hey, Dad," I said happily. He pecked on the keyboard for a few more seconds before looking up.

"Hey, Casper, how's it going?" he responded, then returned to his typing.

I fell back onto one of the wing chairs and breathed out heavily. He looked up at me and smiled, still distracted by the computer.

"Things are okay. I'm a little bored. You mentioned the other day that there's some garden or park near here?" I asked, fiddling with one of the loose red threads on the arm of the chair.

He finished what he was typing and looked up at me again. "Yes, White Point Gardens. It's right across the street," he said, nodding his head. His cell phone rang and I knew that was my cue to leave. When had he become so busy? In the past, he would have taken the afternoon off to go to the park with me.

"Just let your mother know where you've gone," he called out as I walked out of the room.

Great, that means she will try to get me to help her with something.

I was determined to make it by her and out of the house with as few words as possible. I passed her and then called out, "Off to the park, Mother," and walked out the open front door. I glanced behind me. She simply threw up her hand and waved. That was too easy.

I walked down the short driveway and to the sidewalk. There was minimal traffic, so I strolled across the street and into the park, which was also pretty quiet. Only a few people were walking around the park, which was full of giant oak trees, and more of the Spanish moss that I was trying to get used to seeing dripping from everything. Among the trees was a pretty white gazebo. I walked around it and headed toward the edge of the harbor.

I crossed another street and onto a boardwalk, which encircled the park. I stood for a few minutes staring out into the peaceful water, breathing in the heavy air. I leaned against the thin rail and looked over into the murky water. I couldn't see anything, but golden sediment floating away to the ocean. It wasn't the prettiest body of water I had ever seen.

A little sadness crept into my consciousness as I studied my new surroundings. I felt like I was swimming out in the vast, murky water, treading hard to keep my head above the lazy waves. I wasn't used to feeling so isolated, or out of control. My fate was in the hands of the water currents, or at the mercy of a passing boater. I needed to be in control, because it was the only way I could trust the outcome. Whether what transpired was good or bad, I could trace it back to one source, and that was comforting to me.

Here, that comfort was all but gone. I was in a strange city at the mercy of my parents' decisions, and the decisions of strangers who I couldn't completely figure out.

"Hey, Casper."

I turned around to see Cal standing behind me. A smile engulfed his handsome face.

"Hey." I leaned my back against the railing. "Trying to add to your criminal record?"

His face scrunched up in confusion. "Huh?"

"Well, you're already a kidnapper and speed demon; now you're adding stalker to the list."

He pointed toward the street. "I just live around the corner, you know, but I can stalk you if you want."

I couldn't help but stare at his hypnotic blue eyes.

"Well, stalking is a little creepy, unless you're a gorgeous vampire looking to make me your only reason for living," I responded.

"There are so many contradictions in that statement, I'm not even going to try to understand. What in the world are you talking about?" he asked, honest confusion showing on his face.

"You've never read *Twilight?*" I leaned up from the rail, and crossed my arms against my chest.

"Are you kidding me? Do I look like a lovesick teenage girl to you?" He laughed and his dimples danced at the corners of his lips. "Because if I do, then I have bigger issues than I ever thought."

I felt my cheeks flush. "No, but, I mean, everyone has at least heard of it. Vampires are the craze now; you don't watch TV?" I was a tiny bit offended.

I didn't consider myself a lovesick teenager, but I loved the books and Edward Cullen. Admittedly, I had a small poster of him in the far corner of my bedroom—out of view—*and* a Team Edward T-shirt, but that had been a gift from a friend. And, of course, I had the pillow case. Okay, maybe I was a lovesick teenager.

"Sure, but I'm not actually paying attention to the—as you put it—'gorgeous vampires' . . . unless they're female. Even then, I prefer my love interests breathing. I don't find anything sexy about being undead," he said indignantly.

"Hey, I think living forever and never aging is pretty hot," I said flatly.

"Anyways, I'm not a stalker, I promise," he said, putting a hand over his heart.

"I don't know that I believe you. There are so many strange things about you." I turned back around toward the water. Cal walked over to the rail next to me and placed his elbows against the rail.

"Like?" He turned his face to mine.

"You read up about me, you kidnapped me..."

"Wait, you were a willing participant there. I was saving you from our parents. That doesn't count," he interjected.

"Fine. You have mysterious ways with cops," I continued.

"So?" He shrugged his shoulders "Shouldn't that make the cops strange, not me?"

I sighed, and I felt myself becoming more annoyed with his smart answers.

"Ugh, so you have a point," I conceded and met his gaze.

He looked like he belonged in an ad for some fancy men's clothing line. He was wearing a pair of dark jeans, an untucked gray dress shirt, and a shiny Rolex on his wrist. Not to mention his face was perfect enough for the ad, too. Who got so dressed up for a walk in the park? He had more in common with a particular vampire than he realized.

I thought about myself, in a pair of torn, faded jeans and brown T-shirt. My hair was being less than tame in the humidity, curling wildly around my face. I didn't have any makeup on, except a touch of mascara. I suddenly felt inadequate standing next to him.

"But it's your car that made the cop act strange—why's Kythera written on the side of it?" I glared in his direction and waited for another profound answer.

He looked back at the water. "It's one of my parents' companies."

I stared at him, not sure if he was telling the truth. Kythera had come up as an organization in my internet search, but with so little information, I had no idea if it was owned by the Romans.

"Why would seeing a company name make a cop do a one-eighty?"

He touched my shoulder. A warm, tingly sensation traveled through my body. I sucked in a quick breath.

"Hey, you want to go out with me sometime?" A brush of coral stained his chiseled cheekbones. He was gorgeous in every aspect at that moment.

"Uh, you're evading my question . . . but sure," was all I could say.

"What about Friday?" He reached over and put his hand on mine. I stood motionless and my heart skipped a couple of beats.

"Okay," I said. He dropped his hand to his side. I wished he would have let it linger a little longer.

"I'll pick you up around seven?" he suggested.

"Sure."

"See you then; hopefully you'll regain your ability to talk." He started walking away from the harbor.

I suddenly snapped out of his spell, when it finally registered what he had just said.

"You think you're so cool don't you?" I started walking toward the street as well.

"I don't think . . . I know I am. Why else would someone like you agree to go out with me?"

We stood a few feet apart as we waited to cross the busy street. After a car passed by, he walked across the street.

"You *are* a jerk!" I shouted from the other side of the street.

"Then you must have a thing for jerks. See you Friday!"

And before I could say anything else, he disappeared around the block.

~ * * * ~

When I returned to the house, Mother was still standing in the exact same spot, waving her hands wildly. I felt the tension emanating from the chaotic scene in the foyer.

"I didn't say that I wanted the credenza in the living room. I wanted it in the dining room on the opposite wall from the china cabinet. Who puts a credenza in the living room? Could you please have someone move it again?" she said her voice raising an octave as she spoke.

She kept pointing down the hall toward the dining room as an exaggerated gesture. The short, muscular man nodded his head, but kept a steady frown on his face. Obviously, he wasn't too thrilled to be working with my mother. *Join the club, buddy.* Mother wasn't well-liked by many people in the service industry. She lacked a sensitivity that was essential to working with other people, which rendered her a complete pain in the butt to anyone who had decided to work for her. Most people instantly regretted their decision, no matter how much she had paid them in advance.

I picked up a box, raising it to my shoulders, and scooted by her. I hoped she would mistake me for one of the movers and I could walk peacefully up the stairs and to my room.

"Wait right there, Casper Isadora." It was never a good sign if she used my middle name. I turned around and looked at her anxiously.

"Yes?"

"I need your help this afternoon, since these men seem incapable of taking directions. I can't believe the realtor recommended them."

The tall, lanky man who had just entered the living room gave my mother a stern look, and muttered something under his breath.

"I'm not really any good at placing furniture," I said desperately. I had no desire to stand around the rest of the day, directing the movers to and fro as if they were incapable of "moving" furniture.

She looked at me suspiciously. Her lips were pursed, and she tapped her foot at a steady pace. "All I need you to do is make sure they don't scuff the floors, or damage the furniture. I tell them where to put it. Please help me," she said, pleading with her blue-gray eyes.

I exhaled slowly as I contemplated my options . . . which were *none*, if I wanted any peace. "Sure," I said, half smiling.

Her face instantly lightened up and her tiny mouth smiled widely. I could only muster a half of a frown.

I begrudgingly went to the third floor, trudging my feet against each step to watch the moving men do what they did best: move furniture. *How fun.*

I entered the bedroom at the top of the third floor, which had navy wallpaper with a toile design. I was beginning to get dizzy staring at the explosion of toile that engulfed the room. I found a small stool—that, to my shock, was only covered in a plain white fabric—to perch on and "watch" the moving men. Two men came in with a giant dresser. After several deep breaths, they put it down very carefully in the corner near a window. The wiry little man with the bald head took a rag out of his pants pocket and rubbed the sweat from his face. They went over to the large antique dresser that had come with the house and placed it onto sliding pads and slid it out of the room to make room for our own furniture.

As I watched them leave the room, I noticed a piece of paper on the floor where the dresser had been. I walked over and picked it up. It was yellow and brittle. I unfolded the paper carefully and read the messy writing:

Let's meet in Greece and sail to exotic places.
K&

I stared at the crinkled paper and the red ink. "K&." It had to be related to the painting and Cal's car. It had to be related to Kythera. But what in the world could it mean?

I folded the paper back up, put it in my front pocket, and walked out of the room. I thought about going back to the computer to look up the phrase, but something told me that would only aggravate me. I knew I wouldn't find anything. I was going to have to do some more digging outside of the internet, maybe talk to neighbors—or the library was a thought.

"Miss, where does this one go?" asked one of the moving men. He had a large oil painting of the family's first Triple Crown Winner, Casper the Friendly Ghost.

"Oh, um, I think the second door on the right," I responded absently.

Although I hated the task I had been assigned, I was comforted by the arrival of the furnishings that were so familiar to me. The house felt less alien and more like home. Pieces of Kentucky drifted in all afternoon, until just before dinner.

The moving men rushed out of the house wordlessly, happy to not be serving my mother. I was happy to no longer be in her servitude as well, and could only dream of hopping in the moving truck and finding my way back to everything I had left.

~ * * * ~

The next couple of days flew by with little excitement. The moving fiasco continued, with an influx of interior designers who were hired and subsequently fired by Mother. She finally settled on one who was so terrified of her that she simply let Mother pick everything, while she did all the work.

Dad had disappeared, into his world of never-ending work. Dad had always been busy managing the farm, meetings with stockholders in our other companies, and conference calls with employees. But now it felt like he never had a moment free. I had tried to ask Dad what this new business venture entailed, but he had given me some non-descript answer that hadn't explained anything to me. I had shrugged my shoulders and given up on finding out what he was doing. After my unproductive talk with Dad, I had asked Mother about the business, but she seemed as clueless as I was, which made everything even stranger.

I may not always know what's going on in our family business, but Mother always knew everything. She normally refused to be out of the loop and it was uncharacteristic for Dad to have left her in the dark.

I was hoping that maybe Cal could shed some light on the issue. I would see him Friday. I thought about our date and I felt myself become weirdly giddy. I tried to control my excitement, reminding myself once again about all the things I still didn't know about him. But the thoughts about Cal were becoming increasingly difficult to control.

Friday afternoon finally rolled around, and I was happy for the distraction that Charlotte was sure to provide. Charlotte didn't disappoint. She dragged me from store to store, and I had no time to think about Cal or anything besides Gucci, Prada, and Brian Atwood.

I looked at my watch and realized it was almost six o'clock. I was supposed to meet Cal at seven at my house. I stood in line with Charlotte as she paid for her mountain of purchases.

"There's one more store I would like to go to, if that's okay with you?" Charlotte asked, as she handed the cashier her credit card.

"Sure, as long as I'm done by six-thirty." I had failed to mention my date with Cal.

Charlotte signed her name and handed the receipt back to the cashier. She looked at me questioningly. "Have a dinner with your parents tonight?"

"No." I picked up my bags and started walking toward the exit. I rearranged a couple of the shopping bags in my hand trying to avoid her obtrusive gaze.

"Oh, your mother has you helping her?" She picked up her bags and we walked out of the store.

Charlotte was very smart—or, at the very least, super nosy. She knew what I had planned wasn't really any of her business, so she wasn't willing to ask me outright what I was doing. Instead, we were going to play twenty questions, until she either guessed correctly or I finally gave up.

"No," I answered smiling. The game was kind of fun.

"Then all I can think of, since you're new in town, is that you must have a date," she proclaimed, her voice oozing with excitement.

"Yes, but I don't know if I would really classify it as a date. We're going somewhere just as friends," I clarified.

"It's Cal, isn't it?" Her voice went higher, which I hadn't thought was possible at this point. She jostled the shopping bags in her hand as she shook with excitement.

I scrunched my face, not wanting to confirm what she already knew. I nodded and waited for her enthusiasm to spring at me like a happy golden retriever. She stopped in mid-stride, dropped her bags, and grabbed my hand. Fortunately, she didn't start jumping up and down, but she did a little dance that made me think of Christmas elves for some reason.

"I knew it. So, where are you going?"

"Don't really know. It's really no big deal," I answered in an even tone. I didn't want to seem like a silly girl who was giddy over anything and everything, especially an egomaniac guy.

Charlotte looked at me with disdain. "Come on, it is a big deal. I was right, and you should be thrilled," she gushed.

"He's a nice guy that I would love to count as

a friend. It was a friendly invite. He wants me to feel more comfortable being the new girl in town," I explained. I began walking again, hoping to make it to the other store. Charlotte picked up her bags and scooted forward to catch up with me.

"I think you're thrilled, you're just too stubborn to admit it," she said nudging me with one of her bags. She was right.

"I just don't want to get my hopes up. Like I said at dinner, we've just met and it's crazy to think that he likes me from the couple of times I've seen him," I responded—and then breathlessly added, "or that I would like him."

Charlotte walked into the Plaid Poodle, the clothing store she was hoping to shop in, but she didn't pay any attention to the racks of trendy clothes. She was too busy analyzing me. "If you like someone, you don't need to figure them out, you just *know* you like them. You know?" She tilted her head to the side in that parrot-like way she had, and she waited for me to say something.

"I don't believe in love at first sight. That's ridiculous; it's lust at first sight at most," I said throwing my chin in the air.

"Oh, honey." She put her hand over her mouth in an effort to stifle her laughter. "You really have no clue do you?" She gave another pitiful nod toward me. "Love is the most irrational thing in the world. It's not something you can analyze, pull apart, and find logic in. If it were, then it would be less magical, less mysterious. It wouldn't be the stuff of legends, and Romeo would have never killed himself for it."

"He didn't because he's a fictional character," I quipped.

"But you know what I mean," she said, rolling her eyes.

"How did this turn into a story about love at first sight in the first place? We were debating whether or not he liked me as a friend or more. Haven't we totally jumped off track here?" I said, a little annoyance showing on my face.

Instantly, her complexion turned warm red and she bit her lip. Once again, she looked as if she had said too much.

"I don't know, I was just saying," she retorted, with some annoyance splicing her words.

This wasn't making any more sense than anything else I had discovered in this town. I started to wonder if the mysteries were ever going to end.

My cell phone rang, forcing me to throw my bags on the ground in order to fish it from my back pocket. "Hello?"

"Hey, Casper," the familiar voice said. It was Cal and I did everything possible to control my facial expressions. Charlotte didn't need any more encouragement.

"Hey," I said calmly. I looked over at Charlotte, who was studying a short black dress she had pulled from the rack. A sales clerk appeared and Charlotte handed the dress, along with another armful of clothes to the woman, before moving to another rack.

"So, listen, I hate to do this—"

Before he finished the sentence I felt my heart drop into my stomach.

"—something has come up and I can't go out tonight. I've got some business to take care of," he said, regret flooding his voice. I looked at the slick concrete floor to avoid any gaze from Charlotte or anyone else in the store.

"Oh, okay." I was sure that he could hear the disappointment in my voice. I looked around for Charlotte. She had disappeared into the dressing room. I started walking to the back of the store to find her.

"I feel terrible about this. But I'll make it up to you, I promise," he said sincerely.

"Yeah, it's fine. I understand." I forced myself to sound more cheerful than I felt.

"Okay. And I'll give you a call soon."

"Sure."

"Bye, Casper."

"Bye." I clicked the phone shut and sighed heavily, trying to regain my composure before stepping into the dressing rooms.

I plastered a smile on my face as I walked in. Charlotte was in front of the mirrors, studying her figure in a pretty, pale pink chiffon dress. She was holding her strawberry blonde hair up, twisting around so she could get glimpse of the back of the dress. She didn't notice me as she studied her reflection.

I was about to speak when I noticed something on her back. Scrawled in beautiful black script across her right shoulder blade was the word "Kythera." I felt my mouth drop open. "Kythera" seemed to be showing up everywhere, a word until I had moved to Charleston, I had never heard of.

The sales clerk had walked in a few seconds after me and had glimpsed the tattoo as well. But her reaction was radically different from mine. She had audibly gasped, but then became very attentive.

"Ms. Watson, can I get you anything?" she said breathlessly, as if she were saving a life instead of getting clothes. I gave the girl a curious look. She was acting like the cop had the other night with Cal.

Charlotte looked at me in the mirror, and she could see the odd expression on my face. She immediately dropped her hair, covering the tattoo.

"Hey, I thought you were still on the phone?" she asked, ignoring the sales clerk, who had started picking up the clothes that Charlotte had left on the ground. Her face slowly turned rosy red.

"I just came in," I said slowly, as I tried to understand what I had just seen.

"Was it Cal?" she asked, as she stepped off the platform in front of the mirrors.

"I didn't take you as the type to have a tattoo," I stated, ignoring her question. She had disappeared into the dressing room and I could hear her rustling through the clothes. Plastic hangers clattered to the floor.

"It was on a dare. I really didn't know what I was doing," she said nervously.

"What does it mean?"

"It's an island somewhere in Greece."

"Why Kythera?"

Another clattering of hangers fell to the floor and I thought I could hear her mumbling under her breath.

"I was in Greece when I got it. Some of the local boys—who were gorgeous, by the way—dared me to get it. Something about Aphrodite and it being her island or something like that. I don't really remember now." She reappeared from the dressing room, several garments slung over her arms.

The sales clerk rushed to take them from her and took the items to the cash register. Once again, Charlotte didn't seem to notice what I thought was the girl's totally bizarre behavior. She kept her gaze from mine as we followed the sales clerk to the cash register.

"Our house and Cal's each have a painting named after that island," I stated.

Charlotte only glanced in my direction, before rummaging in her purse.

"Really? I haven't even paid that much attention at Cal's and I've never been to your house. That's an interesting coincidence."

I didn't believe her. I wasn't convinced it was a coincidence at all.

"So, what's with the island? Is Kythera special or something?" I asked, leaning against the counter. Charlotte started pouring the contents of her purse out on the counter, rummaging through some gum wrappers, lipstick, and a gold compact.

"Nothing, really. A favorite vacation spot . . . that's all," she said curtly.

"Oh, is it a really nice place?"

"Yeah, sure." From her wad of receipts, she finally pulled out her credit card.

I was about to ask her another question when the girl behind the counter shook her head. "Ms. Watson, I've been instructed not to take your card. The clothes are yours to keep as a gift from the store, according to my manager."

"Oh, thank you," Charlotte responded, taking the bags from the girl without questioning the decision.

I had never had any store give me anything for free and I knew for a fact that the Watsons didn't own this boutique. I didn't think any store gave anything away for free unless the person owned the store or they were a celebrity.

"Are you an actress or something?" I asked, unable to contain my curiosity.

"What?" She looked at me quizzically.

"You have to be an actress or some kind of celebrity for a store to just *give* you clothes."

"Oh, that. No, I'm not. My mom is friends with the owner or something like that," she said in a noncommittal tone.

We walked out of the store silently. The tension was palpable between us. After a few seconds, I decided to let the whole thing go for now. I knew this wasn't the time to argue about it, because I wouldn't get anywhere. Besides, I didn't want to alienate the one of only two friends I had made so far.

"So, you never answered my question. Was that Cal on the phone?" She instantly perked up, breathing easier now that she was shifting the focus away from her.

"Yes, it was. Something came up, so we're not going out," I said calmly.

"Oh, that sucks. I'm sure you're bummed." Her voice was full of empathy.

"It's not a big deal, really." I smiled, but she looked at me doubtfully.

She sighed deeply. "Why can't you admit it bothers you just a little?"

"Because, it doesn't bother me that much. I'll see him again, I'm sure." We reached her black BMW and I waited for her to pop the trunk.

As she searched in her purse for the key, once again I was awestruck by what I was seeing. The numbers were missing on her vehicle and a bright red "K" was in their place. I knew I didn't have to look on the driver's side to confirm what else I was sure was there. Kythera would be plastered in red script above the wheel. I felt uneasy again. Somehow I knew Charlotte, Cal, and Kythera were connected—beyond it being some awesome vacation spot.

"I know you will," she said hopefully, winking at me as she unlocked the car.

The rest of the ride home was pretty quiet. She described a few more details about her high school and promised to introduce me to everyone

I needed to meet. Charlotte was such a sweet and bubbly person, it made it hard for me to not trust her. I felt bad for doubting the one person who had genuinely been nice to me and seemed really eager to have me as a friend, but I couldn't shake the feeling something was off.

Charlotte pulled into the driveway and she helped me bring my shopping bags in through the front door. She gave me a quick hug, promising that she would call later to set up another girls' event—this time with some of her other friends.

I thanked her for the shopping trip and walked into my house, still mystified by the strange day.

Chapter

6

AFTER PUTTING AWAY THE RED blouse and blue jeans I had purchased, I threw myself on my bed. I lay perfectly still and stared at the intricate molding on the ceiling. I needed to find a way to get more information about Kythera, but I knew for a fact I couldn't go to Cal or Charlotte. The internet had left me empty-handed, so how else could I research the issue?

I could spy, I thought—but I quickly realized I had no idea what I would be spying *for*, not to mention I had no experience as a secret agent. Besides, if I were caught, I would look like a total psycho.

There had to be more information about this

group, company, or whatever it was—somewhere. Like a newspaper article or some local magazine. Then it hit me: I needed to find the public library. I could go through the old newspaper articles till I found some sort of details. I was sure there would be some information of interest there, because everyone around me seemed to know what Kythera was when they saw it. To me, that meant that there had to be information available *somewhere*.

I ran downstairs to the kitchen, in hopes of finding someone who could tell me where the car keys were located. As I walked into the kitchen, the chef was busy cleaning a set of very big knives, and the maid was loading the dishes into the dishwasher.

Luck was with me tonight. I was almost positive that the maid would know where the keys were. This meant I could avoid asking my mother and enduring her barrage of questions that would surely follow.

"Miss . . ." I went blank on her name. The petite woman looked up at me, her pale cheeks glowing.

"Christina," she said in a meek voice.

"Christina, do you know where the keys to the vehicles might be?" I asked.

She looked away for a minute, almost panicked and her pink lips dipped into a frown.

"No, miss, I'm sorry, but I don't know. I can find out if you like," she said in a hurry.

"They're in the pantry," I heard my mother's voice calling from the family room. I sighed and entered the room.

She was sitting on the couch, very prim and proper in a blue silk pantsuit, watching the news. She must have been on her way out the door to some country club function or dinner party. *No,* I thought, *she's already been or she wouldn't be sitting on the couch.* It might wrinkle her pressed suit.

"Thanks," I muttered, and moved like lightning out of the room.

"Casper," she called, and I reluctantly turned back around.

"Yes?"

"Where are you going? Do you really think you're going anywhere without telling me?" She turned her beautiful petite face toward mine. Her eyebrows flew up, and her round face was elongated.

"No, of course not," I lied.

"Good. Now where are you going? I thought you had a date with Cal Roman?" she asked, turning back toward the television.

"It wasn't really a date. He had something come up," I said, trying to disguise my disappointment.

"Oh, okay." She paused again, as she watched a news program about the growing concerns over the stock market. "Then where are you off to?"

"The library."

"Interesting. Just be back by eleven." And, with that, I was dismissed.

I raced to the pantry, where I found several pairs of keys hanging on small wooden pegs. I picked a pair at random and ran to the garage. I hit the unlock button, and the red Audi coupe blinked at me. I got in the driver's seat, carefully navigating the car out of the garage and the narrow driveway. I turned on the wipers as a light drizzle pelted the windshield.

I drove slowly on the unfamiliar streets, following the monotone voice of the GPS. The GPS made a noise as I closed in on my destination, but I still couldn't get a visual on the building, especially since I had no idea what it was supposed to look like. It was more difficult to locate the library in the dark and the rain than I had anticipated. I turned the wipers on high, hoping that that would somehow allow me to see more clearly. After a couple of swipes, it only seemed to smear the city lights into streaks of orange, causing me to become even more irritated.

Finally, I spotted a small sign which read "Public Library." I sighed in relief and pulled into the small parking lot. I ran into the building, trying to avoid as much of the warm, humid drizzle as possible. As the revolving door ushered me in, I was greeted by the chilled scent of old books. The air conditioner was on full blast and I was sorry that I hadn't brought a jacket.

I inhaled the stale smell of well-read volumes, which had always been kind of pleasant to me. The lobby was very cavernous, with tall ceilings and two exposed floors of book shelves visible behind the large librarians' desk. I walked past the desk, where an elderly woman covered by a bright red cardigan was busy typing on a computer. She looked up at me and smiled, but didn't offer any help.

I followed the large signs, which directed me to the archives on the lower floor. I walked down the large set of stairs into a room with rows of magazines and newspapers. There was another desk situated in the large room, with a younger woman, who was busy stacking magazines on the counter.

"Hello, miss. Can I help you?" she asked cheerfully.

"Yes, I need to look at back issues of the local newspapers," I said, coming up to the desk and placing my hands on the counter. The pleasantly round woman stopped what she was doing and looked at me. Her shiny gold nameplate read *Shirley Lewis*.

"Sure, I'll show you where the machine is."

I followed her into an even colder, windowless room. The room contained the machine used to look at the microfilm and file cabinets that were crammed with rolls of film. The plain, fold-out table the machine was perched on had several rolls of film strewn across it like black party ribbon.

"Here's the index for you, and all the filing cabinets are labeled. Just leave the film on the table and I'll put it back when you're through." She handed me a crumpled piece of paper, which was overcrowded with numbers, letters, and dates. I realized then that this might be more of a daunting task than I had expected.

"Thank you," I called, as she left the room.

She nodded in response and returned to stacking magazines. I sat down heavily on the squeaky, padded chair. Where should I even begin looking? I thought it would be safe bet to go back a few years, maybe even further, and start the search there.

I pulled the papers for 1991, and methodically started going through them, looking for any signs of Kythera, the Watsons, or Romans.

I reached 1995 and found a front page article entitled, "Kythera: A Charity Event." I read through the material, soaking up what I could. The article described Kythera as being a name of an organization that often was involved in charity work. Every year, they held a benefit ball and other fundraisers for a variety of charities, which were always local. The rest of the article just described all the charities they sponsored or local projects with the city government they were involved in.

According to a quote from Tyson Roman, the organization "deals exclusively with local charities, because it is our belief that by benefiting our own community we will provide support to share that wealth with the surrounding area, the state and the country."

Pretty ambitious, I thought.

The fundraiser was described in depth, all the way to the decorations, dinner menu, and charities supported, but there was no information on Kythera members, or a background on the organization. The only things mentioned about it directly were that Tyson Roman was the current president and that he had been president since 1989.

I went back to the filing cabinets to search for the next few years. I found another article from 1998 entitled, "Kythera: A History in Charleston," but when I went to read the article, it was blurred to the point of being unreadable. How was that possible? Was the film damaged?

I got up from the chair, stretched my tired legs, and went to find the helpful librarian. Ms. Lewis was rolling a cart around the room, returning magazines to their rightful places. I glanced at the clock on the white wall, which read ten forty-five. Wow, I couldn't believe I had been sitting in that room almost four hours. I was sure that meant the library was about to close.

"Ms. Lewis, I have a question," I said, as I walked toward her. She instinctively turned around at the sound of her name, giving me a big smile.

"Yes?" she said in a cheery tone.

"I think there's a problem with the film. It isn't coming out very clear," I said.

Without a word, she walked with determination past me and into the back room. I all but ran to keep up with her. She studied the machine and then took a look at the film. She read through the page and then her face instantly relaxed in relief.

"When the film was made, there must have

been a problem with the page, that's why it's like that," she said very assuredly.

"So why is that the only article that's blurred?" I said calmly pointing at the article on the screen.

"Maybe someone handled the paper there. Got something on it," she said, shrugging her shoulders.

"Okay, thanks." I sat back down in the chair and stared at the blurred page.

I tried to squeeze in a few more issues before I left. The last one I looked at had another article featuring Kythera in the title. The headline read, "Kythera: What do they really do?" I went to the article and I gasped. It too was blurred. This was not a coincidence. I pulled the film out hastily, and threw it on the counter.

"Ms. Lewis, do you know anything about Kythera?" I asked, walking toward her desk.

She looked at me and her face went pale. "No," she said curtly and turned back to her computer.

I thanked Ms. Lewis for her help and left the library.

I was more annoyed than ever. Obviously, I was going to have to do some more digging, because I couldn't trust Cal or Charlotte to tell me the truth. Maybe I could make a trip to the newspaper office. They should have copies of old issues, and hopefully those wouldn't be blurred or destroyed. If they were, I would know there must be something serious going on.

I pulled the car back into the driveway and

hopped out into the pouring rain. I shielded my hair with my hands, but still ended up drenched by the time I reached the front door. My shoes squeaked as I bounded across the slick wood and up the stairs to my bedroom.

As soon as I hit the room, I pulled my wet clothes off, which smelled of salt, and threw them on the floor. I turned the Jacuzzi tub on and allowed the hot water to fill up around me. I laid my head against the tub and closed my eyes. It had been a long day, between the shopping marathon and the library.

I pulled a towel off the bar and wrapped it around me. As I stepped out of the tub, there was a tap-tap-tap sound coming from the window over the tub. It sounded like someone knocking on it, but I knew that couldn't be possible. Another tap-tap-tap.

I stepped back into the tub, opened the window, and craned my neck out. The yard was barely lit, but I could make out a figure standing in the middle of the grass.

"Casper!"

I leaned out the window further. It was Cal.

"What are you doing out here? And how did you know this was my window?" I asked, trying to whisper as loudly as possible.

"I wanted to see if you wanted to hang out with me. And your light is the only one on."

"Why didn't you just call my cell phone?"I leaned a little further out. My toes were barely touching the tub.

"I don't have your number."

"Then why didn't you ring the doorbell?"

"It wouldn't be sneaking out, then, would it?"

I looked at the clock on the vanity. It was twelve-thirty, "I thought you had something to do?"

"I did, but I felt bad for blowing our date off, so I wanted to make it up to you." He walked toward the hedges directly below my window.

I thought for a moment. "My parents aren't going to let me go out this late." In Kentucky, they didn't care what time I came home, because most of the time I was out in the barn or on the farm. But they had become a lot stricter since moving here.

"Climb out the window," he shouted.

I looked down to the hedges below. There wasn't even a ledge I could possibly climb down. "That's crazy. How am I supposed to do that?"

He pointed toward another window in my bedroom. I leaned out further to see the convenient trellis that went all the way to the ground right below it.

"Well, okay, then," I said, shutting the window.

I changed into a pair of jeans, hot pink T-shirt, and tennis shoes. I opened the window near the fireplace and looked out cautiously. I took a deep breath before sending one leg out. One foot at a time, I slowly made my way to the bottom. As I reached the bottom, I realized there was a three-foot drop from the trellis to the ground into the hedges.

"I think I need a little help," I called out

to Cal.

He rushed toward me. "Here, jump back and I'll catch you."

I swung my head around toward him. "That's insane, I'm not doing that."

"Come on, you made it this far."

I took another deep breath and prepared to let go. Unfortunately, the trellis had started to give—and before I had a chance to jump, the whole thing came down on top of me and I was flung into the hedges. The branches scratched up my skin, and sent little stings of pain across my arms. I winced as I tried to push the trellis away from me.

Cal pulled it off of me and helped me up. "Are you all right?"

I looked at him, his eyes full of concern. I couldn't help but laugh. "Yeah, I'm okay, but I don't think the trellis is. Hopefully my parents will think the gardener did it."

Cal broke out into laughter. "Hopefully. Come on."

Cal took my hand as we jogged across the yard and toward the driveway. He pulled me toward the street.

"Wait, where's your car?" I stopped and looked around for his Mercedes.

"No car. But I have this." He pointed to a sleek black motorcycle.

My mouth dropped open. "I can't imagine what kind of maniac you are on that thing. I'm not getting on there with you."

"Are you going to complain about everything?

Just get on already." Cal sat down on the motorcycle, lifted the kick stand, and put on a helmet. He picked up another helmet and held it out to me.

I sighed in defeat, took the helmet from his hands, and jumped on behind him. I put my arms around his waist and felt his muscles underneath his thin T-shirt. "I hope you know what you're doing," I whispered into his ear. Goose bumps formed on his neck.

"Of course."

I put the helmet on my head. The motorcycle rumbled to life, and within seconds, we were roaring down the street. The wind whipped my loose hair that wasn't underneath the helmet. I could feel every muscle in Cal's body as it tensed up or shifted. It felt like we were flying through the air, kind of like being on a horse. Only the motorcycle was a whole lot faster than even our fastest thoroughbred, and a lot more terrifying when we whizzed by a semi-truck that could crush us in an instant.

I buried my head into Cal's back and refused to move an inch until the motorcycle slowed to a stop. Although the helmet muffled sounds, I could tell we had left the city. I lifted my head and pulled off the helmet.

He had pulled to the side of a small, two-lane road lined with massive oak trees. The moon was bright and full, casting beautifully eerie shadows through the gnarled branches covered in Spanish moss. A split-rail fence lined either side of the road. I looked up the lane and saw a massive house at the end of the tree-lined road.

"Where are we?" I asked as I slowly got off of the motorcycle.

"One of my favorite places. A plantation just outside the city." Cal pulled his helmet off and stood up from the motorcycle.

I walked over to the fence and looked out at the large field full of tall grass. It reminded me of our pastures. A sense of comfort filled my body.

Cal hopped over the fence and motioned for me to follow.

"So now we're trespassing? Are there any rules you won't break?" I crossed my arms over my chest.

"No, not really. Comes from being in a family that has so many rules. Makes me want to break everyone I can." He put his hand out for mine.

"I completely understand." I grabbed his hand and jumped over the fence.

We walked across the field, hand in hand, until we reached the edge of more trees. Cal stepped in front of me and led the way through the dimly-lit trees. I pushed tree branches and several spider webs from my face before we emerged into another field. Moonlight reflected off a small pond in the middle of the grass.

The bright night was filled with the sounds of crickets and frogs. The noise of the city was drowned out by the sounds of summer. Cal walked to the edge of the pond and sat down. I sat down beside him, and gazed at the moon reflecting against the still water.

"So, how did you find this place?" I

whispered, afraid that I would drown out the beautiful summer music with my voice.

"I've rode by the plantation a lot, and one night, almost like this one, I stopped on the side of the road. I saw the trees across the field and I wanted to know what was on the other side. Since then, I come here a lot."

"I can see why." I leaned back on my elbows and stared up at the sky. A few wispy clouds filtered through the bright stars and deep navy sky.

"Do you miss Kentucky?" Cal asked.

I breathed out deeply. "Very much. But I don't think it's Kentucky so much as it is the horses. If they were here, I think I'd be okay." I said it without really thinking. As I sat in the plantation field, on a perfect night, I realized Charleston was just as beautiful as Kentucky—but it was the horses that made all the difference to me.

"Maybe you can bring them with you?" Cal pulled a blade of grass and started tearing it apart.

I laughed. "And where exactly would we put them? Our yard's pretty small, and I don't think they'll fit in the garage . . ." I leaned back up and looked at the pond. "Plus, I don't think our neighbors would be all right with us taking our horses for walks in the park."

"Good point," Cal said, and turned to look at me. He smiled and his dimples showed in the soft white light. My heart skipped a beat and I quickly looked away.

"So, how long before the people who own this

place will come run us off?" I asked, changing the subject.

"No one lives here anymore. It's a museum. No one is here this late."

"Good, because I don't want to know the cops as well as you do." I got up from the grass and walked to the edge of the pond, picked up a small rock, and threw it into the water.

"I really don't get into that much trouble . . . unless you're into bad boys."

"Oh, please, you just think you're the hottest thing going, don't you?" I turned around fast to face him. Too fast. My shoes slipped on the muddy bank, and in one swift motion, I plunged into the cool water of the pond.

"Casper!" Cal called, as he splashed into the pond.

I flailed around for a moment, before realizing it wasn't that deep. I stood up, water up to my hips, and threw my wet hair out of my face.

"Man, you need to stop being so clumsy around me. I really must be the hottest thing going for *you*." Cal stood waist-deep in the water, and before he could finish his sarcastic comment, I pushed him down. No reason for me to be the only one completely covered in pond water.

Cal emerged from the water with a gasp. His thin white T-shirt was transparent, and his muscular chest and abs were visible. It was so hard for me not to stare.

Cal began to laugh and I couldn't help but do the same. He trudged through the water toward me, closing the distance between us. I looked up into his deep blue eyes that still sparkled in the dimmest of light.

Wordlessly, he bent down and pressed his soft lips against mine. I didn't resist, allowing his lips to overtake my own. He threaded his hands in my wet hair, and I wrapped my arms around his waist. Adrenaline and excitement pulsed through my body. Finally, he kissed my lips softly once more and backed away from me.

Wordlessly, he held out his hand for mine. I took it and he helped me out of the pond. We walked through the trees and into the field back to his motorcycle. Cal stripped off his wet T-shirt and slung it across the seat. My eyes were instantly attracted to his completely bare chest. As I scanned his gorgeous figure, I focused in on something I hadn't noticed before. He had a tattoo on the right side of his chest, a tattoo of the word "Kythera." I gasped out loud and Cal focused his attention on where my gaze had fallen.

"What? You don't like tattoos?" he asked, shrugging his shoulders.

"No—I mean, yes . . . but why do you have the same tattoo Charlotte has?"

"It's a big joke in our circle of friends," he said, shrugging his muscular shoulders. "When our families went on a trip together to Greece, we thought it would be cool to remember the trip with a tattoo. It was really bad idea."

It was sort of the same story Charlotte had used, but not exactly.

"So, you're telling me that you tattoo your car *and* your body with a name of someplace you went on vacation *once?*" I crossed my arms over my damp chest.

"Yeah, I know it sounds stupid," he said, running his hand through his damp hair.

"I might believe you, except for the fact that that both our houses have a painting named after the place, the cops are terrified of the symbol on your car, and that I found out there's a charity group with the same name here in Charleston."

Cal's jaw tightened. "How did you know about that?"

"I did some research at the library. Didn't get too far, since everything about it was mysteriously blurred out, but I know enough not to believe it's just some amazing vacation spot you and your friends can't forget."

Cal was quiet for a long moment. "You're right—it isn't. But I can't say anything else about it right now. I want to, believe me, but I can't. Give me some time, and I'll tell you everything you want to know, okay?"

I was surprised at how easily he gave in to admitting it was something more. I was disappointed he wasn't willing to tell me anything else, but I was willing to wait.

"All right, but I want to know everything." I stood back from the motorcycle, my arms crossed over my chest.

"I promise—as soon as I can, I'll tell you everything." Cal got on the bike and motioned for me to get on, too. I hesitated for a moment before finally getting on the bike and putting on my helmet. I put my arms around his damp waist and held on tight.

He started the motorcycle and we sped down the deserted road, toward the glow of the city lights.

~ * * * ~

"Do not let the china hit the table without the proper chargers underneath. You'll scratch the wood," Mother was saying as I swung open the door to the dining room.

Mother was prying a plate from Christina's shaky hands and putting it back in the china cabinet. She reached into the drawer beneath the massive glass display of china and pulled out three gold chargers, which she plunked into Christina's hands. The petite girl barely kept them from clattering to the floor. It was clear the only reason they survived was her fear of my mother's wrath if she let them fall on the floor.

I gave the maid a meek smile as she passed. She glanced at me and put her head down as she walked out of the room.

"Good morning, Casper," Mother said in a musical tone, instantly switching gears into her more pleasant façade. Her scowl turned to a bright smile and her rigid body relaxed.

"Good morning, Mother," I responded, as I sat down at the table.

"Casper, do you know what happened to the

trellis outside your room?" She fumbled with a pair of gold earrings before sitting down to the table.

"Um, no, I don't have a clue," I lied.

We had tried to put the trellis back up so I could sneak back in, but it had been no use. Fortunately, my parents' car had been missing from the driveway, so I knew they were at some late night party. For once, I was glad they had left the front door unlocked.

"Strange. I guess the gardener must have knocked it down yesterday. I'll have a talk with him." She wrote a note on her list to talk to him.

Poor guy, I thought, but I couldn't help smiling to myself.

I looked over to where Dad would normally be with his papers, but he wasn't sitting with his cup of coffee, perusing *The Wall Street Journal.*

"Where's Dad?" I asked, still staring at his empty chair. It was very rare for him to miss breakfast.

Mother looked up absently from her daily list to his empty chair. "He had some sort of business meeting with Tyson this morning. They had to finalize their deal," she said, waving her hand in the direction of his empty chair. She didn't like for him to miss breakfast and neither did I. It was one of the rare times I saw him for more than a few minutes.

"Huh," I said, and stared dumbfounded at Mother, who had returned her attention to her list.

"There are a few things for you to do today,"

she mused out loud, tapping her pen against the pad. Her face was tight and her brows furrowed in concentration.

"Cool," I said absently.

"Will you go check the mailbox out front? The butler seems to think it isn't his job to bring in the mail." As I got up from the table, she added under her breath, "So hard to find good help around here."

"Sure," I said, as I walked out of the room and toward the front door. It was already hot outside and I had to squint against the bright light of the sun.

As I opened the lid to the mailbox, someone shouted "Hello!" in my direction.

I looked up to see an elderly woman dressed in her bathrobe, waving her hand at me wildly. Her hair was in pink curlers, and she held tightly to her fuzzy pink robe to keep it closed.

"Hello," I said, with less enthusiasm.

The woman took my reply as a sign that I was open to a conversation. She practically ran to where I was standing. "My name is Mrs. Hamilton. I live next door. Who might you be?" She adjusted her thick black glasses as she looked me up and down.

"I'm Casper Whitley. My family just moved in." I turned back to the mailbox and pulled out the contents.

"Moved in? Wait, where did the Walkers go?" she asked me.

"I dunno." I shrugged my shoulders. As if I would know? I started flipping through the mail.

There wasn't anything too interesting, the usual junk and a few bills.

"Huh, they didn't even say goodbye. Where are you from dear?" She moved a few inches closer and narrowed her brown eyes at me.

"Lexington, Kentucky," I said, hoping the conversation would end soon.

"I've been there. Beautiful horse country. I still can't believe they left. So many people in and out of that house," she mumbled.

"What do you mean?" She had my interest now.

"Oh, I said that out loud? Sorry, it's just people are always moving in and out of the house. It's very weird, and they always have a parade of black cars with strange marks on them." She tapped her forehead, as if she were thinking, "Oh, the cars . . . they always have the letter K on them. What color are your cars?"

"All different colors." I closed the lid on the mailbox absently. "Their cars would *always* have that symbol on them?"

"Oh, yes. You're the first family that hasn't had all black cars since I've lived here. That's been about twenty years." She looked at me curiously. "They must have sold the house . . ."

"Huh?" This wasn't making any sense.

Mrs. Hamilton caught the confused look on my face. "Oh, nothing. Never mind, I always ramble on. Well, it was nice to meet you, Casper. Welcome to Charleston!" She turned and scurried to her front porch before I could ask any more questions.

I stood motionless on the sidewalk, the mail still in my hands. After a moment, I looked up at our house. It looked normal enough, like many others on the street, but I had the strange sense it wasn't like the rest at all.

Chapter

7

I DECIDED TODAY WAS THE day to get some answers. My intuition was telling me I needed to dig deep and find out what was going on, and I never ignored what my gut was telling me. The newspaper office was downtown and I figured they had to keep copies of their newspapers.

I drove downtown and parked in front of the small office, which was wedged between a French restaurant and a law office. I was greeted in the lobby by a short woman behind a black desk, a telephone receiver glued to her head.

"I understand, Mr. Mills, but we can't run a personal ad for your dog. I know he's like your baby and you're upset he's all alone. Have you tried the animal shelter?" The woman hung the phone up and looked at me. "I guess he didn't like that suggestion. How can I help you?" she asked, as she pushed her glasses up her nose.

"I'm wondering if you keep copies of all the old newspapers on file. I'm doing some research for school and need some information from back issues," I said, hoping I sounded convincing.

"I know we keep some of them, but let me get Susan, she would be able to help you better." She picked up the phone and called for Susan.

A slim woman with short blonde hair walked through the door leading to the back. "Hey, I'm Susan and you are?"

"Casper. I'm looking for some back issues of the paper for a school research project."

Susan looked at the woman at the reception desk and then back at me. "I didn't know school was in right now."

"It isn't, but I'm new in town and my new school needed me to do some assignments this summer to make sure I was on the same page." *Crap;* I needed to learn to be a better liar.

She studied me for a minute, her thin lips set in a straight line. "Did you check with the library?"

"Yes, but the articles I need were smudged and unreadable, so I thought you might have a copy." I rubbed my left hand, something I always did when I was nervous.

"So what were the articles on?"

"A group called Kythera," I said innocently.

"Oh," she said, surprised. "Why don't you

come back to my office and we'll see what we can do. Mary Ann, let me know when Mitch gets here for our interview." Susan opened the door and gestured for me to walk in first.

"My office is there on the right," she said, and I turned into a small office stacked with papers and folders all over the desk. A computer was barely visible to the side, and a framed diploma from Tulane University hung behind her desk.

I sat down in one of the green chairs as she sat down at her desk, the chair squeaking as she turned to face me. "So why do you want to know about Kythera?"

"For my assignment."

"I know that isn't the truth, because I know there isn't a teacher in town who would touch that topic. So why are you really interested?" She leaned back in her chair and crossed her arms over her chest.

"Because they are all around me, and I'm curious. My neighbor seems to think I should stay away from anybody involved with them."

"She's right, but I can't help you find out anything. I've been trying to figure that out for years. In fact, if you find anything, you let me know."

"But someone wrote an article about what they're hiding—that's one of them the articles that was blurred."

She turned to her computer screen and tapped on the keyboard. "Yes, but that article was retracted the next day and the girl who no longer works here. She quit that week."

"But don't you have a copy of it somewhere?" I leaned up in the chair, alarmed by what she was telling me. She didn't answer, but the printer started buzzing.

"I do. I had to hide it in my personal files. I don't know how much it's going to help. I never could get anywhere with it, but maybe you can if you know them."

She handed the article to me, and I looked down at the page, everything intact. "Thanks."

I stood up to leave her office.

"And remember—if you find anything, I want to know. Here's my card." She handed me her business card, and I nodded.

I walked out the office, holding the piece of paper like a secret treasure. I got into my car. Before leaving, I looked over the title: *What is Kythera Hiding?" written by Kelly Winters.*

A photo of Tyson Roman standing at a podium accompanied the article. The caption said it was taken at the ground-breaking ceremony for the newest Boys and Girls Club. I scanned the article, looking for anything that might be interesting and useful. It described Kythera as a charity group that dedicated most of its time to raising funds for local charities and the city for much needed public improvements. They had raised the funds for the new Boys and Girls Club and for the new play equipment at the park near Colonial Lake.

But, according to the article—through an unnamed source—Kythera appeared on the payroll for several of the projects after they had funded them, including the renovation of the Charleston police department and a landscaping project at city hall. When the reporter had asked for comments, she was directed to the group's attorney, Martin Charles of Charles & Whitaker, LLP. The statement from the attorney was that Kythera was not on the payroll, but that if a member worked at city hall or the police department, they could choose to have their dues taken directly out of their paychecks.

Ms. Winters had confirmed through public records that Kythera received $150,000.00 from the City of Charleston last year, and could not confirm who the employee was who shared their duties with the city and with Kythera—and her calls to the mayor's office had not been returned.

I put the piece of paper on the passenger seat and turned the ignition on. Something was definitely fishy with this whole thing, but nothing was giving me enough evidence to put it all together. I thought for a minute and realized I needed to find Ms. Winters and do some snooping at the house. If Mrs. Hamilton was right in saying the house was owned by Kythera, then our family was already involved with them.

That meant Dad had to know something.

~ * * * ~

After my little trip to the paper, I walked back into the house and headed straight for the office to look through the drawers and the computer for any information. Suddenly, the doorbell rang, flooding the house with deep, somber tones that reminded me of church bells. I was already in the hallway, so I took a couple of steps to the front door and opened it.

Cal was standing at the door, with a coy half-smile plastered on his handsome face. He had his hands shoved in a pair of dark denim jeans, and his biceps were flexing under the rolled-up sleeves of his plaid shirt.

"Hey Casper," he said.

"Hey, Cal, haven't seen you in a while," I said sarcastically, pretending I hadn't just spent last night out with him.

"Yeah, I know. Sorry about that. I'll try not to deprive you of my presence."

"You're so full of it," I said shaking my head.

"Anyways, I was wondering if you would like to go with me somewhere today?"

"When? Where?" I blurted out. I cringed at how excited I sounded.

"Now and wherever I decide to drive." He leaned against the door frame.

"I have a busy day planned. You know, the usual . . . a luncheon with stuck-up snobs, cocktail hour with fake friends. I can't pass up all that fun," I said sarcastically.

"I promise, what I have planned can top all that." He inched forward, his face very close to mine.

I could feel his warm breath on my face, and his eyes were a deeper blue from this distance. My heart was jumping in my throat. "I've got plans . . . sorry." I shrugged my shoulders and moved to close the door.

"I think you'll really like what I've planned."

I paused for a moment. "Okay, I'll ask."

I was sure that I would get a resounding no to my proposal, and I was disappointed in the thought of not being able to go. I asked Cal to step in and wait.

I trudged myself back down the hallway and into the library, where Mother was reading a book.

"Hey, can I go with Cal?" I said, without any further explanation. Mother looked up at me. I hoped she was able to scratch out any plans on her list she had made for me already.

"Sure, honey. Just be back by four; there's a few neighbors coming over for cocktails, and at seven we are expected at a charity function for the local university."

"Okay," I said, and almost tripped over myself to get out of the room before she changed her mind. She hadn't even asked where I was going, not that I would have had an answer. I reached the front door, where he was dutifully waiting for me.

"I'll be right back," I said, as I climbed the stairs—but then I stopped, turning back around to face him, "Can't you tell me where we're going? I'm terrible with surprises. And, besides, what if I need to be dressed up or something?" I coaxed, hoping he would break over and just tell me already.

"No, but I'll tell you jeans are perfect for

where we're going," he said curtly, refusing to give any more information.

I huffed and continued to climb the stairs. I grabbed my purse and ran back down. I whooshed passed him and out the front door and toward the driveway.

Cal pointed to the black Lexus SUV. Before jumping in, I tried my best to inspect the back and driver's side. I was only able to see the back without going out of my way—and, to no surprise, it too had a red "K," which replaced the letters that identified the car model. I was sure the front wheel well had "Kythera" plastered on it, too. It didn't even surprise me anymore.

Cal got in the vehicle; he stopped at the end of the driveway and turned on the right blinker.

"So, where are we going exactly?" I asked, breaking the silence.

"Somewhere cool," he said, without taking his eyes off the road.

"That doesn't tell me much."

"It's not supposed to. Can't you handle a surprise?"

I sat back in the seat heavily. As I leaned back, I heard a crinkling noise coming from my front pocket. I pulled out the little piece of paper I had found underneath the dresser.

"Hey, what does this mean?" I held out the paper to Cal. He took it and held it on the steering wheel with one hand. It took only a few seconds for him to read the line. His face turned pale and his expression was unreadable.

"Where did you find this?" His tone was deep

and serious.

"It was under a dresser the moving men moved out of one of the bedrooms. Is it some kind of secret code?"

Cal handed the note back to me. I read it again.

Let's meet in Greece and sail to exotic places.
K&

"What does the signature mean?"

Cal was silent, answering none of my questions.

"Greece has something to do with the painting, right?" I asked, hoping he would respond in some way.

"Yes, but I can't explain right now. Remember, I said I would explain it all, but not now." His gripped the steering wheel, his jaw clenched.

"Okay, well, what about the Walkers? The people who used to live in our house? Were they a part of Kythera, too?" I asked quietly.

"How did you know about them?" He finally turned his gaze to mine, shock written all over his face.

"Mrs. Hamilton, the neighbor. She caught me at the mailbox this morning and started babbling about how the Walker's didn't even say goodbye to her and how people were always moving in and out of that house." I folded the note neatly and put it back in my pocket.

"She shouldn't have said anything. I promise

you'll know everything, but can we forget about it for now? I don't want to ruin the surprise and right now I'm not in a great mood. Let's talk about something else."

"Okay," I said, and nodded in agreement. I hadn't seen this side of Cal yet. He was almost scary when he was serious and angry.

I had been so distracted by our conversation I hadn't been paying attention to where we were going. The city had already floated out of view and now we were in the middle of the countryside, with a multitude of trees and open fields surrounding us.

The patches of trees were green and vibrant from the ample moisture in the summer air, and draped in Spanish moss. The air was so thick with humidity that I could basically see it hanging in the air like silky gauze. Rays of sunlight danced across the fields as the clouds moved across the sky. It reminded me a little bit of home, except for the extreme effects of the humidity—and there were no traces of Spanish moss in Kentucky. The moss gave the scene an eerie beauty that reminded me of several scary movies I had seen in the past. I was waiting for our SUV to mysteriously stop and then the zombies to run out of the forest and grab us.

The line from *The Wizard of Oz*, "I've a feeling we're not in Kansas anymore," popped into my head for some reason.

"Where are you taking me?" I demanded again.

"You'll see. You aren't very patient, are you?"

he commented, still looking ahead to the empty road.

"I can be patient, but I like to know where I'm going," I said, crossing my arms against my chest. I was starting to think this hadn't been such a good idea.

"Well, use some of your patience and wait a few more minutes okay?" he said.

"Fine," I said, and turned my attention back to the window.

Cal slowed the vehicle down and turned onto a gravel road. We were now in the middle of the trees, and bumping along on what appeared to be a never-ending dirt path into the middle of nowhere. I decided to keep quiet, and lay my head against the head rest. I thought it was in my best interest not to upset my captor any further.

A few seconds later, the vehicle stopped. We were at a black iron gate that didn't look like it was guarding anything in particular. Cal pulled out a little card from the center console and waved it in front of the sensor. The gate beeped and proceeded to open. I was fascinated by the bizarre scene unfolding in front of me.

We drove another quarter-mile before we came to a brick sign, which read, "Yorkshire Hunt Club."

"Are we hunting?" I asked. If so, he had seriously miscalculated my likes and dislikes. I had no desire to go sit in the middle of the woods and wait for Bambi to pass by so I could shoot him and take him home for dinner.

"Sort of," he said, still smiling. Maybe he meant to torture me and thought that this would be a great form of entertainment for himself.

We finally pulled up to a large building that looked more like a home than anything else. It was a large, two-story blue-sided house with a wraparound porch. It was flanked by a matching blue barn and a gravel parking lot. Cal jumped out of the SUV, and came to open the passenger door for me. I jumped from the SUV and stared at my surroundings. My mind was still racing to figure out what was going on and I was desperately hoping it wasn't hunting.

There was a group of men sitting on the porch in white rocking chairs, smoking cigars and sending billows of gray smoke into the air. The front door burst open, and a couple emerged in matching riding gear, holding hands.

I stopped moving. Without warning tears, began to form in the corners of my eyes. I looked up at the sky to keep them from falling down my cheeks.

I suddenly missed home more than ever—but, at the same time, I was happy. Happy to be somewhere I could possibly see and ride a horse, even if it was not my own. I looked over at Cal, forcing myself not to allow a tear to fall. He looked at me with the most beautiful smile and I felt all the reservations I had about him soaring off into the sticky air.

"Are we riding?" I asked, my voice barely above a whisper.

He nodded. "Yes, but that's not it."

He grabbed my hand and started walking toward the barn. As we approached, my nose was filled with the smell of hay and my stomach felt like butterflies were trying to escape. We stepped into the barn and walked down the hall. Several horses neighed as we passed. Cal stopped in front of a stall on the far end and motioned for me to peek over the door. As I looked into the dark stall, I saw the familiar big brown eyes staring back at me.

"Wendy!" I couldn't get the lock opened fast enough. I pushed into the stall and wrapped my arms around her neck. I rubbed my face against her shiny coat, taking in her horse smell. Suddenly, nothing else seemed to matter, and I felt like part of my soul had been returned. The tears began to flow down my cheeks, but I didn't care—because, for the first time since the move, they were happy tears.

I patted her softly on the neck before releasing her. "How did you do this?" I asked Cal, who was still standing in the doorway of the stall.

"I had a lot of help from your mother. She knew how much you missed Wendy and she thought it would be a great idea if we kept it secret and I brought you out here. She knew you would know what was up if she stepped foot at the Hunt Club."

"Come here and meet Wendy," I said motioning him into the stall.

He looked at me hesitantly. "I'm not that great with pets. I had a hamster once and when I tried to pet him, he bit me. Same thing happened with my iguana."

I laughed. "Wendy isn't like any other pet you've had. She can see right through you and know what you're feeling. She's so smart and so much more than just a pet." I put my hand out for his. He finally took a few steps into the stall. I grabbed his hand and put it on her long neck, against her smooth coat.

I guided his hand down the side of her neck. "See, she won't hurt you."

He smiled, and I was overwhelmed with so much happiness. "You don't know what this means to me. Wendy's a part of my soul that no person could ever fill . . . at least, not until I met you."

Slowly, I dropped my hand from his, but he grabbed it and pulled me to him. "Normally, being compared to a horse wouldn't be a compliment—but in your case, I think it's the best one I could get." He moved in to kiss me, our lips meeting, and I felt the sparks fly again.

Wendy huffed and stamped her hoof, and Cal took a few steps back.

"I guess she's saying that's enough." I laughed.

All morning, we were on the expansive trails of the Yorkshire Hunt Club. I found out Cal was not an experienced rider, and he had trouble keeping his horse under control, almost falling off when the horse reared up. I was starting to think he had never even been on a horse and that made me feel even more appreciative of him.

I became absorbed in the wonderful feeling of Wendy's jostling back and forth and the wind in my hair when I got her up to a gallop. I left Cal in the dust, taking my hands off the reins and putting them up in the air like I was Jack on the bow of the *Titanic.* The feeling of freedom swept over me, and I felt I could breathe freely again.

"Thanks for doing this," I said, coming back to ride beside him.

"I could tell from dinner the other night that riding meant a lot to you. Your eyes light up when you talk about the horses, so I wanted to show you that Charleston had something you would like before you decided to run off." He pulled out a mischievous grin and the horse jostled him. His face flashed full of fear.

"I guess I can cancel that plane ticket I booked, then," I said winking at him.

"Good," was all that he could manage to say before his horse took a rough step into a puddle.

Cal regained his composure and guided the horse toward the trail and back to the barn. He made careful movements, like he was afraid to breathe. His hands were clenched around the reins. He looked terrified, and I felt bad for him.

"Have you ever been on a horse?" I asked warily.

Cal continued to focus on attempting to guide the horse, who was not willing to follow Cal's directions. His silence confirmed what I had suspected.

"You know, horses can sense fear. If you relax, you won't have so much trouble," I instructed. Cal relaxed his body and he released the tension in his jaw. The horse responded to Cal's change in demeanor and settled down into a slow walk.

"Incredible," Cal said under his breath.

"It takes a lot of guts to get out here like this on a horse when you've never been on one. Haven't you ever even ridden a pony at a fair or something?"

"Do I look like someone who has spent a lot of time at a county fair? Have you ever been to a county fair?"

"Actually, I have. When I was seven, my dad took to me to a fair where they had ponies, ducks, and goats. I wasn't allowed to ride on the ponies. Dad told me he wouldn't contribute to the mistreatment of the ponies in their little pens. I think I remember him giving the guy an earful about it, too. Anyways, I've been to a county fair."

"I stand corrected. Well, my parents never took me to a county fair. Did I miss anything?"

I giggled a little at the memory of the greasy food and giant stuffed animals. I hadn't been that impressed by it, but I'd loved every minute of it because it was one of those rare moments I got to spend with Dad when he wasn't working like crazy.

"Not really," I finally said.

"Good, because otherwise I would have to hunt one down for you and me to go to," he said, as his horse picked up speed. He pulled in the reins and the horse returned to a steady walk.

"I think you might be traumatized by this experience," I said, as I jumped off Wendy and gave her a pat on the neck.

"Maybe," he said uncertainly. He sat still on the horse, unsure of how to get down.

"But I'm grateful you were willing to do it for me," I said sincerely as I walked toward him and reached my hand out for the reins. I held his horse steady as he jumped to the ground. There was an instant look of relief on his face, as if he had just survived a scary plane ride. I kept waiting for him to kiss the ground.

"I'll be having nightmares about this for weeks," he said. He then looked up at me and gave me a sly smile. "But it was worth it to see you happy. You have such a beautiful smile and it's even more beautiful when you're riding a horse."

I felt hot blood rushing to my cheeks and looked away from him. I started to lead both horses to the barn, avoiding Cal's glances, but I couldn't control the smile on my face.

No matter how mysterious or difficult I felt Cal was, he had shown another side of himself. He was willing to look like an idiot by riding a horse for the sake of allowing me the opportunity to do something he knew I loved.

~ * * * ~

I ran up the steps of our house and into the foyer. I ran up the stairs to my parents' bedroom and burst through the door. Mother was in her slip and her hair was in curlers, looking at her reflection in the mirror.

She turned around, "Casper! Don't you know to knock?"

I ignored her as I rushed over and put my arms around her. I let my head fall on the soft skin of her shoulder. "Thank you so much," I whispered.

Seconds later, Mother wrapped her arms around me and squeezed. "You're welcome, honey." She took a step back and studied my face. "I know how much that horse means to you and you just haven't been the same without her." She tucked a piece of my hair behind my ear. I could see tears forming in her eyes, but she quickly turned back to the mirror and started pulling curlers out. "Now, go get ready. The neighbors will be here in a few minutes and you smell like a horse."

Wordlessly, I left her room, knowing the moment was over. I went to my room, but couldn't focus on anything but the amazing morning I'd had with Wendy and Cal. I hoped that more days like this would happen in the future—because if so, I might just like Charleston after all.

Chapter

8

I WAS STILL RIDING HIGH off the day before when I realized there was still some digging I needed to do about Kythera. I had been about to leave the house and go for another ride, but I caught a glimpse of the painting and knew that this was something that couldn't wait.

I dropped my backpack in the foyer and headed back up to the office. Dad had been spending a lot of time up here, and if he knew anything about Kythera, it would be in there or on his laptop. Since he kept the laptop with him twenty-four seven, I had to hope I could find something on the desktop computer. I turned the lights on in the empty room and walked over to the computer.

As I waited for the computer to boot up, I started pulling out drawers in the desk. I found files of bills and the usual work information, but as I was about to shut one drawer, a file in the very back caught my attention. It said "House in Charleston" in big black block letters. I put the file on the desk and opened it. It was a lease agreement for the house, which I scanned over for anything out of the ordinary.

Mrs. Hamilton was right; the house was owned by Kythera. As I read the terms, I realized this was much more than a normal lease.

"Hey, kid, what are you looking at?"

I jolted, surprised to see my dad standing in the doorway.

"Oh, hey, Dad. Nothing, I was just looking for a pencil." Fortunately, the computer screen blocked his view of the file and I shoved it back into the bottom drawer of the desk. I pulled out another drawer, searching for a "pencil."

"There should be some in the top middle drawer," he said as he walked over and behind the desk.

I pulled the drawer out and picked up a pencil, "Thanks." Now that I had the pencil, I had no idea what to do with it.

"Were you about to use the computer?" he asked, pulling out his Blackberry.

"Yeah, I was about to check Facebook and my email. Do you need it?"

"I have a conference call in a couple of minutes, and I need to do some work on the computer, if you don't mind."

"Sure," I said, as I jumped up from the chair and walked out of the room. I breathed a sigh of relief once the door was firmly shut.

That was close.

Once my heart started beating normally, I could finally focus on what I had found. The lease didn't mention anything about rent or a deposit. And had I seen a mention of the horse farm on there? I couldn't be sure, since Dad had walked in. If I *had* seen it . . . why would that need to be on a lease?

I walked down the steps, slowly wracking my brain. I picked up my backpack and walked out the front door. As soon as I could get back in the office, I would try to find out *exactly* what I had seen.

~ * * * ~

"Where are we going now?" I asked, as I sat impatiently in Cal's car. He had instructed me to wear a dress and some nice heels, but wouldn't give me any details about where we were going. It was typical Cal behavior, but that didn't stop me from trying my best to break the cycle.

He smiled at me. "You'll see."

I sighed loudly and stared out the window. I decided if he said anything to me, other than where we were going, I would ignore him. We were driving toward downtown, which had become familiar to me. I stared at the historic buildings and well-manicured flowers along the sidewalks.

My stomach growled, and I hoped wherever we were going involved food. I hadn't had anything to eat since breakfast. I had spent all day at the club with Wendy, and by the time I returned home, I only had a few minutes to shower and get ready for Cal's "surprise." I was excited to find out what his next surprise could be, but disappointed I didn't have time to continue my investigation in the office. How many surprises could he come up with?

"You look beautiful," he said, breaking the silence.

"Thanks." I looked over at him briefly, but quickly returned my gaze to the buildings.

"Are you going to ignore me all night?" Cal asked.

"Maybe . . . I might be more talkative if you tell me where we're going."

"I don't want to ruin the surprise. I love the look on your face when you are completely surprised," he answered.

"But I could have a pretty look on my face right now if you told me where we're going."

He looked straight ahead, furrowing his dark brows. He was contemplating giving in. "How about I let you ask three questions, and if you guess, then I will tell you."

I perked up at the suggestion. It was more than he would usually let me do. "Is it a restaurant?"

"No."

"Is it downtown?"

"Yes."

"Is there food there?"

"Some."

"Is there music?"

"You already got your three questions."

"Fine," I responded, and sat back in the seat.

Seconds later, he pulled into a parking lot next to what looked like an abandoned warehouse. The lot was poorly-lit and there seemed to be no life for miles around.

"Are we going to a rave?" I asked, shocked he would bring me to anything like that.

I wasn't really the partying type. I had been forced to attend so many parties throughout my life that I'd be happy if I never had to go to another one. Then again, a rave would be a lot different than one of my parents' parties. They looked pretty crazy on TV, but I couldn't say that going to one was something I was dying to do.

"*No,* are you crazy?" He looked at me, his face full of disdain.

I shrugged my shoulders, "I don't know. What else would be out here? It looks like a crime scene on *NCIS.*"

Cal got out of the car and rounded the front to open the door for me. I took his hand as I stepped out into the thick air. There was a foul smell of fish and salt water penetrating my nostrils.

Cal kept a hold of my hand as he led me to the large, dark building. I looked from side to side for a masked serial killer or muggers waiting to jump out at us. I wished Cal would pick up the pace and get of us out of here.

We finally reached the building and he pulled open a metal door that squeaked loudly. Suddenly, I could hear the booming bass of music coming from somewhere above us.

Four flights of stairs later—*in heels*—we reached another metal door. I huffed and puffed as I waited for him to open the door. He paused for a moment, looking back at me.

"Are you ready?" he asked.

"Sure . . . just promise me . . . there aren't . . . anymore stairs," I said between labored breaths.

He gave me one of his Cheshire grins before pushing the door open. He motioned for me to step out first and, as I did, I stood in shock. It looked like some kind of rooftop club or bar. There were people dancing slowly on a dance floor in the middle; a DJ was situated in a corner on the left and a bar was set up on the right. Twinkling lights were twirled around a tent frame that encompassed the whole area. A simple crystal-beaded chandelier dangled from the middle of the frame.

Cal pulled me forward through the crowd of people and to the edge of the rooftop. There was a magnificent view of the harbor and river. The moon cast a shimmering glow on the dark waves below, which made them twinkle like stars.

"Cal, this is *amazing*," I said, still staring out at the scenery.

"I'm glad you like it." He pulled me against him, his arm wrapped around my waist. Pleasant chills went up my spine and I nestled myself closer to him. "So, you wanna dance?" he asked quietly.

I turned to look at him. "Sure."

He led me to the dance floor, just as the DJ put on a fast-paced Latin song. Couples began moving rhythmically with the music. I didn't expect Cal to know how to dance; my own dancing was limited. My parents had forced me to take ballroom and I had taken a couple of Latin dance classes with some girlfriends from school. I hadn't retained much. I seemed to only be coordinated on the back of a horse.

With ease, he stepped into rhythm, directing me to follow him. I stopped for a moment. "I don't really know how to do this dance."

"Don't worry, just follow my lead."

He pulled me close into him and took a few quick steps, forcing me to follow him. I held my breath, as my heart began beating wildly. Within seconds, we were working the dance floor in rhythm with the music. It was impossible for me not to smile as he turned me into a spin and then pulled me back into his chest.

The DJ switched it up and played a slow song. He held me tightly, in complete control as he led me gracefully across the dance floor. The rest of the people faded into the background, and all there was left in our universe was us and the music. A sense of complete pleasure engulfed my body, and I felt myself falling deeper in love with every turn and exquisite dip on the dance floor.

Thirty minutes later, we were exhausted from

the constant dancing. My feet were aching and tired. We sat down at one of the small café tables, and were served some appetizers and lemonade.

"What's this place called? How did you ever find it?" I asked him. I popped a stuffed mushroom into my mouth.

"It's called the Warehouse. Real original, right? I had heard about it from some friends. I knew it would surprise you." He took a sip of lemonade.

"Cal! What's up, man?"

I turned my head to see a guy with his hand in the air. He moved smoothly through the crowd and up to our table.

"Hey, Alex," Cal said.

I looked at Alex. He was just as gorgeous as Cal, although he was the complete opposite. Alex had beautiful, caramel colored skin, deep brown eyes, and dark pink lips. The only thing they had in common was their jet black hair, even though Alex's didn't have curls and his hair was cropped shorter.

"Hey, I didn't expect to see you here. And this must be Casper Whitley." Alex turned to look at me and winked.

"Yes, it is." Cal pointed to Alex. "This is Alex Alamilla. He's one of my friends." He pronounced Alex's last name "Ala-*mia*."

"Nice to meet you. You're gorgeous, by the way," he said, taking my hand in his.

My cheeks felt hot and I was sure they were blood-red. "Thank you," I said quietly.

He kissed my hand and released it, returning his attention to Cal. "So where were you the other night? I tried calling your cell, but you never answered."

"Out." Cal kept his gaze on the table and his drink.

"Well, your dad wasn't in a good mood. You better not do that again," said Alex.

The waitress stepped over to us and asked if we would like beer or some liquor. She didn't ask for our IDs, which I assumed had to do with the fact she had recognized Cal earlier. The way people reacted to Cal and Charlotte no longer fazed me.

"I'll take a bourbon and Coke," interjected a girl, who I hadn't realized had stepped up next to me. The waitress nodded and scurried to another table.

"Hey, boys," she breathed in a sexy, smoky voice. I turned to see a beautiful girl with smoldering brown eyes. Her hair was dark chestnut and flowing in waves around her shoulders. Her lips were deep red and pouty, and her skin was an alluring bronze shade. She was wearing a skin-tight red dress that clung to her hourglass figure.

She moved around Alex and put her elbows on the table next to Cal, locked eyes with him as if no one else were present.

"How've you been? I haven't seen you much lately," she said, fixing his collar with her hand.

"Come on, sis, give him some space. He's on a date," Alex said pulling on her arm.

She looked at me. "Oh, I hadn't noticed."

"Casper this is my sister, Veronica, and, Veronica, this is Cal's date, Casper." Alex pulled his sister under his arm.

She raised an eyebrow. "Casper, that's an unusual name. Where did that come from?"

"My family's horses," I said hesitantly.

She laughed, and it was just as sexy and glittery. "So, you were named after a horse?"

"I think it's a beautiful name," Alex interjected, smiling at me.

"Thanks," I muttered.

Finally, the waitress came back with Veronica's drink. She picked it up from the table and took a seductive sip. As she lifted the glass, I could see a faint tattoo on her wrist. It matched Cal and Charlotte's tattoos. What a surprise.

"All right, I think it's time for us to get going. Got a long day tomorrow, right Cal?" Alex let go of his sister and punched Cal on the shoulder.

"Right," Cal nodded.

"It was nice to meet you Casper, hope to see you around more often. If you ever get tired of this one, give me a call," he said, winking again.

I smiled at Alex as they both walked away, Veronica swinging her hips and glancing at Cal.

"So what was that about?" I asked, putting my fingers on the straw of my drink.

"Alex is one of my friends from school," Cal said quietly.

"And Veronica?"

"She's his sister, and . . ." He paused, combing his hand through his hair. "We used to date."

I felt a rock drop in my stomach. "How long ago did you date?"

"A little while ago . . . couple of months ago." Cal avoided eye contact with me.

"So . . . how long did you date?" I started tapping my foot against the table.

"About a year off and on." He finally looked at me, but his face was unreadable.

"Oh," was all I could manage to say.

I knew that someone like Cal would have plenty of girlfriends, but I guess I hadn't expected them to be so . . . sexy and obviously way more attractive than myself. Suddenly, I didn't feel too confident about our relationship, and I wondered how I got myself into this mess.

"But it's over for good this time. She cheated on me with some guy from Savannah. She's history, but I have to see her because of her brother and she goes to the same school."

"And she has a Kythera tattoo," I added.

"Yeah, that, too. But I try to ignore her most of the time."

I raised my eyebrows. "She seems pretty hard to ignore."

"All Veronica has is a tight dress and confidence. There's nothing else. You're beautiful inside and out."

I looked at Veronica, who was chatting to a couple of other guys, who were practically drooling. I looked back at Cal, trying to forget about her. "So are all your friends involved with the mysterious Kythera?"

"Most."

"Why are there so many secrets around you?" I asked.

"I was born into them," he said frankly.

He signaled to the waitress for the check and with seconds he paid her and we were heading out the door. It was a signal that the conversation was over and I decided not to push my luck.

Chapter

9

I PEEKED AROUND THE CORNER from the kitchen into the family room. It was pretty late, and I figured my parents would be asleep, but I couldn't even think of going to sleep after tonight. Life was really starting to turn around, and Charleston wasn't so bad.

The TV wasn't on, but a lamp on an end table was lit. The coast was clear and I plopped down on the couch and started flipping through the channels, looking for *Golden Girls* reruns, which were usually on this time of night. I didn't tell many of my friends that I watched the show; it wasn't exactly cool. But they reminded me of my grandparents—or the grandparents I always wanted. There was just something comforting about them. I couldn't find them on, so I settled for *Lost*, another favorite show.

"What are you watching, Casper?"

I jumped a foot off the couch and then looked behind me to see Mother standing just past the breakfast bar, looking at the screen. She had her arms crossed against her chest and her face was scrunched in concentration.

"Oh, um, *Lost*," I answered.

"I never understood that show," she said, with a confused expression on her face. She stepped from the breakfast bar toward the couch. She came to stand behind me, placing her hands on the back of the couch. She stood stoically through the scene. "What's with the black smoke? Is it, like, the devil or something? And what's with the noise? I bet it's a machine of some sorts . . ." she surmised out loud.

I couldn't help but smile to myself at my mother's attempts to figure out *Lost* in five minutes. *Good luck.*

She moved again to sit by me on the couch. She was dressed in dark blue silk pajamas and matching robe. Her hair was up in a bun and her face was clean. She was always the prettiest when she had no makeup on her face and she was not in her fancy clothes. She looked more like a *real* mom. She had a few faint lines and creases at the corners of her mouth and around her eyes, but they were hardly noticeable. Her face was delicate and exquisite like a china doll.

"Did Cal leave already?" she asked, still

staring at the television.

"Yeah, he just dropped me off and went home."

"You're spending a lot of time with him," she responded.

"Yeah." I kept watching the show, trying to not notice the look my mother was giving me.

In my peripheral vision, I could see she had an eyebrow raised and a half-smile on her lips. She probably thought Cal and I were more than friends—which was absolutely right, but I didn't want her to *know* that she was right.

"I think you have a crush."

I snapped my head toward her. "I *don't* have a crush," I said indignantly.

"So you don't like him?" She squinted in confusion.

"I do, but I wouldn't call it a crush. I'm pretty sure he likes me, too." I turned my attention back to the screen. I was sure my annoyance was written all over my face.

"I didn't mean anything by it. I know he likes you."

I perked up at her last statement. "You do?" I cocked my head to the side as I looked at her.

She nodded with enthusiasm. "Yes. I can tell by the way he looks at you." A smile broke out on her face.

"What do you mean?"

"He's always looking at you, smiling, and there's just an air about him. He cares about you a lot," she said, her own blue-gray eyes sparkling.

"Maybe, but he's one of those guys that has all the girls after him. I'm sure he's a player," I said, my thoughts turning to Veronica and her tight dress.

"He may be, but that's not what I see in him with you. This is more for him," she said—and with that, all my hope was placed in her words.

"But how can you be so sure?" I demanded. I had very little experience with boys. I had gone out on a couple of dates with some guys my mother had basically set me up with, but they hadn't interested me. I would have rather spent my time on the farm with the horses that were way more interesting to hang out with—at least, until now.

"I know a thing or two about first love. I've had one, you know. And it's not something that can be described; you just know it when you see it. When you get a little more experience in life, you'll be able to see it, too." She pushed a couple strands of my hair back from my face, like she always did.

Her demeanor was so soft and loving. I didn't believe it was my mother. I was more inclined to believe it was an alien who had hijacked her body. If that were true, I would welcome the alien peacefully into my life.

"This isn't my first love," I said quietly. I felt my cheeks burn hot, and I looked down at the floor. If I looked at her, I was sure she would know I was lying. "Hey, how much is the rent for this house?" I blurted, hoping to distract her from questioning me further about Cal.

"Um, I'm not sure. Your dad took care of it with Tyson. At first, I didn't want to rent, but we didn't want to buy anything before we knew for sure we're staying here," she said.

"And you have no idea how much?"

"What does it matter, anyway?" Her eyebrows were furrowed and her lips were pursed.

"It doesn't, just curious." I shrugged my shoulders.

She looked at me for a moment before turning her attention back to the TV. "What's with the airplane? They crashed right?" she asked me, but continued before I could say anything. "There is no way that that many of them would have survived that kind of crash. You need to go to bed and not fill your mind with such nonsense," she said with disgust before walking out of the room.

I turned off the show, bored since I had seen the episode. The house was silent as I walked up the servants' stairs. I was about to stop on the second floor—until I realized this would be the perfect time to snoop some more in the office.

I opened the office door and closed it quietly behind me. I walked over to the desk and opened the bottom drawer where I had found the file earlier. I searched through every single file *twice* before I realized it wasn't there anymore.

Had Dad seen me with it earlier or was it just a coincidence it was gone?

Chapter

10

FTER THE NIGHT IN THE office, the trail went cold. For the next month, I couldn't find anything about Kythera. I researched more on the internet, looking for Kelly Winters, the newspaper journalist who had mysteriously disappeared, and I made a couple more trips to the library—but *nothing*. I tried talking to people around town, but once I mentioned the word "Kythera," it was like I was a leper and they didn't want anything to do with me.

"What are you doing for the Fourth? Is your family going to Kentucky?" Cal asked, breaking my train of thought. He had come over early to hang out, and we were sitting at the breakfast bar in my kitchen.

"The fourth?" I said absently, finally looking at Cal.

"Yeah, as in the Fourth of July? You know, Declaration of Independence, the Revolutionary War? Any of this ringing a bell?" he said sarcastically.

"Oh, um, no, I don't think we have any plans to go back for a while. We might go for Christmas, though. Why?"

"My family always has a big party on the Fourth. I wanted to know if you wanted to go with me?"

"Sure, sounds interesting. I'm not going to say fun, because if your parents throw parties like mine, then you're asking me to keep you from being bored to death." I picked up a handful of grapes from the fruit bowl the chef had sat in front of us.

"This party isn't too bad. At least . . . most of my friends will be there, but I can't guarantee we won't be required to talk to all 'the important people,' as my dad would put it." Cal picked up an apple and bit into it.

"That's funny, that's what I call my parents' friends, too." I plucked a couple more grapes from the bowl.

"So you'll save me from dealing with the important people on my own?"

"I guess I'll go. But won't there be a lot of girls upset? I know you have to have a Facebook fan page or something." I popped a couple of the grapes into my mouth. The tartness made my lips pucker.

"You just think I'm some real playboy, don't you?"

"Of course." I smiled at him.

"Maybe I am, but I can reform, can't I? Isn't that a turn-on for girls? The reformed playboy, looking to be with one girl at a time." He took another bite out of the apple and stared at me as he chewed.

"Please."

"Even if you don't believe me, I'm a serial monogamist. I only flirt on the side."

"Such big words, for such a small brain . . ."

The chef slid a hot omelet onto a plate and placed it in front of me. Steam rose from the spicy eggs. He put another omelet on a plate for Cal.

"Since I like you so much, I'll let that one slide."

"Will Veronica be there?" I picked up a fork and cut a piece of the omelet.

"Yes, but so will Charlotte and a bunch of other people from school."

"Will all the Kythera people be there, too?"

A loud metallic sound ringed against the floor. I looked down, startled by the noise. Cal had dropped his fork.

"Damn it," he said under his breath, as he picked up the fork from the floor. He sat back down, but his jaw was tight. "Listen, can you not mention anything about that in front of the help?" he whispered, leaning into me.

"Sure," I said, taken off-guard by his reaction.

There was a long silence as we both ate our omelets. I suddenly felt really uncomfortable, and pushed the last couple of bites around on my plate. I had no idea mentioning Kythera in front of anyone would bring such a quick and angry reaction from him.

The chef put the empty skillet in the sink and left the room.

"I'm sorry for acting that way. I just don't want the help to know I'm with Kythera. Forgive me?

I nodded. "Okay."

"You want to go riding again this week?" he asked as he took the last bite of his omelet.

"Are you sure you can handle another round on Lightning?" I pushed my empty plate away and sat back on the bar stool.

"Can I request a different horse?" He smiled, and I felt the tension melt away.

"I'm not sure. They may let you have one of the little ponies to ride," I said teasingly.

"That might actually be a great idea," he said, looking straight at me.

Breakfast ended, and we handed our plates to the maid. We got up and walked to the front foyer.

"Thanks for breakfast," he said, as I opened the front door. "I would hang out, but I've got business to handle today."

"You're so funny with all your business talk. You sound like some thirty-year-old professional. What is it exactly that you have to do?"

Cal grabbed my hand and pulled me to him.

"Go to some board meeting with my dad. Sometimes I feel like I'm thirty," he said, letting out a heavy sigh.

I couldn't help but feel like he was taking on some big burden that was beyond the usual teen angst. If only he would let me in.

Wordlessly, he kissed my lips, threading his hands through my hair. As we kissed, I stepped closer to him until his body was next to mine. I wanted to get as close to him as possible, our bodies almost melding into each other's. I wanted more, but I knew we were in the front foyer where the butler or a servant could walk in at any moment. Seconds later, he untangled his hands from my hair and placed them on my face, holding his gaze to mine.

"See you later, okay?" he said, his face softening as he smiled.

"Yes," I said breathlessly.

"Good." He dropped his hands from my face, pulled me toward him, and kissed my cheek.

Cal headed for his mysterious black "Kythera" car. I lingered motionless in the front doorway for a few seconds more, watching his car disappear down the driveway and onto the busy street.

"Casper! Is that you, dear?"

I looked toward the street, startled by Mrs. Hamilton's loud voice. She was in her pink bathrobe and curlers, walking as fast as she could up the front steps of our house. By the time she reached the front door, she was huffing and puffing.

"Here's some mail for your house. They accidentally put it in my mailbox. I thought I should bring it over right away." She handed me a large postcard. It was an advertisement for a furniture sale at some store where Mother had purchased a couch. Important mail? Who was she kidding?

"Thanks," I said with a quick smile, and turned to go in the house.

"Oh, um, did I just see the Roman boy leaving your house?"

Would this lady ever quit asking questions? "Yes," I said, as nicely as I could manage.

"He's such a nice-looking young man, and well-dressed, too. Not many teenagers dress that nice anymore. They all want to wear baggy pants or pants that are too tight . . ."

"Uh-huh." I crossed my arms against my chest.

"I'm sorry dear, I tend to ramble. Are you dating the Roman boy by any chance?"

Mrs. Hamilton wasn't very good at pretending to not be nosy. "Yes."

"Oh, well, that's nice. He really is a nice boy, and he has such great manners. His family has been to my house a couple of times for dinner. And his mother is a member of the same country club. I see her occasionally when I go to meet the girls to play canasta or have tea. Gorgeous woman, did you know she was a model?" She wiped the beads of sweat from her forehead with the sleeve of her robe.

"No." When was this going to end?

"Oh, she was. I think she spent some time in Milan and Paris, too. Nice family . . ." I was about to walk away, but Mrs. Hamilton grabbed my hand. There was a look of concern on her face, which was magnified by her thick glasses. "But you need to speak to the Walkers."

"The people who lived here before? Why?" I said, irritated.

"Just do, dear. Look up Callie Walker on the internet. I heard someone at the club say that they live in California now."

I stared at her a moment. Her expression was so intense that something in me knew I needed to take her seriously.

"I will," I said with complete sincerity.

"Good, dear. Well, have a nice day." She smiled and shuffled down the front steps and onto the sidewalk, then she went next door.

I stood on the porch and watched as she opened her front door. She looked at me through her bottle cap lenses, no trace of a smile on her face. Chills ran up my spine, and I realized I needed to find Callie Walker . . . fast.

~ * * * ~

Upstairs in the office, I turned on the computer and started my quest for Callie Walker. I had no idea where to start and I knew this wasn't going to be an easy task. Walker was a pretty common last name, and Callie wasn't exactly unusual either.

I decided to start with Facebook. Almost

everyone had a page, so maybe if I typed in her name and California, I might get something. My search resulted in over sixty-five Callie Walkers in California. *Great.*

I tapped my fingers on the mouse pad as I tried to think of how I could narrow my search. Then it hit me. I put in her name, California, and Charleston as her hometown. I got two matches. Fortunately, both profiles were open and I didn't have to request either as my friend to see their pages.

Callie number one's profile picture was of her on the beach in a pretty pink bikini. She had blonde hair, tan skin, and huge black sunglasses on. Callie number two's photo was a close-up of two girls, their faces covered in icing and big goofy smiles. I couldn't help but smile at the photo.

I searched both pages, looking for phone numbers. Callie number one didn't have her number posted, but Callie number two did. I jotted down her number and decided to email Callie number one. But what would I say? "Hey, some crazy lady I live next to told me to give you a call," just sounded ridiculous. But that pretty much summed up why I was calling or emailing.

Oh, well, I didn't know either one of them. If they didn't like me contacting them, what could they do to me? I wrote a quick email to Callie number one and turned off the computer. I picked up my phone and dialed Callie number two's number. It went straight to voicemail. I left a message and ended the call.

As I walked down the steps, my cell phone began ringing. I pulled it out of my pocket, flipped it open and answered.

"Hello?"

"Hey, Casper, it's Charlotte," she chirped into the phone.

"Hey, what's up?" I said, disappointed it wasn't Callie.

"Are you going to the Fourth of July party with Cal?" she asked curiously.

"Yeah."

"Okay, I just wanted to prepare myself," she responded.

"Why do you need to prepare yourself?" I asked, laughing at her comment.

"Because Veronica will flip when she sees you with Cal, and I just need to be prepared for her whining and complaining," she added matter-of-factly.

"Oh, I didn't know you were friends." I sat down on the bed and leaned back to look at the ceiling.

"It's a small school, so everyone is friends— or, at least, pretend friends. You know how it is. I don't really like the girl, but she is a lot of fun to shop with."

"So she said something about seeing me with Cal the other night?"

"Oh, yeah, she was really mad. Veronica has a bad temper," she said heavily.

Suddenly, the call-waiting kicked in on my phone. "Hey, hold on a minute," I said, and clicked over before she could answer.

"Hello?"

"Is this Casper?" asked a sweet, girlish voice.

"Yes, it is. Is this Callie?"

"Yes, but I think you have the wrong girl. We haven't lived in Charleston for a long time. We moved before I started high school, and we never lived near White Point. Too ritzy for us," she said with a laugh.

"Oh, well, sorry I bothered you. But thanks for calling me back," I said, with some disappointment.

"No problem. Hope you find the person you're looking for!" she said and hung up.

I clicked back over to Charlotte. "Hey, sorry."

"Who was that, Cal? Was he whispering sweet words into your ear and telling you how much he misses you . . ." She giggled.

"No, and hopefully he won't ever do that," I said with disgust.

"Then who was it?" Charlotte didn't know the meaning of privacy.

I hesitated. "Did you know the girl who lived here before me? Callie Walker?"

Dead silence.

"Charlotte? You still there?"

"How do you know her?" she asked, all the playfulness in her voice gone.

"I don't. Mrs. Hamilton mentioned her to me and . . ." I paused, realizing I shouldn't explain my reasoning for contacting her. Charlotte had a tattoo just like Cal's.

"Hah! That crazy old lady? Listen, she doesn't know what she's talking about half the time.

Don't listen to her . . . there's no need. Listen, I got to run, but I'll see you at the party, okay?" she said abruptly. The conversation was over.

"Okay. Bye." The phone connection ended and I laid the phone on my chest.

Charlotte's reaction, made me all the more desperate to find Callie. She said Mrs. Hamilton was crazy, but there was panic in her voice. The investigation just got a boost and I knew I was onto something they didn't want me to know.

Chapter

11

"YOU READY FOR THE PARTY tonight?" Cal asked, throwing himself onto my bed. He flung his arms back and almost disappeared into the mountain of pillows.

"I almost forgot about it. I was so busy with Mother's party last night," I said, while I studied my reflection in the mirror. I had spent all day out in the humidity and now my hair didn't want to cooperate. I pulled it up into a ponytail and went to jump on the bed beside Cal.

"Oh, yeah, how did that go?" he asked, as I laid my head next to his.

"The usual—tons of rich people, little bits of food on crackers, and loads of champagne. Don't they ever get tired of it all?"

"I know I do. For once, I would like to do something for the world, make a difference. I'm thinking about applying to the Peace Corps after college, but I doubt that's going to happen," He paused for a minute, as if he was talking to himself. "I'm sorry I couldn't keep you from being bored, but I had other plans I couldn't get out of," he said, totally switching tracks.

"Yeah, thanks a lot. Although I did get a little entertainment out of watching Mother go berserk on several waiters and the chef. She wanted the party to be the perfect debut into Charleston's best party circles and the staff just wasn't getting her vision," I said, then stopped. "That's really awesome that you want join the Peace Corps. Why won't it happen?" I placed my head on Cal's chest and listened to the rhythmic thump of his heart.

"For the same reason you can't do the things you want to do," he said, his voice echoing through his chest.

"I'm determined to make my own decisions. I just haven't figured out how to do it yet. But when I do, there won't be any going back."

"I hope you get your wish; you deserve it." He leaned up and pressed his soft lips to mine. I kissed him back slowly, the intensity building at a rapid pace. He reached his arms up underneath me, easily lifting me toward him. I felt weightless as he lifted me up on top of him, my lips never leaving his. More than anything, I wanted to unbutton his shirt and feel his hot skin on mine, but something kept me from doing it. Was it nervousness? Or fear because I didn't know everything about Cal that I needed to know? Whatever the reason, I broke my lips from his and slowly rolled to the other side of the bed and stood up.

"What's wrong?" he asked, propping himself up on his elbows.

I shook my head. "Nothing, I'm just not ready for that."

"Oh, I understand," he said, running his hand through his hair.

I walked into the bathroom and started brushing the tangles out of the ends of my hair, needing to break the awkwardness of the moment. I put the brush down and picked up my cell phone. It was almost four o'clock. Another hour before I had to start getting ready for the Romans' party—but something else came to mind.

I'd heard from Callie number two, but nothing from Callie number one. I had left her my number in my email, and I hoped she would give me a call soon. It had been almost a week and a half since I sent her the email.

"What are you thinking about?" Cal asked. I turned to see him standing in the doorway.

"What? Oh, nothing . . ." I said, but felt the urge to ask about Callie. "Hey, did you know Callie Walker really well?"

"Yeah, why?"

"No reason, just Mrs. Hamilton mentioned her awhile ago and I was—"

"Mrs. Hamilton? The old lady next door?" Cal

asked, without letting me finish. He laughed and walked over to sit on the edge of the tub.

"Yeah," I answered timidly.

"Don't listen to anything that woman has to say. Callie was a cool girl, but her family moved. That's it. The old lady thinks something else happened, but nothing did. She's always looking to start drama."

"Okay." I shrugged my shoulders.

Cal looked at his watch. "I've gotta go. But I'll be back in a couple of hours to pick you up."

Cal got up and walked out of the room before I could even say goodbye.

~ * * * ~

I slipped on the dress I had bought on my last shopping trip with Charlotte, and looked at myself in the mirror. It was a cobalt blue sleeveless dress with a tiered skirt. A wide black belt with crystal beads was wrapped around my waist in an effort to give my boyish figure more of an hourglass shape. I was never into the super-short skirts, revealing necklines, and exposing as much flesh as possible.

I pulled my hair into a sleek ponytail, put in diamond stud earrings, and found a pair of strappy black heels. My normally-translucent skin had a bronze glow from the time I'd spent on the riding trails at the Hunt Club. The sun must be stronger here—it was the only explanation I could come up with for the change. It was just enough warmth to keep me from looking like a cold vampire.

I walked down the stairs in my towering stiletto heels, tapping a steady beat on the wooden floor. My parents were already at the party, because they didn't want to barge in on my date. Nervous butterflies engulfed my stomach. I became panicky, thinking of all the new faces I was going to have to deal with and impress. It didn't bother me at my parents' parties, because they were always attended by their friends, and people I only needed to smile and look pretty for. This party would include, from Cal's description, almost the entire student body of my new high school. This was my one chance to make an impression with them and I had no idea what to expect.

Thankfully, I would be arriving with Cal on my arm. Hopefully, that would be more of a blessing than a curse.

I walked into one of the front rooms and looked out the large front window. The street was quiet, and a few people were walking around the park. In the distance, I could see dark, purplish clouds over the harbor. A flash of lightning crossed the dark sky. I *hated* thunderstorms. It always meant that I couldn't go out for a horse ride or really hang out with the horses. They would always get spooked and jumpy.

Finally, the thundering doorbell sounded through the halls. I ran to the door so fast, I almost tripped on the thick Persian rug. I regained my composure as I opened the door for Cal.

"You look beautiful," he said immediately, and he handed me a bouquet of beautiful white roses.

"Thank you, these are beautiful" I responded with a smile. He was dressed in a sleek black suit, with a white dress shirt and dark blue tie. The suit was perfectly fit to his slim, athletic body. His normally unruly waves were messy in a way that reminded me of Robert Pattinson as Edward Cullen. I was only a little obsessed . . . *really*. His blue eyes stood out against his pale complexion, sparkling like ocean waves.

I walked out into the balmy air, instantly feeling a layer of moisture encompassing me like fairy dust. Unfortunately, this layer of "fairy dust" would eventually turn my smooth ponytail into a messy mane of curls, and my makeup would go from dewy-looking to an oil slick.

Twenty minutes later, we pulled up in front of the country club. It was a beautiful, red brick building with white columns. The usual fountain flanked the front entrance and circular drive. Cal pulled the car underneath the portico, where a valet promptly opened my door, and, in a flash, sped off in Cal's car.

The doormen opened both doors simultaneously, and I was instantly met with a burst of cold air. The lobby was as elegant as the outside, with a white double staircase leading to a landing. In the center of the room, a large chandelier hung with hundreds of sparkling crystals. A light pink and navy rug was centered underneath the chandelier, and a round pedestal table which held a crystal vase filled with white roses.

Cal grabbed my hand as we climbed the stairs to the landing. It was an expansive space, with light pink carpet and a few upholstered benches flanking the white walls. The far end of the room was dominated by several sets of French doors. Beyond the doors, I could see a large terrace with lots of people in dresses and suits.

The doors opened, and once again I was hit with the balmy, salty air. The terrace was packed with what I was sure was Charleston's "finest" families. Groups were gathered around tables covered with white linens and towering flower arrangements. Decorative lights twinkled in the potted palms and along the railing against the back of the terrace. Beyond the terrace was the harbor, and a view of Charleston across the way. Rows of colorful homes and buildings dotted the background.

As we entered the party, it felt as if every pair of eyes was on us. Several people looked at us blatantly, while others simply made casual glances our way. I held tightly to Cal as we started to make our rounds to inevitably meet *every single person* at the party.

After meeting a dozen or so local politicians, their wives, children, and mistresses, we came to a familiar face in the crowd. Charlotte was standing near the terrace railing, laughing and dancing with two other girls. Her eyes locked on mine for a second, and then she quickly looked at one of the other girls. We hadn't spoken since the whole Callie Walker fiasco, and although she had tried to act like it was no big deal, it was clear she still was upset I had brought it up.

I looked at both girls and instantly recognized Veronica. She was wearing a skintight black dress that clung to her flawless hourglass figure. Her dark hair was pulled up in a messy bun, curls framing her beautiful face. She moved forward and, without giving me a second glance, went straight for Cal.

"Hey, Cal," she breathed in her sexy, smoky voice. She moved into his personal space, looking up into his eyes longingly, as if I didn't exist.

I looked at Charlotte, who looked at me helplessly and shrugged her shoulders.

"You remember Casper, don't you," he said, backing up a couple of inches. He swallowed hard, and ran his hand through his hair nervously.

Instantly, Veronica set her piercing gaze on me, fluttering her long, dark lashes. She smiled, revealing her blindingly white teeth. I thought for sure she might growl at me like a predatory cat, but her smile wasn't the reaction I had been expecting.

"Oh, yes, I remember you. You're the one named after the horse, right?" she said, a hint of a sneer on her lips.

"Yeah, that's the one," I said flatly.

She continued to look at me, still smiling and all friendly. I didn't know what to do, but before I had time to think, she had returned her attention to Cal.

"So, what have you been up to?" she asked him, bubbling over with excitement.

She fluttered her eyelashes at him and reached her hand out to touch his tie. As delicately as possible, he pushed her hand away and glanced in my direction. I smiled back, trying not to reveal my own tension.

"Casper and I have been hanging out, going out to the Hunt Club, riding," he rattled off.

"You? Riding?" she said, sincerely surprised. "You must have done a number on him. Cal's never ridden a horse a day in his life," she said looking at me, still smiling.

She was playing a game with me. If that's how she wanted it, I could play, too.

"Yes, he knows it's a passion of mine. It was his idea, actually, to take me there. He knew how much I missed riding."

She looked at me, still holding her smile, but her eyes became hard, losing their luster.

"Casper is all about horses," Charlotte finally piped in. Veronica looked at her, loosened her grip on Cal and turned around to look at me.

"That's what I've heard. Your family owns horses, right?" Veronica said, with a little indignation in her voice.

"Yes, lots of horses. We have more Triple Crown winners than any other farm. Not to mention, we're the favorite place for the Queen of England and the Crown Prince of Dubai to buy their thoroughbreds," I added coolly, but with a smile.

"That sounds exciting," said the other girl,

who had been lost in the chaotic scene. She was a very petite girl, with soft green eyes and mousy brown hair. Her features were too small for her face, and her neck was long and elegant. She looked like one of those tiny ballerinas twirling in a pink music box.

"My name's Sara Lansing," she announced sticking her hand out for me to shake it. I grabbed her delicate hand, afraid I might crush it in my palm. "Did you ever get to meet the queen?" she asked, seconds later.

"Yes, when I was ten. We were invited to London. I played with Prince William in the palace garden," I told her.

I heard a huff come from Veronica. I looked over at her, but she still had a that stupid smile on her face.

"That's amazing!" exclaimed Sara. I was surprised such a delicate person could have so much enthusiasm without shattering into pieces on the floor like fine china.

Seconds later, Alex sauntered over to us, a cell phone held up to his ear. "Yes, I'll be there tomorrow. No worries, you know me," Alex said, winking in my direction. He ended the call and stuffed the phone in his jacket pocket.

"Hey, Casper, how's it going?" he said in a warm, liquid tone.

"Good." I didn't know what else to say as I took a step back.

"So how's the horse-racing business? Did you know I won a bunch of money because your horse beat the odds? I told Cal I'm quitting poker and sticking to horse racing," he said, as he jabbed Cal in the shoulder. "You know, that's where Cal first saw you, in the circle after the big win. He thought you were beautiful and I totally agreed."

"I never knew you saw me on TV. Is that how you knew everything about me?" I asked, shocked he hadn't mentioned this earlier.

"No, he researched you after he saw you. He had to ask me your name and everything—which, of course, I already knew, since your family is the reason I won big," interrupted Alex. He was bent on airing everything he knew about the situation. And from the look on Veronica's face, she wasn't happy with her brother, either.

"Yeah, well, thanks, Alex, for making me look like a complete idiot," Cal said, his tone harsh.

"Oh, come on, I thought she would be flattered that you took such an interest in her," said Alex, in an attempt to plead his case.

"I am," I said earnestly. I hadn't realized how much interest he'd had in me all this time. I was flattered—but a little unsettled by the fact he had never mentioned anything about seeing me on TV at the Derby.

"See, Cal? I did you a favor," Alex said proudly. A cell phone started chirping and everyone started looking in their purses and pockets.

"It's me," said Alex, flashing his phone in the air. "My offer still stands if you get tired of this guy," said Alex, winking at me and smiling mischievously before putting the phone up to his ear.

My heart skipped a beat. I looked at Alex as he walked away from our group and disappeared into the other party guests. Cal seemed to sigh in relief.

"Let's go meet some other people." Cal pushed me forward with his hand on my waist, propelling me into the rest of the crowd.

I waved at Sara and Charlotte over my shoulder as we scooted away. Veronica had her eyes locked on me, her hands on her sexy Shakira hips.

Within minutes, we were immersed in another conversation with a group of adults who worked with our dads. They did the usual doting on our appearances and how wonderful our families were. We stayed the obligatory amount of time before moving onto another group. We continued this game for what felt like hours.

We met some other students from my soon-to-be high school, including a guy named Xander Chen. He had a striking eye color of watery blue-green, Asian features, and a lingering scowl plastered on his face. I got the impression that he either was an unhappy person or he did not like me at all. I was leaning toward the latter choice after speaking with him. He had little interest in me, except for my name.

Once I had told him my name, his scowl deepened and his black brows knit together. He abruptly turned the conversation to next year's soccer team, and acted as if I were not physically present, but a ghost in the backdrop of the conversation. Guess he hadn't noticed my slight tan.

I felt anger rising in my chest at this guy. I didn't expect him to be enthralled by my presence or intensely curious about me, but he could have pretended to be nice like everyone else did at these things.

Adding to the insult, he asked Cal about Veronica and why she wasn't with him tonight. My heart sunk and my fury broke out blood-red on my cheeks. He was on "Team Veronica," a sympathizer to the enemy, and I immediately wished we had been standing closer to the edge of the terrace.

After that unpleasant encounter, we were moving to what I would be an equally unpleasant encounter . . . my parents. Before my mother could even get a word out, I excused myself to the bathroom to regain my composure after the Xander experience.

I walked back into to the upstairs lobby and began searching for a sign for the restroom. I opened the door to the restroom in the hall, sat down on the pretty floral loveseat, and took a deep breath. These stupid parties were always draining, and they weren't exactly my favorite way to spend a night. Adding to my dislike was the fact that it was a whole new set of people I had never met. Also, his gorgeous ex-girlfriend, who was *obviously* not over him, was here. Not to mention I already knew she had a connection to Cal through Kythera.

I thought again about the tattoo on her wrist

and how it was identical to Charlotte and Cal's. I wonder how many people here have those tattoos and marked vehicles.

The door to the restroom opened and the quiet room was engulfed in the sharp, staccato steps of high heels.

"Casper?"

I looked up and Veronica was standing in front of me.

"Yes?" I said in an unfriendly tone. *Couldn't she just disappear or something?*

"Why are you just sitting in here?" she asked, as she walked over to the mirrors.

"I was feeling kind of sick. I think I may have the flu or something," I lied. She raised a carefully manicured eyebrow. She didn't believe me.

"Then maybe you should go home. I don't want the flu and neither does Cal," she responded.

"It's probably nothing. I've just been out in the sun too long today at the Hunt Club."

"So is that what you do all the time with Cal? Ride horses?" she said, a little disgust in her voice.

"No, most of the time I go by myself. He doesn't do so well with horses. They sense his fear," I said, thinking back to his stormy first ride.

"No, he doesn't. He's never really been into them, but he's willing to try anything to impress a new girl and get her into bed." She pulled a tube of lip gloss from her purse and smeared it all over lips.

"You think that's all I am to him?" I stood up, irritated by her words. She was like an annoying bee who refused to go away.

"I don't just think it . . . I know it," she retorted, dropping the gloss back into her purse and looking straight at me.

"Really?" I responded, placing my hand on my hip. I wanted to go over and pull her hair out, but didn't think a cat fight would be the best thing to do at a party with a bunch of people I didn't know.

"He does this all the time, but he always comes back to me." She took a few steps toward me, swaying her hips as she walked.

"He's not coming back this time," I said with confidence, even though I had no way of knowing if that were the truth or not.

"He'll come back to me. We've got a bond, something in common that you don't. Something you could never be a part of . . . you could never be one of us," she pronounced as she walked by me, grazing my forearm roughly as she passed and went out the door.

Great. I'd only been here a couple of months and I already had an enemy. I felt the need to see Wendy and go for a long ride, but it was too late to go out to the Hunt Club. I was done with this stupid party. At least I could go home and take a long bath. I walked out of the bathroom and searched the terrace for Cal. He was talking to a couple who looked old enough to be our grandparents.

"Hey, can I talk to you for a minute?" I said, tapping his shoulder.

He excused himself from the couple he called the Donaldsons. "Sure, what's up?"

"Listen, it's been great hanging out with you here, but I'm tired of the party. I'm feeling a little sick and wondered if you could take me home?"

"Are you okay? My parents need me to help them with something, but I'll see if they'll let me go with you," he said and turned to look for his parents.

"Oh, no, that's okay if you have to stay. I'll just hang out downstairs or something until you're through."

"Don't be crazy . . ." He looked around the crowd again, "Hey Alex!" he shouted and motioned for him to come over. "Do you mind taking Casper home? She's not feeling well and I can't leave right now."

Alex nodded. "No problem," he said with another wink.

"I'll come by and check on you as soon as I can," Cal said and gave me a quick kiss on the lips.

He draped his arm around my shoulders, his warmth radiating through my body. "Let's go."

The valet pulled up a black Porsche with a license plate that read "Al's #1"—and, of course, it had the red "K" on the back. I got in, buckled my seat belt, and prayed Alex didn't drive like Cal.

I stared out the window. The sky was an ombre of blues, stretching from light blue to a deep navy. A few stars were twinkling like well-polished diamonds, and the moon was barely visible. A rumble of thunder sounded overhead, and a flash of lightning streaked across the sky.

All I wanted was to soak the salty humidity from my body. I wanted to forget about Veronica and all the other stupid people at the party. I couldn't wait for the day that this circus would be over and I would be able to live my life the way I wanted. College couldn't come soon enough.

Alex pulled up to my house and I opened the door to get out. "How did you know where I lived?"

Alex got out of the car and came over next to me. He hesitated a second. "Cal told me. You live just around the corner from him, and I'm just a couple of blocks in the other direction."

"Oh," I said, "thank you for the ride home. Sorry to make you leave the party."

"No, it's no problem at all. That party's always a drag. I wouldn't go if my parents didn't make me. But it was worth it this year to see you again, you were the highlight," he said, his voice smooth and silky.

I muttered, "Thank you."

"Let me walk you to the door," he offered. "I hope to see you again. You were the highlight of the party for me." He put his hand on the door frame and leaned toward me. I felt my heart thump hard in my chest. I had to admit he was totally *hot.*

"Goodnight," I said quickly, hoping to avoid

his next move.

"Goodnight," he said, without moving an inch closer. He winked at me and went down the front steps. I breathed a sigh of relief, but I had the sudden urge to watch him walk back to his car.

He wasn't as graceful as Cal, but he moved with purpose and force. He had a certain strut that made him seem capable of destroying anything in his path. As he opened the door to get back in his car, he looked back toward the door and waved at me. I waved and closed the door.

I kicked off my heels with more force than necessary, causing one of them to fly into the table in the foyer. I rushed over to the table to make sure there weren't any scratches or cracks in the glass statue that Mother might notice. Thankfully, nothing was out of place, so I turned around and went up the staircase.

As I walked up the stairs, a flash of lightning shone through the stairway window. It was a bright white flash which caused me to jump. Seconds later, thunder caused the house to shudder.

I hate thunderstorms. I think they're creepy and ominous—even more so in this hundred-plus-year-old house, which was pitch-black. I ran up to my bedroom, shut the door behind me, and rushed to turn on a light. I breathed a sigh of relief as the room became engulfed in bright light from my bedside lamp.

I stripped off my dress and threw it on the floor. I walked into the bathroom and turned on the tub, letting the steaming hot water begin to fill the tub up. I pulled out my scruffy bathrobe and went back into the bedroom. I needed to unwind and release some of the anger that had built up through the crazy afternoon.

My cell phone rang, causing me to jump. I picked it up off the bed and looked at the caller I.D., hoping it was Cal—but it wasn't a number I recognized.

"Hello?"

"Is this Casper?" asked a cautious female voice.

"Yes."

"This is Callie Walker."

Chapter 12

"HELLO, CALLIE. I DIDN'T THINK I was going to hear from you."

"I wasn't sure if I should contact you. I put everything in Charleston behind me and I didn't want to get involved again . . ." She breathed deeply. "But I think you need my help."

A loud crash came from downstairs, like glass shattering on the floor. "What was that?" I asked out loud.

"What? Are you home?" Callie asked.

"Yes." I walked to the bedroom door and out onto the landing.

I took a step down the stairs, but stopped when I heard an unfamiliar male voice. It was not my parents, and all the house staff were gone for the day. *Maybe it's the driver,* I thought, and continued down the stairs.

"Are you alone?" Callie's voice sounded strained and scared.

"Yeah, my parents are still at the party," I whispered.

I reached the bottom of the stairs, where shards of glass were shattered all over the floor. I didn't take another step, because the glass would shred my bare feet to pieces.

"There's broken glass all over the floor." I was stunned.

Without moving, I looked for the source of the mess—which, to my horror, was the small window by the door. The door jamb was broken and the door had been left slightly ajar. I was overcome with panic, but was unable to move. I was literally frozen in fear.

"You need to leave! Get out of the house now!" Callie said frantically.

I didn't answer her, afraid to move or speak. My heart thumped so hard that it felt as if it was going to force me off balance and onto the floor. My breath quickened, but I tried to slow it, in fear that I was breathing too noisily. I heard more noise coming from the kitchen. Things were falling to the floor, glass and metal objects clattering on the marble. I could see the door to the kitchen, and my intuition told me I needed to move and get back up the stairs, but I couldn't force myself to take a step. My brain was shouting feverishly for me to get out of there, but my body was too petrified to respond.

The kitchen door swung open and a figure in black clothes and a mask walked into the hall. He hadn't seen me. I ended the call with Callie without a word, and put the phone in the pocket of my robe. I finally willed myself to move and quietly started up the stairs. Unfortunately, the stairs were not as quiet as I needed them to be, and on the second step, a loud creak sounded through the silent hall.

"Hey, somebody's here!" I heard the man shout, and I was finally able to move. I rushed up the stairs. His pounding steps were rushing toward the front door and over the glass behind me. I had reached the top of the stairs when he grabbed my ankle and forcefully pulled me down. My legs hit the steps hard, sending sharp spurts of pain radiating through my knees and shins. I braced my arms against the landing in an effort to keep my head from hitting the hard steps.

I struggled to get my foot free from his vice grip, trying to kick him in the face. I struggled a few moments before kicking him squarely in the jaw. Instantly, he let go of me, moaning in pain as he grabbed his chin. But he recovered too quickly for me to get far. As I stood up, he grabbed me again and forced me, once again, down onto the steps.

With a quick and painful move of his wrist he twisted my ankle, and I let out a cry of pain. I was forced to turn onto my back, afraid that he was going to snap my ankle in two. From this position, I had less leverage on the top step. With little effort, he was able to pull my body down the steps and closer to him. My hands dragged across the wood steps as I tried to stop myself, but it was no use—I ended up almost underneath the masked man. I squirmed and kicked as best I could, but he now had a hold of my forearms, squeezing them so hard I had to cry out in pain.

"Where is it?" he demanded in a gruff, strained voice.

I ignored his questions, and continued struggling to get away from him. He shook me hard and pushed his gloved hands further into my flesh. I was barely able to move my upper body. I looked at the masked face of my attacker, my lips trembling.

"Where is it?" he demanded again.

"Where's what!?" I shouted, my voice cracking as I spoke.

I tried to hold the tears back, because I knew the minute I let them go, I would cry hysterically and without end. I didn't want that happening, because it could cause the man to lose patience with me, and I didn't know what he would do to me.

"The painting," he barked.

I stopped struggling, because I was so shocked by what he wanted. Didn't most burglars want money or jewels, things people like us have plenty of? Why would they want a painting?

"What painting?" I retorted, my voice full of pain from the tight grip he had on me. I bit my lip in an effort to keep from screaming.

"The painting . . ." He paused, searching for the right words. "Their painting . . . the one of the island and the ship, your group's painting," he said hurriedly, shaking me as he spoke. My mind was blank and I couldn't put his request together in my head. My mind was racing to find the answer, in hopes he would let me go.

"I don't know what you're talking about!" I shouted, and started kicking again.

There were hurried steps crunching on the glass at the bottom of the steps. Time was running out to for me to escape. I moved my body as hard as I could against his strong grip. I began kicking my legs, until my foot finally found flesh. He let go of me with a deep moan of pain.

I rushed across the landing and into my bedroom, as the man crumpled on the stairs. I slammed the door shut and locked it. I pulled my cell phone out of my pocket. As I held it in my shaking hands, it was hard to dial the numbers on the tiny key pad. I messed up several times and had to start over. Three little numbers had never been so hard to dial.

There was a faint noise at my door and I stared at it. The knob was twisting slowly as they were trying to open it. I felt like I was in a scene of a horror movie. It was locked, but I knew that it wasn't going to hold them for very long.

I ran to the bathroom, clutching the phone in my hand, and locked the door behind me. The tub was still running and was almost overflowing onto the floor. I reached for the faucet and turned the rushing water off. I sat down on the edge of the tub, trying my best to concentrate on the phone. I dialed the number again and pushed send. As the phone rang, I heard the splintering wood as they kicked down the door into my bedroom. The loud burst startled my already-wrangled nerves; I let out a scream and dropped the phone on the side of the tub. I watched in horror as the phone, in slow motion, plunked into the full tub.

I plunged my hand into the scalding water, but it was too late. The water had already fried it.

I clutched it in my hand, despair running through my veins. *Now what?* I looked around the room to see if there was any object that I could use to defend myself. I found a large decorative vase that was sitting on the floor. I sat it on the side of the tub, then looked toward the window over the tub. I held up my robe, and waded into the water. It was so hot that it instantly burned and numbed my calves. I bit my lip to keep from crying as I held onto the edge of the windowsill, pushing myself onto my tip-toes to look below.

There was no way I could climb out of the window and safely down the side of the house. The trellis I had broken had not been replaced, and I couldn't reach it from this window even if it had been. I thought about that night with Cal, and wished he was here.

I looked down again, knowing if I jumped, I would risk falling onto the hard ground below. I didn't like my chances. Either way, there was a possibility I wasn't going to make it out alive. My heart sunk down into my twisted stomach.

I went back to the edge of the tub, pulled my reddened legs from the water, and wiped at them with my robe. I felt tremors creeping up into my chest, but I refused to let them come to the surface. I knew I needed to be strong. I was going to have to fight back and hope that I could get out of the room and down the stairs.

The knob on the bathroom door started twisting. I gripped the vase in my hand and moved forward, but the door burst open, flinging me to the ground and shattering the vase on the tile. I scrambled to get up, but I felt a strong grip on my legs. My heart was beating so fast, it was hard to catch my breath. I squirmed and moved against him with as much strength I could muster.

"You weren't supposed to be home," said a baritone voice, which was calm and collected. The controlled measure of his voice scared me. I knew he wasn't going to let me get out of this alive, which made me fight even harder. I had nothing to lose.

"Stop it!" he shouted, so loudly that it made my ears ring. I stopped immediately and looked up at him. His face was covered with a mask, but I could tell it wasn't the same man from the stairs. He was smaller and his grip was stronger.

"Where's the painting?" he said, calmness returning to his voice.

"I have no idea what you are talking about!" I

shouted back, my voice cracking like the vase beside me.

"Yes, you do. You're one of them, you have to know what I am talking about," he retorted, digging his fingers deeper into my already scalded flesh. I winced in pain.

"I have no idea what you are talking about. Who's 'them'?" I demanded through a now-flowing stream of tears.

"Kythera," he said quickly.

"I'm not one of them. We just moved here. I have no idea what you want," I said, a little more calmly. As I spoke, it finally occurred to me what they were looking for, the peculiar painting in the downstairs front room. Why couldn't they find it? It wasn't hidden. It was proudly displayed over the mantle.

"You do know, and you're the newest one. Where is the painting? We want it now!" he said, once again shouting at me. I cowered at the sound, and then breathed in deeply so I could speak clearly.

"It's in the downstairs front room on the right, over the mantle," I said, hoping the information would end this terrible ordeal.

Although I couldn't see his face, I could see he was smiling as the rough material shrugged up his face.

"Now, was that so hard?" he asked, loosening his grip on my legs, but still holding them. I didn't answer.

"You're such a pretty thing. I could see why they would want you, although that has nothing to do with it. Your family has more money than the government, as I understand it," he said, going off onto some sort of tangent. I lay on the floor motionless, hoping this monologue would continue long enough for me to think of a way out of here.

"Does Kythera want me?" I asked, hoping he would continue explaining. One, because he was giving me time to fight back—and, two, he actually had given me more information than anyone I knew who was involved with Kythera. How ironic.

The masked man laughed. It was a deep, guttural sound that made the hairs on my arms stand up.

"Why do you continue to pretend you don't have a clue? You're caught like a trapped animal. You may have brought my partner down—who, by the way, may never have kids thanks to you— but you can't get away from me. There is no point in lying to me any longer," he said in a vicious tone.

Why was he toying with me?

"That doesn't change the fact I'm clueless about Kythera. They haven't told me anything, I swear," I pronounced, staring into his dull gray eyes.

He narrowed his eyes. He was contemplating whether or not I was telling the truth. "You will protect it till the end, won't you? Even in the face of certain death." He laughed again. "I will have to give you all this—you're consistent," he continued.

I felt the air go out of my lungs as he said the words "certain death." All the hope I had left was slipping away.

"I hate to have to do such a thing to a pretty girl, but I can't let you get away. I have to send them a strong message," he said, his mask shrugging up again. He was either smiling or snarling. Both choices sent chills up my spine.

He let go of my legs with one hand, but kept the other hand firmly on both of them. I kicked violently, forcing him to let go of my legs. He lunged forward to grab my waist, but I was too quick. I got up to my feet and jumped over him, but he reached out a hand and caught my foot as I sailed over him. I tumbled to the floor again, my head hitting the ground. The room started spinning; I tried to get up again, but failed.

The man got up and, with a growl, lunged at me. He grabbed my waist and pulled me up to my feet.

"You little *bitch*. You think you're going to get away!?" he screamed angrily, shaking me like a rag doll.

I was so dizzy that I thought I was going to throw up. All the strength I previously had seeped out of me. I let him shake me, unable to stop him. He threw me and I landed on the bed, the springs squealing in protest. I bounced back, weightlessly, adding to my feelings of dizziness. Once I stopped bouncing, I laid motionless on the soft bed. There was nothing else I could do.

I heard his heavy steps toward me as if he were the grim reaper himself. I breathed raggedly, trying to push myself up on my hands. I managed to pull myself up just as he grabbed my hair. He pulled violently and there was nothing I could do to keep from screaming at the top of my lungs. My neck snapped back as he pulled me to his body. His breath was hot against my ear.

"Kythera can't keep its hold much longer. Your death will be proof of that," he whispered in my ear.

I felt a cold blade at my neck. Tears began streaming freely from my closed eyes. I took in shallow breaths in an effort to keep my vulnerable neck as far away as I could from the blade. I braced myself for what was coming next, saying a quiet prayer.

"Let her go!" said a forceful voice from the door of my bedroom.

Without moving my head, I opened my eyes to see Cal standing in the doorway with a gun in his hand. His beautiful features were furrowed and hard. His jaw clenched and his blue eyes trained on the man behind me.

"You shoot me, you kill her, too," the man said acidly. He pulled on my hair again, and I screamed; the pain from my scalp was excruciating. He positioned me directly in front of him like a shield.

Fire blazed in Cal's eyes as his anger rose, but he held his ground. The gun in his hand was unwavering. "Let her go," he demanded firmly, ignoring the man's comment.

The man didn't move his position, but his

breath was quicker, and I could feel his heart beating wildly against my back.

"You really risking her life to keep your secret?" the man asked, his rough voice loud in my ear.

"No, there's no risk involved. I'll kill you and save her. There's no doubt about that," he said confidently. "Ask your partner," he added. I'd wondered why the other one hadn't come running in to help. Cal must have gotten to him at the stairs.

The man gulped, but still did not let up on the knife pressing against my neck. Without another second passing, I heard the loud pop and crack from the gun, instantly smelling the acrid smell of gun powder.

The man was startled and stumbled back, but the knife grazed my neck as he moved away. A second shot rang out, and the man fell to the ground without a word. Warm drops of blood sprayed across my neck and ear. I clasped my hands against my neck, afraid it was my own blood. I sighed in relief when I realized there was only a small nick in my skin. After the relief of realizing I wasn't hurt, I shuddered in horror that it was the man's blood covering me.

I looked at Cal, who was still standing at the doorway with the gun. He looked stunned, as if he couldn't believe he actually had accomplished his goal without killing me. I stared into his wide eyes before finally collapsing onto the floor.

All the calm fell away and the fear and horror took over. I began crying—for several reasons. All the emotions that had been building up came flooding out in a pool of salty tears on the stained rug. I sobbed so hard, my body shook uncontrollably.

Cal walked over to me and bent down, encompassing me in his strong embrace. This sent even more sobs through my aching body. My head was pounding from the crying and the hair-pulling. I tried to stop sobbing so hard, but I couldn't catch my breath. I didn't like crying in front of anyone, especially not guys. There was no stopping it today, but I figured it was okay . . . I had almost died.

Cal was down on the floor beside me; I was lying curled up in a ball, hiding my face in the rug. Once I was sitting upright on the floor, he pulled me into his arms, cradling me like my dad would when I fell off a horse or got a bruise. The sobs from my chest finally slowed down; I felt safe with his arms around me, but I still let the tears flow freely down my face and onto his shirt.

He bent his head down to my ear. "I'm so sorry," he whispered, sending chills down my spine. I wanted to ask why he was saying sorry, but was too tired to ask out loud. I would ask him later, when my mind was clear and the images of my possible death weren't floating in my mind every time I closed my eyes.

There was the faint sound of sirens penetrating the silence. Their shrill sound was like a soft lullaby. It was the best sound I had ever heard in my life. I lay motionless in Cal's arms, too exhausted to do anything else. I didn't even care that I was furious with him. His heroic and somewhat irresponsible way of saving my life wiped out his past transgressions . . . at least for now.

"I need you to do something for me, Casper," he whispered gently in my ear. I opened my eyes and looked up at his face. His face was still set in a hard line, and his eyes were flat and hard like stones, the blue becoming a muted sea green.

"Just tell them you came home and they were in your house. They were looking for money and jewelry. Don't mention Kythera, okay?"

I furrowed my brows, and tried to comprehend what he was asking. Then it hit me all at once that he wanted me to cover for Kythera.

"Why?" I asked, my voice hoarse from screaming.

"I don't have time to explain now. I hear the cops downstairs and I need to get you to them. You need to go to the hospital, but you have to promise me you won't mention what they were really looking for," he said seriously.

"When will you explain?" I asked, my mind becoming less foggy.

"Tomorrow. I will come by and will talk about everything. I need to tell you everything," he said, and my heart dropped. It was only more confirmation of what Veronica had said in the parking lot.

"Okay," I responded, laying my head against his chest. In one swift motion Cal stood up with me in his arms. I felt the smooth movements of his stride, until we reached the stairs. The constant jolting from the stairs made my head ache even more.

"Are you all the only ones here?" I heard a high-pitched voice ask.

"No, the two men are upstairs. One is on the stairs, and the other is in the first bedroom at the top of the landing," he said, still holding me tight in his grip. Suddenly, I felt that I was being pulled away and was reluctant to let go. Two sets of hands had me as they stomped across the crushed glass, and placed me on a gurney.

"Are they alive?" asked the woman.

"No," he responded.

The room became blurry and black, and the voices of the policeman and paramedics floated off into the distance. Finally, everything turned black and quiet as I was wheeled into the ambulance.

Chapter

13

THE NEXT FEW HOURS WENT by in a blur as I went in and out of consciousness. I could only remember bits and pieces of the chaotic scene of arriving at the hospital. There was the pleasant steady beat of the monitors, which lulled me to sleep, and then the inevitable wailing of my mother, which jolted me awake. She was beside herself, throwing one of the best dramatic performances I had ever seen her give. Although she was theatrical, I believed she was deeply upset, worried that I had almost died.

After hugging me and patting my arm, she pulled Dad out into the hallway, leaving my room's glass door wide open, and started to blame him for everything. She told him she'd gone along with this crazy idea, but now look what it had led to in the end.

"You almost lost your daughter tonight. Nothing like this would have ever happened at the farm. We're not staying here any longer," she said in a berating tone.

He was silent for a moment.

"Listen, it's terrible that this happened, but this could've happened anywhere. You can't blame this on Charleston—or on me. We have money, and that makes us a natural target wherever we go. I feel bad enough without you making this out to be my fault. If you hadn't have begged to stay at that party, then we might have been at home and avoided all of this," he said, his voice strained and ferocious.

I tuned out the rest of the argument, trying to focus on the steady rhythm of the heart monitor. I felt terrible that my parents were fighting about who was to blame when I knew it wasn't their fault at all.

Kythera was the reason for my current situation.

Blood-red anger filled my face and the heart monitor picked up noticeable speed. I wondered—could I tell my parents the truth about why our house was invaded? It would end all the arguing, which was becoming higher-pitched out in the hallway. As much as I hated it, I decided to wait until I had gotten the full story from Cal before saying anything to my parents.

My parents arguing were asked to keep it down by a nurse. They apologized, and Mother quietly came back into my room, while Dad stood in the hall.

Mother came to the side of the bed and began stroking my tangled mess of hair. I opened my eyes and looked up at her groggily. She still had on her dress from the party. It was a very pretty white, one-shoulder number with a full, knee-length skirt.

"How are you doing, Casper?" she whispered, her eyes peering into mine, searching for an answer. She fluttered her ebony lashes several times, blinking away tears.

"I'm fine, Mother," I said, my voice raspy and dry. I smiled, trying to reassure her I was okay. I needed some of my own reassurance, but it would have to wait till I spoke to Cal. Something told me the secrets he would reveal to me would either satisfy my curiosity or only deepen the pit of fear already building in my stomach.

Mother grabbed my hand, careful to not disturb the IV as she intertwined her fingers with mine.

"You're going back to Lexington," she said, and my heart skipped a beat as she spoke. "You wait and see. I'll convince him or I'll leave him," she said with determination.

I was shocked—and although I really wanted to go back to Kentucky, I didn't want her to leave Dad.

Mother's maternal instinct had never really been all that pronounced, but now it was developing right in front of me. Her eyes, which were normally cool, were lit with a fire I had never seen, and that same fierce protectiveness was set in the lines of her face.

I didn't respond to her statement; instead, I looked at her in amazement.

The sliding glass door opened with a whoosh, and a tall, blonde woman in a white coat stepped in. She had a toothy grin, with prominent wrinkles around her mouth. She took several steps toward us in her sensible white doctor shoes.

"Mrs. Whitley, I'm Dr. Green," she said in a heavy and melodic British accent, extending her hand to my mother.

Mother got up from the chair beside me and shook her hand. She stepped a couple of feet from the bed and crossed her thin arms against her chest, waiting for Dr. Green to speak.

"Casper suffered a minor concussion, and some heavy bruising on her legs and right side, but nothing too serious. We want to keep her overnight for observation," she said, looking at my mother as she spoke. The door whooshed open again, and Dad walked in. His face was beet-red, as if he had been running. He walked over to where Mother was standing, but didn't physically touch her, keeping a noticeable space between them.

"So what's wrong with her?" Dad asked, his voice tense and just below demanding.

"As I explained to your wife, Casper has a minor concussion and some heavy bruising.

We're going to keep her overnight for observation," Dr. Green explained patiently.

"Okay," Dad said, breathing out deeply as if he had been holding his breath. He was visibly better; his face was less tense and the redness was dissipating.

Dr. Green looked at me. "I'm going to recommend you schedule an appointment with Dr. Milan, the psychiatrist on staff. You've been through a traumatic experience—not only physically, but mentally as well." She scribbled something on her clipboard and handed the piece of paper to my dad. "If you need anything, just let the nurses know, and I'll check back in on you in the morning," said Dr. Green as she patted my foot. She smiled at me before turning around and walking out of the room, her shoes squeaking on the tile floor.

Instantly, it felt as if the temperature had been turned up a hundred degrees. Mother stood awkwardly beside Dad without saying a word, only intensifying her position, her face screwing up into a frown and her eyebrows forming a single line.

"It looks like you're going to be okay," said Dad, swiftly moving away from Mother and picking up my hand carefully.

He looked bewildered and scared, in a way that I had never seen him. He was always strong and sure of everything he did. But now he looked small, and the creases lining his face were more pronounced.

"Yeah, I know," I said quietly, even though I

felt far from being okay.

Life had been turned inside out, and it felt as everything was crumbling around me. My protected, beautiful world was disappearing. My heart had been ripped in two, and then my life had been threatened and almost ended for a reason I still couldn't totally understand.

He patted my hand softly, looked over at Mother, and walked out of the room. She followed suit, hopefully to work things out with him without another embarrassing screaming match.

I closed my eyes, and listened to the soothing rhythm of the machines and worked to clear my mind of all the memories of the most dreadful Fourth of July *ever*. I wasn't sure I could look at the holiday the same way. Would it always bring dread into my stomach from now on? Would every Fourth party we attend cause me to fight the memories of the masked men, the sharp knife, and the fear I had felt from head to toe? Hopefully I was strong-willed enough to block them out, but I was clueless as to whether I really could.

The door whooshed open again, and I popped my eyes open. I assumed it was Cal and I instantly perked up—and then realized it was Alex. He was still in his shirt from last night, but his handsome face looked forlorn. I sat back against the pillows, my heart sinking a little.

"I'm so sorry, Casper," he said, his hands shoved in his pockets. He looked at the ground, before turning his gaze on me.

"Why does everyone keep telling me sorry?" I said, a little irritation in my voice.

"If I hadn't taken you home, if . . ."

"It's not your fault, Alex. You didn't know. I don't blame you," I said.

He nodded, immediately becoming more animated, and he walked with a lighter step over to the bed.

"In that case, can I say that I'm very glad you're okay?" he said, smiling brightly. Without warning, he bent his broad shoulders over me and grabbed my body in a hug. I was surprised, and winced in pain as his jacket caught on my IV. My head was crushed against his hard chest, and my heart fluttered. His skin was taut, and excruciatingly hot even under the crisp cool blue shirt.

He let me go and leaned against the rail of the bed. "You've had a rough night, haven't you? What exactly happened?" he asked.

I thought about what Cal said, and I wondered if I should tell Alex the same story he told me to tell the police. I was positive Alex was one of them and would be able to answer my questions just as easily as Cal, but something told me keep quiet.

"I came home, went to my room, and was running a bath when I heard something breaking downstairs. I assumed it was one of the staff being clumsy, so I went to investigate. That's when I realized it wasn't the staff or my parents. I ran back to my room, but one of the men grabbed me." I winced at the memory of my shins against the stairs, and the rough, calloused hands of the masked man. "I struggled and got free, got to my room, tried to call 911, but dropped my phone in the bathtub.

"There were two men, and the second one broke the door to my bathroom and attacked me." I looked down at my hands, rubbing around where the IV entered my skin. It was swollen, bruised, and sensitive; I rubbed it carefully. I breathed deeply, trying to hold back tears that were welling up again.

"I got loose from him, but he caught me again and that's when I fell on the floor and hit my head. He got a hold of me and had a knife to my throat," I said, the last few words coming out slowly and with a lot of effort. I continued to look down at my hand, afraid to look at him.

"What were they after?" he asked, ignoring my fragile state.

"Money, jewels, anything they could find," I lied, remembering their demands for the painting.

I looked up at him now that I had the tears under control. He looked thoughtful and confused, as if he somehow knew that wasn't the truth. Cal had probably already informed the other members, which would include Alex, but I decided it was best to not back down on my story for now.

"How did you escape? Did the police show up?" he said, genuinely clueless. That's when I knew he hadn't spoke to Cal yet, which deepened the mystery as to why he wasn't convinced it was a run-of-the-mill burglary.

"No, neither." I shook my head. "Cal showed up."

"Oh," he said, arching his black eyebrows. His eyes lost their glitter, appearing lifeless and black like a dolls.

"He didn't tell you?"

"No, I just assumed that the police got there in time. What did he do?" he asked, engulfed in this new revelation.

"He had a gun. He shot them both," I said, staring intently at his face. His face tensed, but I couldn't figure out what emotion he was feeling. Was it disappointment, shock, disgust? It could have been any of those emotions.

"Wow." He looked at the floor.

"Yeah," I said in response. The room felt heavy, as if it had been filled with the muggy humidity just outside the window. He stood motionless, mulling this over.

"I had no idea," he finally said, breaking the awkward silence.

"He saved my life," I whispered aloud. The realization of this hit me hard as I thought about the scene again. He'd been millimeters from killing me, but by the grace of God or his aim, he had missed me and ended the life of the man who was threatening mine. I sucked in a quick breath. I owed Cal my life.

Alex had let go of the bed rail, and was fidgeting with something in his coat pocket. He pulled out a cell phone and began texting away. He was no longer interested in our conversation.

"Well, I have got to go home. I'm sure the parents are wondering what I'm up to," he said in a nonchalant manner, as if nothing at all was out of the ordinary. He leaned over and kissed my cheek. Heat rose to my skin and I smiled at him as he glided to the door.

"See you soon, Casper. Hope you're feeling better tomorrow," he said as he departed, winking at me as he walked out of the room.

The minute the door closed, he was on his cell phone, talking as he cruised by the nurse's station. Several of the nurses stopped and stared him up and down with lustful looks on their faces.

I breathed deeply, drained from the conversation in all possible ways. First of all, Alex left my heart leaping at twice its normal pace, which was embarrassing because I was hooked up to a heart monitor. Second, his behavior was unusual. The sudden happiness or unhappiness that he seemed to float between left me disoriented. He was hard to read. Was he upset that Cal had saved me? If so, I had a feeling it was his pride talking and he had wanted to be the one to save me. He had flirted with me at the party, and he was all too eager to take me home when Cal asked. He thought he had been my knight in shining armor at the party, but Cal had stolen his spotlight.

I shook my head, laughing at my silly thoughts. What in the world would make me think like that? I was reading too much into everything. I thought it was best to put it all aside and finally drift off into some much needed sleep, praying I wouldn't dream about the men in the black masks.

~ * * ~

I woke up the next morning with a jolt. I stared up at the fuzzy figure in front of me, panic running through my nerves. I felt the need to try to run away. I sat straight up and started to get out of the bed.

"Sorry, honey. I didn't mean to startle you. It's time to wake up, sleepyhead," she said cheerfully. It was Nurse Colleen. Relief soared through my achy body, but I felt the need to tell the nurse to *go to hell*. But then I remembered it wouldn't be a nice thing to say to someone who had way too much power over my life.

I covered my head with the sheet and tried to ignore her happy voice. There was a knock at the door. I threw the cover off, looked up, and saw Cal in the doorway.

"Come on in. I'm almost done here," said Nurse Colleen as she checked the monitor. She looked at my IV bag before she walked briskly out the door, careful to shut it behind her.

Cal leaned against the far wall. He was still dressed in his suit from the night before, which was wrinkled, and had a few dark red stains on his dress shirt. His hair was wavy and going in all directions; his eyes were darker than normal, and a haze of purple surrounded them.

"How are you feeling?" he said in measured

tone. He didn't move any closer, and his beautiful face looked tired and tense.

"I'm feeling much better," I said, forcing a smile on my lips.

If it weren't for the fact that he could solve the mystery of what happened last night and the mysteries I had been chasing since I'd been here, then I wouldn't have given him a second glance. At least . . . that was what I told myself.

Cal didn't respond. He moved forward and went to sit on one of the furthest chairs in the corner of the room. He was gloomy beyond anything I had ever seen before. His normally square shoulders were slumped forward, and his normally pale skin was paler, if that was even possible. He looked like he had been through hell.

"Good," he finally said, staring absently out the window.

I kept looking at him, hoping he would return my gaze, but he did not even glance in my direction. My heart sunk as I anticipated what could possibly be his news and whether it could be worse than what I had already experienced in the last twenty-four hours, even though I couldn't imagine how that was possible.

"Okay, so are you going to tell me what last night was about?" I said, breathing in deeply.

He stared at the wall for a minute and then turned to look at me. "I care about you a lot, in a way I hadn't planned on. But I'm not a noble guy. My motives weren't exactly pure, but when I met you, it changed everything. You took my breath away, and . . . I felt different. I wanted to be with you and protect you from everything that I am," he said.

He was telling me the truth, even though it didn't exactly make sense.

"What does that mean?" I said, raising an eyebrow. "For someone who was so against the vampire thing, you sure as heck sound like one," I added, trying to lighten the mood.

He just looked at me. "This isn't a joke. It's serious, Casper." He paused, and returned his gaze to the window. "I wish it was just a stupid vampire, but I'm a real-life bloodsucker," he whispered, and fear and panic engulfed my mind.

"What?"

"I'm not a cannibal or anything, or a vampire. I don't drink blood; I was using it as a metaphor . . ." he said, running a hand through his hair. His pale cheeks became flushed.

"You're confusing me, just spit it out already," I said, crossing my arms over my chest—careful to avoid the tube protruding from my hand.

Suddenly, the glass door slid open. Cheery Nurse Colleen was back, and she was smiling broadly."How's my patient?" she asked, picking up my wrist and searching for my pulse.

"Fine," I said flatly.

"Good. The doctor wants to run a couple more tests today before we release you."

"Okay."

"They'll be here in a couple of minutes to take you to x-rays," she said, looking back at Cal. She gave me one more smile, and walked out of the room.

I looked at Cal, who was now texting on his cell phone. He got up from the chair as he typed.

"So?" I said, after he stood there for a minute without saying a word.

"I can't say anymore right now," he said, returning his gaze to mine.

"But you were just explaining how you're like a bloodsucker but not," I said, frustrated that he wasn't going to tell me everything he had promised.

His eyes were no longer translucent like the beautiful Caribbean waters they reminded me of. They were dark and stormy, like a raging hurricane. "I'm sorry, but it will have to wait."

"You promised to tell me . . ." I fiddled with the white cotton blanket stretched over my lap. Tension and frustration was building in my chest. "*Why* am I in Charleston?" I finally blurted out.

He stopped texting on his phone and put it in his pocket. He focused his attention on me again. "Because I wanted you here."

He looked brooding and mysterious, like I had envisioned a vampire lusting for my blood.

"You wanted me here?" I asked completely confused. "So because you wanted me here, my parents changed our entire lives? That just makes no sense."

"It would if you knew what I used to get you here."

I felt the blood draining from my face. What

devils had he made a deal with to get me here—
and at what price to me? I was slowly starting to
connect the dots and it sent chills up my spine.

"What did you do?" I whispered.

"The less you know, the better." His breathing
was heavy, and pain suddenly twisted his face. "I
shouldn't have done it. I used whatever—good or
bad—to get you here, without thinking about
you," he said, his brutal honesty making my skin
go cold.

"But what does all that mean? I know about
Kythera, I know they're more than a charity
group. Please just tell me, I can't take all of this
anymore." I stopped because I was beginning to
get choked up. Why did I always want to cry
when I was really angry?

"Yes, Kythera is definitely a lot more than a
charity group. That's all a front for what really
goes on. The less you know, the better."

"So you aren't going to tell me anything else.
Don't you think I deserve to know? I almost died
last night for them. Shouldn't I get to know why?
You almost killed me," I said.

Cal clenched his jaw, "I'm good with a gun,
and I wouldn't—couldn't—miss."

"Your eyes said otherwise," I whispered,
staring at his face.

Wordlessly, he moved over to the bed, putting
his hand on the rail. "I could've missed," he
admitted, pausing, "but there was too much at
stake for me." He brought his face only inches
from mine. "I couldn't let myself miss. I care
about you too much and my life wouldn't be the

same without you in it. You make my life worth living."

Without hesitation, he pressed his lips against mine, and I responded to the energy that flowed between us. His lips were soft, but crushing and authoritative. Finally, he lifted his lips from mine and looked at me. My heart was beating so fast, I was amazed the heart monitor hadn't set off warning bells.

"Never doubt the way I feel about you, Casper. I was a self-interested soul that had very little motivation to be anything different until you came along." He pushed back my loose hair and kissed my cheek as he stood up. He took my hand carefully in his, making sure to avoid the IV.

"There's some things I have to straighten out, but I'll come see you tomorrow." He let go of my hand.

"With Kythera?" I asked.

He nodded as he walked toward the door and opened it. "There are some things that need to be undone, so you never have to worry about them again."

"I love you, Casper," he said, his voice barely above a whisper, as he slid the door closed.

I sat motionlessly, staring after his beautiful form as he walked down the hall, his head still hanging low. I finally took in a breath as he disappeared around the corner. My heart was racing and the normally steady beat of the monitor was more like the unsteady pounding of horse hooves at a breakneck pace.

He was telling me the truth. I could feel it in his voice. I loved him, too, but I also now feared him. Or . . . maybe not so much him, but whatever he had done to get me here. He'd looked so scared, so . . . *sorry*. As if he had done something terrible. That look had frightened me.

Something inside told me this wasn't over. The men in my house were just the beginning.

Chapter
14

I WATCHED THE CLOCK IMPATIENTLY. Seconds ticked by at a snail's pace. I had been sitting in the hospital lobby for what felt like an hour, while Mother finished the paperwork and Dad pulled the car up front. The wheelchair was uncomfortable and I was ready to return to normal life—or what I hoped would be a normal life.

But I doubted it could be. Every little noise I had heard at night in the hospital, I had jumped up out of the bed, sweat dripping off my forehead. I was terrified to close my eyes. I was afraid I would open them and see the man with the mask staring down at me again.

I needed to go see Wendy, and feel her

warmth. I wanted to make sure she was okay, that I was okay. I felt that being with her, in her stall, was the only place where I would be able to feel safe.

"Ready, sweetheart?" Mother asked.

I jumped at the sound of her voice, but tried to act like it hadn't bothered me. She wheeled me toward the exit in the wheelchair, the doors sliding open. The heat hit me like all the air had been sucked out of my lungs, literally taking my breath away. I felt miserable, as I instantly started pouring sweat.

Dad rushed out of the driver's seat and opened the passenger door for me. I got up stiffly from the wheelchair and attempted to scoot into the vehicle. Dad took my arm as I struggled to pull myself up into the front seat.

"Here," said Dad, as he lifted me at the waist into the SUV. I swung my legs into the seat in one quick motion to minimize the movement of my muscles. Mother hopped in the back without a word, which surprised me. She didn't like riding in the back. She said it made her carsick, yet it never seemed to bother her when she was in a Town Car or limo.

"Can we go to the Hunt Club first?" I asked, as Dad buckled his seat belt.

"You can't ride right now. You could barely get into the car," he said, putting the SUV into drive.

"I don't want to ride. I just want to see Wendy. I need to see her right now," I said, my voice shaky.

The car was silent.

"Okay, but no riding," said Dad, and I felt like some weight had been lifted off my shoulders.

Twenty minutes later, we pulled up in front of the main house of the Hunt Club. Dad rushed to help me out and into the barn. Just the sounds of the horses and the smell of the fresh hay made me feel ten times better. As we approached, Wendy put her head over her stall door. I wanted to rush to her and throw my arms out around her neck, but my sore muscles prevented me from making any fast movements.

Dad opened the stall door and I walked over and put my face on her cheek.

"Oh, Wendy, what's going to happen to me?" I whispered.

I removed my face from her cheek to look into her eyes. I remembered that in second grade, I saw photos of great white sharks and their lifeless black-hole eyes. That's when I had realized how different Wendy's eyes were. Hers were full of life and movement, like she could see through any outer shell someone had and into their core. There was so much peace knowing I couldn't pretend with her and that, without words, she knew everything about me. I felt like she could see my pain and the way my whole body felt like it was crumbling.

Wendy snorted and moved her head up and down. I stroked her neck and her back, placing my face against her side, where I could hear her heartbeat and her steady breathing. The world faded and I stood there, listening to her breathe, for several minutes.

"Honey, I'm sorry, but we need to leave. They need to groom her," Dad said finally, but I didn't move. I couldn't leave her, not yet. She felt so safe compared to the rest of the world. When I didn't move, Dad gently pulled on my arm.

"No!" I shouted, pushing him away.

"Casper, please," he said, as he attempted to move me again. I pushed him again, but he was too strong. He put his arms around me and literally picked me up and out of the stall.

"No! Please, Dad, don't," I said through the tears that were now flowing. He closed the stall door still holding onto me. "Daddy, please. I need her!" I screamed.

Wendy nickered and reared up in her stall. Several workers rushed to the door and tried to calm her down.

"Please!" I screamed again, trying everything that I could to pull away from him. As Wendy continued to fuss, the other horses started to become unsettled, stomping their hooves and snorting.

I pushed harder, hoping I could break his grip and get back to Wendy. The tears were so thick, they blurred my vision and I was getting choked up. I cried harder and my knees felt weak.

"She needs me, please, Daddy!" I begged as I collapsed to the dirt ground.

He finally released me, so I could sit on the floor of the barn. But then he helped me get back up and hugged me tightly.

"I'm so sorry, but you can trust me. I'm not

going to let anything else bad happen to you. I promise," he whispered in my ear.

I continued to cry on his shoulder. I felt like I was a little kid again, when I would get hurt outside and come running for my dad. He would hold me and let me cry and I had felt safe in his arms—but that feeling had faded over the years. The more I felt like he wanted me to be something that I wasn't, the less I relied on him and the more I relied on the horses.

In this moment, he was my safety again. He felt like the Dad I used to know.

~ * * * ~

I was numb and quiet as we drove back to the house. The car ride went by fast, too fast. Before I could blink, I was back in front of our house— where my nightmare had begun. I held my breath as I looked up at the sweeping porches and palm trees along the street.

I took in a deep breath and I was unable to let it go. I was frozen, and I started to feel my heartbeat flutter as I withheld the oxygen it desperately needed. Finally, I took in another breath. My mind was blank and frozen in fear as my parents helped me out of the car and up to the front door. The glass window had already been replaced, but it still was broken in my mind.

Chills ran up my spine and I stiffened as I prepared to enter the house, waiting for the sound of crunching glass under my feet. But as I walked in, I saw that everything had been cleaned and there were no traces of what had happened just a day ago.

"Go on in, honey," Dad coaxed from behind. I looked at him, a painful expression holding his features up. It was the same look he had had at the barn and the hospital. Remorse, fear, and pure anguish were written on his face as clearly as a map. Each line and crease led to his deep green eyes, which were glassed over and impenetrable.

Once again, I took another anguished breath and stepped forward. I'd never dreamed it would be this hard. The men's bodies would have been removed the day before, and all traces of their presence would be whisked away by some expert crew. I thought, with their endless scrubbing, the memories could be cleaned away as well. I was wrong.

I looked around the foyer. Everything was in order, as if nothing had happened. The only reminder was that the crystal vase filled with fresh flowers was no longer on the round table in the middle of the foyer. It had been replaced by a crystal figurine.

I looked toward the staircase. There were no splinters of glass, or blood where the man's body had lain strewn like a broken marionette doll. I faced the stairs and steadied my shoulders in an air of defiance, and—with a lot of help from the hand rail—made the slow trek up the stairs.

"Wouldn't you rather come into the kitchen, Casper?" Mother called from the bottom of the stairs. I turned slowly around to see her petite face staring up at me, the fear written all over her face. She didn't attempt to climb the stairs, as if she were afraid of what lingered beyond them.

"No, I need to do this or I'll never be able to set foot back up here again," I answered, and continued my slow ascent up the creaky stairs.

Finally, I reached the landing. I paused and took another deep breath, looking back at the stairs. My bedroom door was shut and I put my hand on the knob. I stood for a minute, trying to decide if I could actually go in or if I should turn back around. I opened the heavy door and was shocked at what I saw.

It had been completely redecorated. Not even the original furniture remained. The ornate, dark wood bed had been replaced by a more spindly bed frame with gauzy white canopy curtains floating above. The decorative pillows had been replaced by two oversized white ones, and the bedding was pristine white. The room had been painted a soothing shade of green that was very earthy. The rug, which had been stained red with my attacker's blood, had been replaced by an oriental rug, with shades of green and beige.

I opened the door to the bathroom to find the same dramatic remodeling. The same color of green adorned the walls, and all the decorations had been changed out to match the color. A vase of fresh pink roses stood on the bathroom sink, and a small vanity stool was in the corner where the vase I had smashed during the attack had previously sat.

I walked over to the sink and touched the soft pink petals. For a moment, I felt I'd beaten the fear and escaped the memories that had replayed in my head a hundred times. I picked up the new silver vase—and, without warning, the memory of the door crashing open flooded my mind, along with the feeling of fear.

I screamed.

"Casper! Are you all right?" I heard a soft voice say from the bedroom. Soon, Charlotte was at my side, putting her arms around me. I fell into her embrace, wrapping my arms around her body. I was choking back sobs, refusing to let another person see me cry.

"Yes, I just . . . I just remembered something . . . that's all."

"Why are you in here?" asked Charlotte, her tawny eyes searching my own.

"I needed to face it right away."

"Wouldn't you rather have a different bedroom now?"

"It would be harder to sleep down the hall and walk past the door every day. I can't leave things like that. If I can get past the demons now, then they can't take hold of me." Tears began welling again, and I was unable to keep one from sliding coolly down my cheek.

"Oh!" said Charlotte, pity penetrating her voice. She wrapped her arms around me again and squeezed tightly. I was glad she was the hugging type, because it allowed a few more tears I was unable to hold back to slide unnoticed down my cheek and onto her white shirt.

After a few prolonged seconds, she released me again. Her face was so soft and pleading. "I'm so sorry, Casper," she said sincerely.

"I'm fine," I said, managing a smile.

"I heard what happened and then I saw Cal and . . ." She paused, choosing her words carefully. "He was a mess." She didn't explain further.

I thought about Cal, reliving the moment of him standing a few feet in front of me with a gun pointed right at me. There had been a cool blue fire in his eyes. He had been in control of the situation, against the odds, and even the would-be killer had been well aware of that, his heart racing against my back. I had felt so powerless and small in that moment, my life strings held like a taut wire between the man with the knife and Cal with his steady gun.

I shuddered as the sound of the gun echoed in my mind.

"You're not okay," said Charlotte.

"I'm just tired," I said.

I looked at the bed, but was frozen in fear as I relived the moments I had spent on it, helplessly waiting for the man to end my life. It was a different bed, but that didn't ease my mind.

"You are, but that isn't the only thing wrong with you," she said firmly. I looked at her face and saw the same determination I had seen in Cal the night before.

She grabbed my elbow and pulled me toward

the bed. She pulled the covers back and motioned for me to get in. I obeyed, but hesitated before allowing my head to hit the pillow. She pulled the covers up over me—but instead of leaving, she strutted to the other side of the bed, threw the covers back, and got in. I lay on my side, facing her.

"Good night, Casper," she said sweetly, and rolled over, away from me. Normally, I would have thought it was a strange thing to do, but now it was comforting to know that I had someone here with me.

"Good night," I whispered.

My eyelids became heavy and I let out a deep breath. My eyes wondered over Charlotte's strawberry blonde curls, and down to her shoulder blades, where her tattoo showed through her thin white shirt.

I read the word "Kythera" with disgust. I turned over so that it wouldn't be the first thing I would see when I woke up.

~ * * * ~

The sound of strained voices crept into my bedroom. I was suddenly awake and out of the bed. I looked around for the masked man, but there was no one standing in the darkness. My heart beat wildly as I strained to hear the voices in the hall.

It was my parents, in another tense conversation. I looked over at where Charlotte had been sleeping. She was no longer there; she must have gone home already. I tiptoed to the door and put my ear against it.

"She's going back to Lexington," I heard Mother say in a strained whisper. They must've been standing right outside my bedroom door.

"You want her to go back by herself? You didn't see her in the barn like I did—she's a mess and she needs to be with us here in Charleston," said Dad.

"My daughter was almost murdered in that room," she retorted, the malice in her voice still obvious, even though she was whispering.

There was silence in the hallway.

"She can't go back. She needs to be here with us," reasoned Dad.

"I'll go back with her."

"No."

"Why not?"

"We all need to stay here," he said vehemently.

"Why?"

"We just do." He paused, then his voice got louder. "Stop questioning my decisions. I'm doing what is best for this family, and that includes staying in Charleston. If you want to move into another house, that's fine, but we are staying here," he said firmly.

"Of all times for you to decide to put your foot down. Your daughter's life was hanging in the balance in this very house. You're willing to make her stay here for a business deal? You aren't the same man I married," she said, her voice soft and mournful.

"This isn't just a business deal. We need this to save our company, our family, and the farm. The economy has hit us like everyone else. If you want to maintain the lifestyle you're accustomed to, then you will stay put."

"What do you mean? We just won the Kentucky Derby, and we have a successful publishing company . . . production company," Mother babbled, her voice fading as she tried to recall all the family's holdings.

"It's still not enough. When the market crashed, it took a big chunk of our money with it. We have a lot of debt."

My mouth fell open, shocked at what I was hearing.

"How close are we to losing everything?" she asked, her voice trembling like a child's.

"We're on the cliff. If it wasn't for the Derby win and the deal with Tyson, we would be selling the farm along with everything else—and the deal with Tyson isn't set yet," he said, defeat laced in his voice.

"Oh," my mother gasped.

I took a step back from the door, now completely awake and in shock. That explained a lot about why Dad had decided, all of a sudden, to move. But what kind of deal did he have with Tyson and why wasn't it done yet? My head was spinning and I walked over to the bed and sat on the edge of it.

"I guess we have no choice, then," Mother said, breaking the tense silence between them.

Father didn't say anything, and one of them

walked back down the stairs. There was a light knock on the door.

I walked over to the door and opened it. "Yes?" I said, groggily, pretending I had just woken up.

"Casper, are you feeling okay?" she whispered in the dark, moving into the room without turning on the light.

I stretched my arms, and evaluated my current status. My head was still pounding, despite the nap, and my ribs were still painfully sore as I stretched.

"I'm all right, but I still have a headache."

"I'll get Kirsten or Christian to get you something for the headache," she said, throwing up her hands as she tried to remember the maid's name. She started to walk out of the room to call for the maid, but she paused at the door. "I'm sorry, Casper, but it looks like we're going to be staying here," she said hastily, shrugging her motherly persona off her proud shoulders.

I should have been hurt that she would give up my defense so quickly, but I wasn't. I completely understood her decision. In fact, I respected it. She didn't want to lose everything— and neither did I, even if it meant staying here.

Chapter

15

AFTER A QUICK SHOWER, I returned to bed, where I stayed until the following morning. I woke up to the buzzing of my alarm. The incessant pressure in my head had finally subsided, but as I reached to turn the alarm off, my ribs still ached. I grimaced as I stretched to reach the off button. Finally, the happily chirping alarm was silenced and I proceeded to get out of bed.

I brushed my hair, washed my face, brushed my teeth, and made my way downstairs. I descended as fast as I could without looking at the steps or the front door. With my eyes downcast, I walked into the dining room. As usual, my parents were at their usual places performing their normal routine. Mother was busy scribbling on her yellow notepad, and Dad was hidden behind *The Post and Courier*. I figured they would be at opposite ends of the room, pretending the other one wasn't there, but they were acting kind of normal.

As I entered the room, I received a scathing look from Mother. "What are you wearing?" Her eyebrows were lifted high on her forehead and her red lips were pursed.

"My pajamas," I said flatly.

I proceeded to sit down. Kristina sat a plate with an egg white omelet and a bran muffin in front of me. I picked up my fork and dug into the omelet without looking at either of them.

"Why are you wearing your pajamas at breakfast? You should be dressed already." Mother tapped her manicured nails on the table impatiently.

"Because I couldn't get my shirt off because my side still hurts and I just wanted to wear them, okay?" I answered grumpily. I never was a morning person, which was another disappointment for my mother.

"Don't talk to me like that," she warned, but I continued peeling the paper cup off the muffin and ignored her.

"Dear, she's not feeling well. Leave her alone . . . besides, it won't hurt for her to not be dressed for one day, will it?" Dad interjected, folding his paper down to look sweetly at Mother.

"Fine." She went back to her notepad, but her red lips were still pursed in disapproval.

Dad continued to read his paper in silence, occasionally picking up his coffee cup. We spent the rest of the morning in silence. There was tension building ominously in the air.

Dad had been aware of the situation for so long, but had never shown any real worry in his face. He didn't show emotion very well, and always exuded confidence, but now that Mother knew about our misfortunes, the tone had changed. She wore her emotions on the sleeves of her designer clothes, and in the expressions of her face. Whatever she was feeling, she always projected it into the air, and everyone was affected by it.

My parents were usually on top of the world, but now it felt like they were fighting to stay afloat.

As I got up to leave the room, Mother called, "Casper, there's a special Women's Club meeting today that you need to attend." I turned around to look at her in awe, as she went on. "It's a meeting for you and for me. They want to reach out and help us get through this rough time. You'll need to wear a skirt suit or something in black or gray."

"Does it have to be today?" I protested.

I didn't like hanging out at the Women's Club when I was in a good mood—what made her think I would want to hang out with them after being attacked?

"Yes, they really want to see us and it's important we be there. They're concerned," she said, her tone becoming harsher.

"Then why don't they come over *here?*" I asked, my voice getting louder.

"They want to have a luncheon at the Yacht Club, and several members of the police force and a few local officials will be there as well." She tapped her pen anxiously against her notepad.

"It sounds more like a press conference or political meeting than a show of support for someone who was almost murdered."

Mother's mouth gaped opened instantly, and her eyes widened at the word "murdered."

"Casper, these people care about us. That's why they are making a big fuss. Can't you just go along with it? For me?" she pleaded.

I felt blood rushing to my cheeks and my heart started beating faster. *"For you?* Why would I do this for you? I was the one almost killed, and I don't feel like being surrounded by a bunch of fake aristocrats. They're only concerned that will leave Charleston and take our money with us."

"Casper Isadora Ghost Whitley, you better watch your tone with me. I told you that we are going and that's the end of the story. So go upstairs and get dressed and ready to go." She returned to her notes and began scribbling so hard on the pad that her petite knuckles turned white around the pen.

I turned to walk out, but then I was struck with some steely nerves. I had found out that my life flashing in front of me had the ability to do that.

"No," I said flatly.

Mother stopped mid-writing, slammed her pen down, and got up from the table. "I've had enough from you this morning. If you don't go, then you'll regret it. You won't step foot out of this house until school starts except to go to these meetings." Her nostrils flared like she was an angry bull preparing to charge at the matador.

Father finally piped up. "All right, everybody. Calm down. Listen, she's had a rough couple of days. Do we really need to drag her out in public? She's still not recovered. I'm sure they will understand." His tone was pleading, but loving. He was trying to soothe Mother, which was a difficult task, like taming a wild animal. It took plenty of practice to change her mind, unless there was something at stake for her.

"It will take all day for them to cancel it," she whined.

"What's more important here? Your daughter or a bunch of people we just met? Besides, wouldn't it be better if we invited everyone and had the luncheon here? Set it for tomorrow morning." He lifted an eyebrow and cocked his head to the side.

Normally, he would have let our argument escalate further, and then he would have taken her side—but not today. I had a hunch he was protecting me because of the guilt he was feeling about what had happened to me. He was trying to find little ways to make it up to me, in hopes that I might forget it ever happened and continue along with his plan to save the family fortune.

"Yes, that should be fine. Is that okay with *you?*" she said, her voice high-pitched and strained.

I took in a deep breath. "Sure." I walked out of the room and into the family room.

I turned on the TV, found some *NCIS* reruns to watch. That would have normally cheered me up, but it didn't. In fact, when they showed the dead body, I had to change the channel. *NCIS* may never be the same again for me. *I* may never be the same again, I realized. I tried to think about something else, turning the channel to the Food Network, where I doubted any dead bodies would show up.

I settled into the leather couch, pulling a blanket up over me. I felt drowsy again and fought to keep my eyes open. I was afraid of what I might dream. Nightmares were becoming a part of my new norm. If I could get away with it, I wouldn't sleep at all, which made me wish even more that I was a *Twilight* vampire. But I felt like even Edward Cullen couldn't save me from what I was feeling.

I was tired of reliving the horrible moments in my room over and over again in my mind. And, now, my parents' hushed conversation was haunting my dreams as well. Things were falling apart fast, and I had no way to stop it. For once, I wished I wasn't a teenager, and I wished that we had never come here. Even if that meant I would never have met Cal.

But I wasn't sorry that I had met Cal. He

made me feel alive and happy in a way no person had ever been able to do—but he had also caused me more pain than anyone before, too.

Kristina came into the room and sheepishly stood next to the couch, her hands held together in a nervous grip. I looked up at her expectantly. I didn't care if I was turning into my mother at that moment.

"There's someone here to see you," she said quietly, only lifting her gaze to mine for a split-second.

"Who is it?"

"Alex Ala . . . Alam . . ." She fumbled to pronounce his name.

"Oh, okay." I looked at my attire and felt the ratty condition of my hair. "Tell him to sit in the front room. I'll be there in a second."

I jumped from the couch and ran up the servant staircase to my room, my ribs still aching as I moved. I changed into a pair of jeans and a white polo. I pulled my hair into a ponytail and then walked back downstairs.

Alex was pacing in the room, his phone glued to the side of his head. He was wearing dark blue jeans and a white dress shirt with the collar open. Why didn't anyone around here dress normally? I felt like I was living in an episode of *Gossip Girl*. His short black hair was messy in a sexy way. He was animated as he spoke loudly on the phone.

"Of course I'll be there. Don't worry. I'll have everything you need. Give me a couple of hours, okay? No worries," he said. When he glimpsed me out of the corner of his eye, he said a quick goodbye and hung up the phone.

He turned to me and gave me a hug, which hurt my ribs, but I kept silent.

"Casper, are you feeling better?" He smiled broadly in my direction, flashing his blindingly white teeth.

I rubbed my right forearm. "I'm feeling some better. Still a little sore, though."

"I'm sure. You took a serious bruising. Is your head still aching?"

"No, that finally went away."

"Good," he said with a curt nod. He didn't immediately launch into why he was here, but stood, looking thoughtfully at me. I sighed heavily, fighting the urge to tell him to hurry the hell up.

"Listen, there's something I need to tell you," he said, breaking the silence. What a shocker. Those were not words I liked hearing, but I had come to the realization that they were a part of my life. They always seemed to follow something that would probably totally ruin my day. Well, bring it on.

"Okay," I said, holding my breath.

"I really like you," he said matter-of-factly.

"Huh?" I replied. I was completely shocked—and it was surprising to me that he would admit so freely that he liked his best friend's girlfriend. He now had my full attention.

"Ever since Cal pointed you out . . . then, when I saw you again at the party, I couldn't deny it. You're gorgeous. And I hate to admit, but I was jealous when I found out that Cal was the one who had come to your rescue, especially since I was the one who left you alone at your house. I feel terrible about that."

"No, don't feel bad, you had no idea," I interrupted.

Alex moved a couple of inches closer to me. I couldn't look away no matter how hard I tried.

"But I should have walked in the house, or something. But I didn't and I'm sorry. I wasn't much of a gentleman. You made me so nervous, I just didn't know what to do."

"Oh." My face was getting hot and I bit my cheek nervously.

Alex stepped an inch closer, putting his hand against my lower back. He sure didn't seem nervous, but at this point, I would believe anything that came out of his perfect, full lips.

"I know you've been seeing Cal, but he's got a tangled past with my sister. It will only lead to heartache in the end for you, and I hate to see that happen. He's not the most stable when it comes to relationships."

I awoke suddenly from Alex's dreamy spell at the mention of Cal's name. I pushed Alex back a little as guilt started to ruin the moment.

"Isn't Cal your friend?"

"Yeah, that's how I know him so well. He's the same with every girl. Plus, it's in his job description to be that way," he said.

"His job description? What's that supposed to mean?" I took a couple of steps back, and crossed my arms over my chest.

Alex walked over to one of the loveseats adjacent to the fireplace. He sat down casually, his arm slung across the back. He motioned for me to sit with him. I stood motionlessly in front of the fireplace. He shrugged his shoulders.

"Did Cal explain anything about that painting?" he asked, pointing to the Watteau "Kythera" painting with the red writing. The same painting the men had been looking for that night and hadn't been able to find.

"A little."

"He explained to you what Kythera is?"

I couldn't respond; there was complete silence. I looked at Alex.

"Figures," he said under his breath. "Kythera is an organization made up of all the wealthy people, and people with power in this city. We use the money to get whatever we want, from a change in city code to a free pass with the law." He looked at me for some kind of reaction, but I didn't have any. "We *own* this city," he said with pride, a smile coming across his lips.

"How's that possible?" I moved toward the loveseat, sitting on the edge furthest from him.

"A long time ago, Kythera formed in New Orleans . . . when it was just a part of the Louisiana Purchase. They took over, built the city up, and ruled it like royalty. Over time, they wanted to spread their influence and they moved into other cities."

"But what does all this have to do with me?"

"Didn't Cal explain that basically in charge?"

I shook my head. He hadn't mentioned

anything about that. "No, but how can a teenager be in charge?"

"That's where we are trained and brought into the organization. Membership in Kythera is passed down family lines. Once you're a member, your whole family are members for life."

"What about Callie Walker?"

He looked at me in surprise. "How do you know about her?

"Mrs. Hamilton mentioned that she used to live here. From what I've found out, Kythera owns this house and she had to be a part of it to live here, didn't she?"

He looked at his shirt, and brushed something off his shoulder. "We wanted her to be a part of it, but her family moved. Mrs. Hamilton sure is nosy. She needs to stay out of other people's business," he said, and I suddenly got chills up my arms.

"So Cal's in charge?" I said abruptly, hoping to change the subject. But I also was having a hard time buying that a high school senior was in charge of what he was describing as a powerful organization.

"Being in charge pretty much means you're a recruiter. You're constantly looking for new members for Kythera, bringing in new blood. He finds people everywhere he goes. Trips to New York, Los Angeles, on the news, talk shows . . . the Derby." Alex looked at me expectantly. It took a second for it all to click in my mind.

"He brought me here *for* Kythera?" I said aloud, staring at the wall, unable to look at Alex.

"I'm afraid so."

"But that can't be—I mean, I thought . . . this doesn't make sense," I mumbled, unsure of what I was trying to say.

"Don't be too mad at him. He was just doing what he's trained to do. He's been brought up to be what he is," Alex said flatly.

I looked up at his face. There wasn't any emotion, just acceptance as if this were normal.

I sat silently, letting it all sink in. In the silence, I heard a car door slam outside. I got up and went to the door, hoping it wasn't my mother back from the salon. I wasn't in the mood to deal with her. I pulled back the heavy velvet curtains. Cal's black Mercedes was in the driveway. Mother would have been better than this.

"He's here," I whispered.

"Good, he can explain it himself."

I jumped when I realized Alex was standing directly behind me.

The doorbell rang and I hurried to answer it, but the butler was faster than me. I was sure he had been directed to become a sprinter or lose his job. The butler threw me a glance of victory as he opened the door slowly. I didn't hear Cal speak, but the butler nodded and let him in.

Cal walked into the hall with a bouquet of white flowers in his hands. Cal glanced in our direction and his face instantly took on an angry look. He walked forcefully in our direction and Alex put his hand on my shoulder as he stood behind me. Cal's eyes flashed steely blue and his jaw tightened.

"Why are you here?" Cal asked Alex, completely ignoring me.

"I came to check on Casper. I wanted to make sure she was feeling better," Alex said smoothly.

"Sure," Cal said sarcastically.

"I did and she is and I was just having a little chat with her about things."

"Things?" Cal lifted his eyebrows and stared at Alex.

I couldn't take it any longer. I felt like the child in the room who everyone ignored; they were literally talking over my head.

"Stop it," I fumed, "I'm right here. Why don't you both have this discussion with *me*?"

"Yes, let's have this conversation with Casper. You came just in time, Cal. I was just about to tell her about Kythera and your plans."

At those words, Cal blanched white in anger. "What do you mean?"

"Don't pretend you don't know what I'm talking about. Go ahead and tell her that you brought her here to be a part of Kythera."

"That's not true," Cal protested.

"Yes, it is, and the rest of them will back me up on this. You came to us to get help in bringing her family here. You wowed us with stories of their wealth and their prominence in the thoroughbred world and how it would open new doors for us."

Cal looked at me. "I did, but that's not everything . . . they don't know the whole story."

"So what he's saying is true?" I said, interrupting him.

"Yes, but it's not the whole story—"

"I don't need to hear the rest," I said, glaring at him. The anger continued to build in my chest. "Get out," I demanded.

"Casper, listen to me," he begged, bewilderment filling his face.

"I don't want to hear anything else you have to say. You ruined my life and pretended to be in love with me. All so that you could use me and get me into your little group." I motioned for the butler.

"Casper, you don't understand. Alex and the others, they don't know the whole story. I used *them,* not you," he pleaded.

The butler appeared in front of me. "Show Cal to the door, please," I commanded, and turned back toward the fireplace. I couldn't stand to look at him for one more second.

I thought about what he had said in the hospital and I was hurt all over again that he could profess such things, and supposedly tell me about Kythera, but that he failed to mention that pretending to care about me in order to get me to join.

"Casper, please," Cal pleaded.

"She asked you to leave," Alex said in a stern voice.

"You've won for now, Alex, but I'm not giving up," Cal proclaimed as he walked out of the door.

I lifted my head up and the painting was staring back at me. "What the hell is this painting anyways?" I blurted out of anger.

I felt the urge to pull it down and rip it to

shreds. I reached my hand out and touched the corner of it. I pulled forcefully against the painting. But it didn't budge. Alex rushed over to me.

"Don't," he said putting his hands on my shoulders. I felt tears rushing to my eyes again. I blinked a couple of times as the anger welled up in me.

"Why were these men looking for the painting?" I asked, no longer caring that I wasn't supposed to tell what the men were really looking for.

Alex stepped back, his mouth flying open. Cal must have never revealed what they were really after.

"They were looking for the painting?" he asked, his words heavy and thick.

"Yes. Why were they looking for it? Is it worth a lot of money?" I crossed my arms against my chest.

"No, the frame is worth more than the painting," he said with a laugh.

"Then why would they have wanted it?"

"It's a symbol. They were trying to send us a message by taking the painting."

I looked at him in amazement.

"You mean I almost died over a worthless symbol? Over some mob feud?" I felt the heat rising up my neck and into my face.

"We're *not* the mob. We don't deal in drugs or anything like that," he said indignantly. He moved back to the couch and sat down.

I looked at the painting once again and back

to Alex. "Neither did the original 'Godfather.' Doesn't mean he wasn't a criminal." My breathing became shorter and I felt adrenaline pulsing through my body.

Alex opened his mouth to speak, but before he could get the words out, I grabbed a crystal vase from the fireplace and hurled it at the painting. It shattered into a thousand pieces.

"Casper, what are you doing!?" Alex jumped from the sofa, avoiding the spray of glass that fell on the couch.

"Letting you know what exactly I think of your stupid little club." Before he could reach me, I ran around the other sofa and into the hallway, where the maid and the butler were both looking in shock at the room I'd just bolted from.

"Casper!" Alex called from the hall, but I had already made it to the kitchen, grabbed a set of keys out of the pantry, and headed for the back door.

I walked into the garage, and got into the red Audi coupe.

Without thinking, I pushed the gas to the floor and sped down the driveway and into the street. I felt the tears creeping up again. I was so tired of the secrets and the betrayals. I felt numb—physically and emotionally. My body and spirit had taken some serious blows this week, and I wasn't sure how much more I could take without cracking up.

Chapter
16

I HAD NO IDEA WHERE I had ended up, but I knew it was in the middle of nowhere. I had been planning on going to the Hunt Club to see Wendy, but somewhere along the way, I had gotten lost. I crossed over a large bridge and onto a two-lane highway. I pushed the gas pedal down again and watched the speed zoom past ninety and toward one hundred. Something about the speed made me feel free and made me forget about the nightmare I had woken up in. It worked in the same kind of way as a horse ride.

Unfortunately, my need for speed also caught the attention of a policeman sitting on the side of the road. I saw his blue lights flashing behind me and I put my foot over the brake to pull over, but something in me snapped. Old Casper was gone, and new Casper felt like giving the cop a run for his money.

I shifted the car into "S" mode, which allowed the car's engine to push freely into dangerous territory. The lines on the road blurred and the trees on the side of the road appeared to be one long line of green. I didn't dare look at the speedometer. The cop's blue lights were barely visible in the rearview mirror. I smiled to myself.

The cop was gone from my field of vision and I started to slow down. It felt great to do something crazy. I laughed out loud, and brought the car down to a normal speed.

As I rounded a sharp curve, I could see a roadblock up ahead with two cop cars' bright blue lights flashing. I knew they were waiting for me. Where's a black Kythera car when you needed one?

~ * * * ~

All the adrenaline I had gotten from running from the law evaporated after several hours of sitting in a holding cell at the Charleston Police Department. I sat in the corner, with my head against the cool cinderblock wall, dreading the moment when my parents walked in. What could I have been thinking? Like the cop was just going to let me go?

Geez, I'm an idiot. This is going to look great on my college application. Do you have to put your criminal history on a college application? Are felons allowed to apply to college? And once I turn eighteen, will I still be able to vote?

Questions swirled in my head, making me dizzy. I stared at the dirty concrete floor, holding my head in my hands.

"Casper," someone said, and I instantly looked up. I was shocked to see it was Cal's father, Tyson.

"What? Um . . . why are you here?" I got up from the bench and walked toward the bars separating us.

"I'm here to get you out," he said sternly, not smiling.

"Oh, they sent Kythera here to save me," I huffed.

"Yes, and I'm the only thing keeping this off your record and out of the newspapers. And try not to mention the K-word out loud in the *jail*," he said.

I felt embarrassed as he looked down at me angrily.

"And here I thought you would rub off on Cal, but apparently he's rubbed off on you. He's always been irresponsible—even more so lately. Maybe you were never a good influence to begin with. He's been turning against *everything* I want him to do. You two aren't good for each other," he said, shaking his head.

"So are you banning him from seeing me? Go ahead, I never want to talk to him again." I grabbed the bars, pulling my face as close to them as possible.

He laughed, but it wasn't the kind of laugh that sounded happy—it was menacing. "No, because I've got more important things to worry about, and no matter how ticked off I am at Cal, he's still a part of this." He looked at me, his jaw clenched.

"I want nothing to do with your little club," I said, my teeth clenched together.

"What a sense of appreciation for the 'little club' that's saving your reputation and your family—and, believe me, I could let you sit in here for a good long time, but that does me no good. You see, I could let your whole family go down without a cent to your name, but your father has the Queen of England on speed dial and swaps birthday gifts with the Sultan of Brunei."

I stared at him, unable to move.

"And that's almost worth more than any money we could get from you. So, I'm going to get you out of here and you're going to cooperate in order to save your family's money, aren't you?" he asked, a fake smile on his lips.

I looked at him, mulling over my options—which were none, at the moment. "Yes," I finally said.

"You mean, 'Yes, sir,'" he said, and waited for my response.

I bit my cheek and stared at him for a minute before reluctantly muttering, "Yes, sir."

"Good. Deputy, release this young lady."

The deputy raced to the cell and unlocked the heavy bar door. It squeaked loudly as it opened, the sound echoing off the gray walls. I walked out slowly, following Tyson toward the exit. He never turned around to look at me as he got into his black Bentley. He cranked up the engine and revved it impatiently as he waited for me to get in the car. I looked around the parking lot for my car. Tyson honked the horn and I sped up to get into his car. As soon as I jumped in, he pushed the gas and swerved out of the parking lot. Now I knew where Cal got his insane driving skills. I held onto the door, but didn't say a word.

A half-hour later, Tyson pulled up to my parents' house. I opened the car door, but hesitated when he said, "Now, remember what I told you. If you cooperate with us, you'll save your family. If you don't, you can kiss your horses' goodbye." He didn't even look at me as he spoke.

"Yes, sir," I said, as I nodded in acknowledgement. Then I slammed the door shut.

Tyson's threats didn't really bother me. I wasn't convinced that Kythera had as much power as he, Cal, or Alex had been saying. It just seemed ridiculous to me.

I walked through the front door and started up the stairs to my room. Maybe I could hide out for a couple more hours before I had to face my parents.

"Casper Isadora Ghost Whitley, you stop right there."

No luck, I thought, and turned around to see Mother standing at the foot of the stairs. Her red lips were pursed and her forehead was wrinkled.

"Follow me to the dining room. We need to have a discussion with you." She swiveled around, walked briskly down the hall, and pushed through the double doors. I walked a lot slower, feeling like I might be able to savor a few more seconds of peace before the inevitable yelling began.

I entered the dining room to find both parents patiently sitting at the table. I had a sense of déjà vu, and I was transported back to the morning when they told me we were moving to Charleston. My empty stomach filled with dread.

I didn't wait for them to ask me to sit down. I picked a seat a few places down from them and I waited for the lecture to begin.

"Did Tyson bring you home?" asked Dad, his voice measured and calm.

"Yes. What happened to the car I was driving?"

"We sent someone to pick it up. Did Tyson talk to you about . . ." he paused, not wanting to say the word.

"Kythera? Yes, he did." I crossed my arms over my chest and sat back in the stiff chair.

"And?" He leaned forward on the table, clasping his hands together in front of him.

"And what?"

"And what did you say?" he coaxed.

"I said I would think about it," I lied. I hated to lie to him, but I needed time to think about everything. This was just too much for me to deal with in a week's time.

Dad shifted a worried glance to Mother before focusing on me again. "You didn't give him an answer about Kythera?"

I was getting sick and tired of that name. It was unusual and had no meaning to me until a couple of months ago. I hoped there would be a point where I would never have to hear it again. And had they completely forgotten about me getting arrested?

"Not an absolute answer. Why?"

"I'll come straight to the point. We want you to join . . ." He paused. "Actually, we aren't asking, we're telling you that you have to join." His words were forceful and desperate.

"You want to be a part of them, then why don't you join? Why do I have to?" I said, looking up at the ceiling.

"I can't join without you. You're the heir to our family fortune and they need a guarantee from you."

"What kind of guarantee?" I asked, sitting up and putting my hands on the table.

"They need a guarantee that you'll continue to commit our money and resources to Kythera in the future. If I join without you, they have no guarantee that you will cooperate with them after I'm gone."

"What about when I have kids? Aren't they worried *they* won't want to go along with it?" I said, feeling like I had found a pretty convincing loophole.

"They don't care about heirs who don't exist yet. As long as all living heirs in the family join, any heirs in the future are already committed."

"Oh," I said, pausing to think. "What if I don't want to commit my life to them?"

He shook his head. "It's either you join or we lose everything we have. The recent economy has taken a toll on our holdings, and we are left with a lot of debt. We had a lot of stock in corporations now in bankruptcy. The last Derby win saved the farm, but it's not enough, especially when we didn't do so well at the Belmont or Preakness this year. I came to Charleston because of Tyson's offer and we need them to save our sinking ship. I promised you would go along with everything."

I could tell from the strained lines of his face that it was hard to admit. Dad had always prided himself on being a shrewd businessman and he didn't like to admit defeat or let someone else help.

I didn't say anything as I tried to think about my options. Defeat hung in the air, as I realized my fate had already been sealed. We would lose everything if I didn't do what he was asking.

"Let me think about it?" I asked, fidgeting in my seat, hoping I could stall a little while longer.

The angry lines deepened in his face. "We don't have time for that, Casper. We'll lose the horse farm, if nothing else."

"Why?" I asked shocked.

"I used the horse farm as sort of a down payment to them, and on the lease for this house. If we back out of Kythera, we have to leave this house, and will lose the horse farm if that happens . . . including Wendy."

So I *had* seen the horse farm on the lease. I was nauseated. *"How could you do that?"*

"I had to offer something up front to even be considered for membership. They've had a couple of people back out in the past; this was a new requirement to keep that from happening. The farm was the only thing that had any equity and value left in it that I could offer them."

"So I really don't have a choice. Why are you asking me to join when it sounds like the decision's already made?"

I got up and walked out of the room. I felt dazed and numb. What had just happened? Not only did Cal have ulterior motives for bringing me to Charleston, but so did my parents. I felt a sense of betrayal. Why was everything resting on my shoulders? I should be worrying about prom, school, or the recent jail time I'd spent for speeding like a maniac, not protecting my parents' money by selling my soul.

So many questions were swirling around my mushy brain as I made my way up the stairs and into my bedroom. The room that had been a sanctuary the first couple of weeks here was now just as much a prison as the rest of the house.

I picked up my cell phone from the bed and stared at it. I felt the urge to call someone, but who? Everyone I knew was a part of Kythera, and they weren't going to be much help.

Then it hit me: Callie. I had hung up on her a couple of nights ago during the break-in, and I had never called her back. Now seemed like the perfect time to talk to her.

I looked through my received calls list, looking for her number. It was easy to spot, since it was the only call I had received that wasn't in my contacts list. I pushed the send button and anxiously waited for her to pick up. I hoped she would pick up.

"Hello?" said a sweet, girly voice, and I breathed out in relief.

"Callie, it's Casper. I'm sorry about the other night. You won't believe what happened to me . . ."

"Yeah, I was wondering about that. I thought about calling back, but I was afraid of what I would find out," she said, her voice becoming low.

"What do you mean?"

"I don't know how much you know about that house, or who owns it, but you need to get out of there if you can. You are stepping into the middle of a war."

I felt the hairs stand up on my arms and the back of my neck. "What kind of war?"

"Listen, I'm just going to tell you. I'm sure you've heard of the name Kythera and that they're a group of wealthy people with a lot of power. That's all true, but they're not the only ones. There's another group looking to take over their territory."

"Like a mob or gang war?"

"Yes, and if you step into Kythera, you become a target—and by the sound of the last time I talked to you, you're already on their hit list."

"Is that why you left?" I asked, walking over to the window overlooking the backyard.

"Yes, we didn't want any part of it. My parents thought about joining because of the way it was described to them. A group of wealthy people who could become even richer and do anything they want and live above the rules. But when things started happening, they didn't want anything to do with it. So we moved to California, where my mom has some family."

I stared out at the oak trees in the backyard, barely lit by the fading sunlight. "What happened to you?"

"Hey, Callie, it's time for dinner!" I heard in the background.

"Hey, I've got to go, but I promise to call back sometime tomorrow," Callie said quickly.

"Sure, but can I ask a quick question?"

"Yeah, what?"

"How did you get out?"

"Callie . . . I mean it!" said the now-angry voice.

"Cal helped us . . . call you later," she said and the line went dead.

Chapter

17

I SHUT THE PHONE AND put it on the bed and headed to turn on the tub. I needed a long, hot bath. As I walked into the bathroom, I heard a sharp tap on the window above the tub. I turned to the vanity and looked in the mirror. Then I heard the noise again. I stepped into the bathtub and pulled up the window. A pebble flew into the window and whizzed by my head. I looked down to see Cal standing in our backyard.

"You know I have a cell phone, right?" I called down to him.

"Yeah, but I figured you'd see my name and ignore the call. Besides, this is way cooler than a phone call," he said, his smiling face clearly visible in the darkly-lit yard.

"Fine, I guess I'll let you in. Come to the back patio door."

He nodded and started walking to the back of the house.

I flew down the stairs, through the kitchen, and into the family room. Cal was already at the door when I reached it. My heart started pounding as I opened the door for him.

"Come in," I said. I would have just slammed it in his face, but after talking to Callie, I felt the need to let him explain.

He paused in the doorway, "I'm glad you'll talk to me."

"I thought about just leaving you out there or slamming the door in your face. You don't really deserve it, since you're the reason my whole world has gone to hell." I stood in the doorway, unwilling to let him into the house.

"So what changed your mind about letting me explain?"

"Callie Walker."

He looked at me, puzzled, but I didn't explain any further.

"Listen, I know I was wrong to bring you into this, but I've got an explanation. I told my dad about your family and said that you would make a great addition to the group, but I really didn't care if they accepted you into Kythera or not. I just wanted a way to meet you." He moved toward me and I moved a couple of steps back allowing him into the house. "So I really used Kythera, not you."

I searched his eyes, and I knew he was telling the truth. "But that doesn't change the problems I have now. I'm stuck. There's nothing I can do but join the stupid group. You've left with me without a choice."

"I tried my best with them last night, but there's no way my dad's going to let your family go—at least, not without a fight, not once he found out all the connections your family has. But I tried, I promise." He put his hands on my shoulders and their warmth radiated through my bones. My heart pounded so loud in my ears I couldn't hear anything else.

"Like you did for Callie?"

Cal looked at me, surprised I knew that information. "Yes, but Callie's family didn't have anything to offer Kythera but more money. They let them go without a huge fight when I asked, although my dad didn't really like me after that. I'm not high on his list anymore."

"Well, I wish I wasn't so high on his list either." I felt the anger beginning to build. This wasn't fair.

Cal pulled me to his chest and wrapped his arms around me. At first, I wanted to resist, but then I laid my head on his shoulder and took in his thick, woody scent. I wrapped my arms around him as tightly as I could. I closed my eyes, focusing on his warmth, which now radiated against my body.

"You could leave here, run away like you said when we first met—and I'll go with you," he suggested.

I opened my eyes and looked up at him. He was serious. "*What?* Have you lost your mind? First of all, where would we go? We're only seventeen, so not only are we underage, but we couldn't make it a day on our own." I was flabbergasted by his suggestion that we become runaways.

He looked at me thoughtfully, no hint of a smile on his face. "I'm eighteen, and I have access to a trust fund. We could go wherever you want. We couldn't go to Lexington, for the obvious reasons, but we could go out west to Montana or somewhere like that, where they have horses and you can ride every day."

No matter how insane his idea was, it was music to my ears. He was promising freedom, something I wanted more than anything. I seriously contemplated his suggestion—but then I returned to my senses.

"I can't just leave my family like that. They need me to become a part of your group to save the horse farm. I can't abandon them now. And I *refuse* to abandon the horses." I crossed my arms thoughtfully against my chest and stared at him, hoping he could see how determined I was to save the farm.

He didn't immediately answer. He looked down at the floor, as if he was searching for something. "I love you and I don't want Kythera to change you. There's someone coming for Kythera and I don't want them coming for you," he said, still looking at the ground.

"They're already after me and Kythera can't

change me. I'll agree to be a part of it, but inside I'll be fighting every step," I said.

"You don't understand. What happened to you is just the beginning. It's only going to get worse." He finally looked up at me.

"Who's after you?"

"I don't know. My dad knows something about it, but he hasn't told me anything." He shook his head and ran his hand through his hair.

The room was silent for a few minutes. I stared out into the backyard. The shadows of the trees covered in Spanish moss were swaying against the dark green grass. The Spanish moss looked like the tattered cloak of the reaper on his gnarled arms. It was an eerie scene. I shivered and returned my gaze to Cal.

"I don't know what to tell you. I have no choice," I said calmly.

He breathed out heavily and his jaw tightened. "Fine—if you're going to go ahead with it, then I'm going to protect you the best that I can."

"I don't need your protection—thanks for the offer, though," I countered.

"You might want to think about that again," he said, smiling and raising an eyebrow.

"Oh, I guess I did forget you saved my life. Can I ask why you just happened to have a gun when you came to my house? Do you always carry a weapon?"

"I do, at least in my car. I could see the broken glass from the driveway, so I brought it in with me."

"Do I need a weapon, then, if I'm going into war?" I turned to go into the kitchen and flipped on the lamp on the island. I was tired of standing in the dark like two ghosts. A soft, buttery glow ensconced the room.

"If I thought I could be here twenty-four seven, I would say no, but every girl needs some kind of protection. Maybe not a gun, but at least a steel bat."

I laughed. "You don't think I could handle a gun?" I walked over to the cabinets and pulled out two glasses.

Cal walked to the island and sat down at the counter. He shrugged his shoulders. "I don't know. You're pretty jumpy. Do you really trust yourself with a gun?"

I went over to the fridge and pulled out the bottom drawer, which was full of vegetables. I rummaged through the carrots and lettuce until I found the can of Coke I had hidden underneath them and pulled it out. I filled the glasses with ice and poured the soda over them. I sat one of the glasses in front of Cal as it still fizzed and bubbled.

"I hate it when you're right." I sat down on the stool next to him and took a sip of the Coke, the sugary liquid tingling in my throat.

"You're sure you don't want to run away? I'm not kidding about that one." He took a long gulp of Coke.

I looked at him for a minute, tapping my fingers on the cool granite counter. I wanted him more than anything and the thought of us running away together made me ecstatic. But reality took hold and I knew I needed to save my family . . . and the horses.

"I'm positive."

Cal looked at me, but said nothing. He reached out to the bowl of fake fruit and started moving around the oranges and apples.

"Okay, but if you change your mind, you'll let me know?" He picked up a fake apple, tossed it in his hand a couple of times, and put it back in the bowl.

"I promise." I leaned my elbows against the counter and put a hand on my face. He swung his stool around to face me.

"So, we're good?" He reached out for my hand and I willingly let him take it.

"For now."

"That's all I can ask for under the circumstances." He let go of my hand and leaned in to kiss me on the lips. I didn't pull away, and I kissed him back, excited to feel his lips again.

He stood up from the stool and started walking to the back door. I got up, too, and followed him, holding onto the door as he walked out.

"See you later, Casper. I love you." He kissed me on the cheek and held my face in his warm hands. "I really do . . . don't forget that." He let his hands fall from my face and I nodded.

"I love you, too," I said, my heart beating a thousand times a minute.

He strolled across the backyard toward the driveway. I closed the door and went back into the kitchen and opened the fridge. I pulled open a different drawer, full of organic cheeses and yogurt cups. I sifted through the very back of the drawer where I had hidden a Hershey's bar. I unwrapped it and broke off a couple of pieces and put them in my mouth. I finished off the soda, rinsed our glasses out, and left them in the sink.

I let out a long sigh as I walked slowly up the stairs. What was I doing? I knew he was the reason I was in this situation, but I couldn't help but fall in love. He was stupid and impulsive—but, for some reason, that didn't matter to me. I opened my bedroom door and went over to the stand-up mirror in the corner. I wasn't ugly, but I didn't think I was drop-dead gorgeous either. I shrugged my shoulders. The horses had never complained about the way I looked.

I couldn't believe that someone would go that far to meet me, but I couldn't deny that I had felt the sparks between us the minute we met.

Chapter

18

FTER BREAKFAST THE NEXT MORNING, I
went upstairs to get ready for the
dreaded luncheon with the Women's
Club. I couldn't wait for this dumb thing to be
over. Mother had laid out the dress she wanted
me to wear on the bed. Without bothering to look
at it, I pulled the frilly thing over my head. I
went over to the mirror and frowned. The deep
blue frilly dress looked like something out of a
bad eighties movie. My heart sunk at the thought
of walking down the steps to let people come
gawk at the girl who was almost murdered and
pour their fake pity on our family. Of course,
there would be cameras present to capture their
party, and show the rest of Charleston just how

empathetic they all were to our situation . . . *please*. It took everything I had not to puke just thinking about it.

But I was doing this for Mother. I had never realized *why* she cared about the parties so much until yesterday.

I adjusted the blue bow on the front of the dress and walked out of the room. I could hear the buzz of all the people downstairs as I made my way down the steps. I could feel sweat already forming on my forehead and my back. The material was so hot and stuffy, I wanted to just rip it off. I would have, too, if it hadn't been for the cameras.

As I emerged into the foyer, everyone turned to look at me.

"There she is. Casper, how are you feeling? Poor thing," said one woman as she approached me. She was petite, with long black hair and deep maroon lips. She pulled me into an embrace as though she knew me personally. I had never seen her before in my life.

She released me and put her hands on my shoulders. "I'm so sorry, honey."

There was an audible "Aw" from the audience.

Wordlessly, I walked further into the sea of guests full of "Sorry," "Glad you're safe," and, "Your poor mother" comments. The crowded rooms made me feel claustrophobic and I fought the urge to run and scream.

I reached the buffet table and scooped up several crackers with hummus. I stuffed them in my mouth, not caring if crumbs covered my ugly dress.

"Nice dress," said Charlotte, as she approached me at the table.

"My mother made me wear it," I said, tugging on the bow, trying to flatten it against my chest.

"It's . . . different," she said, in an effort to be nice.

"I know it's beyond hideous; you don't have to pretend it isn't." I picked up a chocolate-covered strawberry and took a big bite.

"Okay—in that case, it's pretty bad," she said laughing.

I couldn't help but smile. "Hey, I never got to thank you for the other day," I said, touching her shoulder with my free hand.

"It's nothing. Just glad I could be of some help." She leaned over the table of food and picked up a blueberry muffin. "Seen Cal lately?"

"Are you, like, his spy or something?" I asked.

Charlotte took a big bite out of the muffin and shook her head. "No, why?"

"You're always asking about him. And I know the truth, by the way."

She chewed slowly, her already-rosy cheeks turning blood-red. "Oh."

"So you don't have to pretend anymore. I know why I'm here and what I have to do." I went to the punch bowl, picked up a crystal glass, and filled it to the brim with the light pink liquid.

"So you're joining?" she asked, moving closer to me at the end of the table.

I sighed. "Yes. What choice do I have?"

"It's not that bad, Casper. Cal can exaggerate

things. Things aren't that bad and the perks are great."

"So Cal and Callie are both exaggerating? She thinks things are pretty bad and she thinks they are only going to get worse. What happened to her?" I turned around to look at the crowd of women and I was not happy to see Veronica walking toward us. It was too late to run in the other direction. She had already seen me and she was heading straight for me, strutting like a sexy model in a Victoria's Secret commercial. She was wearing a lacy white dress and towering black stilettos that made her look five inches taller.

"So nice to see you, Casper," she said, her voice sickeningly sweet.

I bet.

"Same here," I said flatly, as I imagined slapping her pouty lips right off her face. I turned back to the punch bowl and got a refill.

"Sorry to hear about what happened. Lucky for you, Cal got there just in time. He's always had such good timing," she said with a little laugh.

I felt the blood rush to my face. How could she be laughing about me almost dying?

"Yeah, he does," I responded, trying not to start a fight.

"He took me home after the party. We had a really good time . . . like we used to. He wanted to come by and tell you about us getting back together. He's really thoughtful like that."

I couldn't stand it any longer. I slammed the

crystal cup down, almost shattering the handle on the table. I whirled around and looked at Veronica.

"Is that what you think I'm worried about right now? First off, I don't believe a word coming out of your mouth. Second, I almost *died,* and the last thing on my mind is a fake war with you. Just goes to show how shallow you really are. Now I understand what he was saying about you. Shouldn't have been such a bitch and maybe he wouldn't have left you," I said, shrugging my shoulders and smiling.

She stared at me, her brown eyes blazing. "You think you're so cool, but this game's just begun. I hear they're actually going to let you into our group. I bet you'll be running the minute something doesn't go your way."

"You obviously have no idea who I am. I can handle Kythera and beat you at your own game. Just watch me."

I started to walk away from the table, ignoring Charlotte, who had stood by me quietly. As I passed Veronica, I kept my gaze on hers. She didn't intimidate me anymore. No one did.

I walked as fast as I could to the other side of the room, ignoring the people trying to talk to me. I walked into the kitchen, which was a chaotic mess.

"Those don't go there! Hurry up with the champagne!" shouted Mother from across the room. I caught a glimpse of her in her pale yellow skirt suit. Her hair was up in a neat bun and her diamond earrings shined brightly.

"Casper, why are you in here? You should be out there, talking to everyone." A worried glance crossed her face.

"I just don't feel like talking to anyone. I think I've taken enough pictures for the newspaper." I picked a celery stick out of the bowl on the counter and took a bite.

"But they're here to see you and it's rude not to take time to talk to them." She crossed her arms against her chest and pursed her lips. She was trying to be nice, but I didn't care.

"I'm tired of all your fake friends giving me hugs and acting like they even have a clue what I went through. I'm done. You go entertain your guests," I said, and before she could even respond, I walked out of the room and into the library.

I threw myself across one of the loveseats and breathed out heavily.

"Casper, don't walk away from me like that in front of the staff," said Mother, who had walked in behind me.

"Sorry, but I can't take them anymore." I dangled my legs over the arm of the loveseat.

"I know you don't like them, but this is the only thing I know how to do." She walked toward the other loveseat and sat down quietly. The room was silent.

"What do you mean?"

"You're hurting and it's painful for me to see my only daughter like this, but I don't know what else to do for you. You run to the horses or your father when you need comfort. Throwing parties is the only thing I seem to be good at, and I know you hate them, but I thought maybe, in a strange way, it might help you." She looked down at her arm and rubbed her bracelet.

"I didn't know you felt that way. I'm sorry."

"That's what terrifies me about losing the money. What would I do? I don't have a job or any other skills. This is the only thing I know how to do. It's the only way I know how to *be*."

I had always thought of my mother as strong-willed and capable. I had forgotten she had grown up a blue blood, trained to be a socialite and gracious hostess.

"But you have so much more than the parties to offer. You're the strongest person I know," I said sincerely, sitting up on the loveseat.

She wiped a tear from her cheek. "I don't feel strong right now. My family is falling apart, and I almost lost my daughter." Another tear slid down her cheek, and she reached up to quickly wipe it away.

"But you didn't lose me, and I'm going along with the Kythera thing."

"You are? We didn't know if you were or not, with the way you walked out of the room."

"Yes, it's the only way to keep everything, and you're counting on me." I picked up the book on the coffee table and fiddled with the spine.

"If I had known how bad our finances were, I would have found another way. But he didn't tell me. I had no idea what was going on. But it's too late now. Thank you for being so strong, too," she said, and got up from the loveseat. She kissed me on the forehead and walked out of the room.

After she left the room, I threw the book down on the coffee table and walked out of the room. I ran up the servants' stairs to my room and slammed the door shut. I jerked at the sound of the door slamming, but shook it off.

I grabbed the photo of me and Dad in the winner's circle with Ghostly Trio that was sitting on the mantle, and threw it on the ground. The glass shattered across the floor into thousands of barely visible flecks. I stared at the shattered pieces, unable to move.

~ * * * ~

The room was brightly lit, and nothing like what I had been expecting it to look like. We were at our first Kythera meeting and my initiation into the group. There were about fifty people standing around in the open ballroom that was above the French restaurant downtown, their voices bouncing off the high ceilings and thin glass windows.

There were long tables with chairs arranged in rows that faced a massive desk, much like a classroom. Tyson clanged a bell on the desk, and everyone started moving to their seats. My parents took a seat at one of the last tables, but Tyson motioned for me to step up front. There were two chairs facing the rows of tables in front of the desk Tyson now sat at. My throat was dry and my palms were sweaty. I didn't know what to expect. Cal had tried to fill me in, but it wasn't easing my mind now that the moment had arrived. I looked for him in the crowd, hoping for some reassurance, but I couldn't find him in the sea of faces.

I sat down and smoothed out the black skirt I had been instructed to wear. All the members wore black dresses or black suits to the meetings.

"Today is a special meeting, as we bring a new family into the fold. As most of you know, the Whitleys are an affluent family from Kentucky, with a great legacy, which they'll be bringing into our group," said Tyson, as he got up from behind his desk. He came over to me and put his hands on my shoulders. I wanted to squirm away from him, but I felt paralyzed in my seat.

"This is Casper Whitley, their only daughter. She will take part in our initiation ceremony, pledging her life and inheritance to Kythera forever."

"Kythera forever!" the room shouted, startling me.

"Now, as part of her pledge she will get a symbol of her allegiance tattooed on her body, so that she will forever be reminded of and bonded to our group."

I gulped; the tattoo artist walked into the room and took the empty seat beside me. He was a skinny man covered in tattoos, including on his head. The tattoo machine was wheeled into the room, along with a tray of other equipment.

It looked like I was going in for surgery.

"Now, where would you like the tattoo?" asked the tattoo artist. I stared at the huge silver tongue ring in his mouth.

"Near my ankle," I said quietly.

"Which one?" he asked, as he pulled on a pair of blue gloves.

"The left one."

He picked up my leg and put it in his lap. My heart was racing and sweat was forming on my forehead. I wanted to get up and run out of the room, but Tyson still had his hands on my shoulders, his grip tightening. He probably knew exactly what I was thinking.

The tattoo artist rubbed antibacterial soap on the skin my inner leg near my ankle and then took a disposable razor and shaved the area. He put some more antibacterial soap on the spot and then turned to flip on the machine. He opened a pack of needles and placed on one the end of the machine. I closed my eyes as I watched him bend down with the needle to my ankle. It sounded like a dentist's drill and I tensed up. I gripped the sides of the chair in anticipation of the pain. It felt like it took several minutes before he actually made contact with my skin, but the minute he did I could feel it. It felt like I was being stung over and over again by an angry bee. I bit my lip in order to keep from screaming.

When I thought it was never going to be over, the stinging pain ended. I looked up to see the man reach for a paper towel, squirt it with liquid and wipe my ankle with it. I winced as the scratchy material touched my raw skin. The man covered the area with a piece of piece of gauze that he secured tightly with tape.

He signaled he put my leg down and got up from the chair, signaling to someone to come wheel the machine away. It was over. I took a deep breath, sighing in relief.

Tyson took his hands off my shoulders and stepped to the side. "Congratulations, Casper, welcome to Kythera!" he said, and the whole room got up and started clapping.

I got up from the chair and walked to the back of the room, the tight tape of my bandage pulling at my skin. My parents were waiting for me, concerned looks on their faces.

"Are you all right?" asked Dad.

"I guess." I looked down at my bandaged ankle. "So why don't you two have to get one?"

"You're considered the first generation of our family to be a member. According to the rules, we're not allowed to get one."

"Oh," was all that I said, because I couldn't say what I was really thinking out loud.

Why did it seem like I was getting the worst end of this deal? Maybe it was because at least my parents had had lives before Kythera took them over. My life was just getting started and already my fate had been decided—or had it?

I looked to the front of the room to see Tyson chatting away with several people, laughing and carrying on. I felt anger rise up in me—but not just anger. Determination was also flowing through my veins. Tyson looked in my direction and just stared, probably thinking he was intimidating me.

He had no idea what I was *really* capable of and he would regret not letting me go.

Chapter

19

I WOKE UP FEELING LIKE I'd never fallen asleep. I had tossed and turned all night, twisting myself up in the sheets, dreading the first day of my senior year. The end of August was already here and I wasn't ready for it. This year wasn't going to be like any of the others. This year, I was in Charleston, and walking into school as a new member of Kythera. I had no idea what would happen this year—or, rather, what Kythera would allow me to do, although I was determined that they wouldn't rule every part of my life.

With a lot of effort, I pulled myself from the bed, and walked unsteadily to the bathroom. I went through my usual routine, and by the time

I had my hair brushed, I felt fully awake. I put on my new school uniform and surveyed the outcome. I didn't look too bad. The white, collared shirt was a little too big in the boob area, but that wasn't really the shirt's fault. The black blazer was a little large. The only thing that fit just right was the pleated skirt, which hit just above my knees.

I pulled on a pair of black flats and accidentally touched the brand new tattoo on my ankle. I didn't have a clue how people stood getting their whole bodies tattooed. I figured they had to either like pain or be stupid drunk. I hadn't been either and promised I would never get another one. I looked at the tiny scroll letters that weren't readable unless you got close up. I'd wanted the smallest tattoo they would allow, so I would feel less like a branded cow.

I picked up my new purple backpack and walked downstairs. Mother was waiting at the foot of the stairs with the butler, who had a camera in hand. Before I had time to realize what was going on, the butler had snapped a picture of me, the flash blinding me with white light.

"Oh," I said startled by the sudden flash. I teetered on the edge of the step, but reached out for the banister. I reached it in time, but not without my mother screaming.

"Casper! Don't fall!" she shouted, and the butler rushed toward me to help me down the rest of the stairs.

"You aren't wearing those shoes are you?" asked Mother, her hysteria gone as quickly as it had appeared.

"Yes, they're comfortable. And I need to be comfortable today," I explained, knowing where she was going with this line of questioning. I was refusing to go back upstairs and change into what she thought was a more "suitable" pair of high heels.

"But those shoes do nothing for your legs." She was staring at my knobby knees and short calves.

"I'm not that concerned about how my legs look today. I'm more concerned about surviving the school day at all."

"Those aren't the shoes you want to make your first impressions in, are they?" she asked, ignoring my last response. Her mouth was turned down in a frown and her brows were close-knit as she continued to stare at my legs.

"I'm only going to see these people for a year, and I already have a couple of friends—and they don't seem to have a problem with my legs," I said sarcastically.

"Wouldn't a pair of heels—"

"No, these are the shoes I'm wearing," I stated, and walked down the hall and into the kitchen. I went into the pantry to grab a set of keys.

"What about those new pair of Jimmy Choos your grandmother sent you? They would look cute with your skirt," Mother said, as she appeared in the kitchen.

"I like my shoes." I grabbed the first pair of keys I could find and rushed out of the pantry, whizzing by Mother and out the back door.

I didn't say anything else to her as I slammed the door and walked speedily to the garage. I hit the unlock button on the brand new black Audi sedan that had replaced my favorite red Audi coupe. When I joined Kythera, every car was taken and replaced with shiny new black ones, with the red "K" symbols on the back and on the wheel wells. I missed the red one.

I had looked up the address to the school and I put in the GPS. The electronic voice told me that the school was about twenty miles away. *Oh no,* I thought, *I'm going to be late for the very first day.*

I put the thought out of my head as I put the car into drive and sped down the driveway. I listened carefully to the directions I was given, finally crossing over the channel on the James Island Expressway. I breathed in a sigh of relief when I saw the sign for St. Mary's School. I pulled into the parking lot and squeezed between Alex's Porsche and Marcus Gray's black Land Rover.

I jumped out of the car just as Marcus flung his door open. "What's up, Casper?" he called, as he pulled his backpack out of the backseat.

I looked at Marcus, a smile instantly crossing my face. Marcus had joined Kythera a couple weeks after me, and he had quickly become one of my best friends. He was an easygoing guy, and nothing ever seemed to faze him. Plus, we had a lot in common, because we were both starting our senior years as the new kids in town.

I walked around my car and over to his open back door. He turned to look at me as he shut the door and put his backpack across his shoulder.

"Ready for this?" he asked as he walked toward me. Marcus stood almost a foot taller than me, had gorgeous, deep brown eyes, and perfect skin the color of espresso. I looked up at him and shook my head.

Marcus Gray's family owned multiple accounting firms in New York City. They were regularly featured during the business segments of one of the news channels, and had caught the attention of Tyson Roman, which lead to his family being shipped to Charleston, just like mine. Marcus was an excellent football player and had already been scouted by some of the top universities, but all that went away when his family had moved to Charleston. His life would now be dictated by Kythera, and football probably wasn't in their plans. But, unlike me, he saw it all as a new challenge and a new door opening. He wasn't terrified of our new school or of what being a part of Kythera meant. I couldn't be so optimistic.

"It'll be all right, and if anyone's mean to you, they'll have to face me," he said, hitting his chest with his fist.

I laughed. "Sounds good to me. You might have to start right now." Veronica was walking toward the school, within a few feet of where Marcus and I stood. She looked over at us, stared for a moment, and continued walking.

We hadn't spoken since the day of the stupid luncheon, which didn't hurt my feelings. I had seen her at my initiation, but she had kept her distance. She was one less person to worry about.

"Veronica. She's *so* hot. You sure she's on the bad list?" Marcus asked, while he watched every swing of Veronica's hips as she went into the building. She could even make the long, ugly, plaid skirt look sexy.

"I'm sure. What about Charlotte? She's really nice and pretty," I suggested. Charlotte had made it known to me during one of our shopping trips that she had a huge crush on Marcus.

"I like her," he said, smiling.

We walked across the parking lot and up the steps to the two-story brick building. It looked like any other school I had seen. We opened the double glass doors and walked into the hallway. Students were crowded together, chatting in front of rows of lockers. The floors were black and white tile, and the walls were dark wood paneling. The taupe-colored metal lockers looked out of place in the otherwise upscale hall.

I opened the front pocket of my backpack and pulled out the yellow slip of paper with my schedule and locker number on it. "What class do you have first?"

He unzipped his bag and pulled out the crumpled sheet of paper. "I have French II first period. What's your schedule?"

"I have Political Science first period, Calculus II second period, and Spanish IV right before lunch. After lunch, I have P.E., and last period is Renaissance Literature." I studied the list carefully. "Do we have any of the same classes?"

He looked at the list. "We have Calculus and P.E. together."

"Bummer. At least we have a couple classes together and I'll see you at lunch." I looked down at the shiny tile floor.

"You know you'll be all right without me. You did a pretty good job before I showed up, and you got Cal . . . remember?" he said nudging my shoulder with his forearm.

I took in a deep breath and exhaled. "You're right. I've just never had to start over, you know?"

"Yeah, I get it. Me either, but at least we're both the new kids in town." I looked up at him, and, for the first time, he looked a little sad. His lips curled into a frown.

I realized then that he was just as sad as I was to have left the lives we had known. The opportunities that had been waiting in our other lives were forever altered—my life as a champion jumper and horse breeder and his life as an NFL superstar. Those opportunities and dreams were gone, and replaced with ones controlled by someone else.

Everything had changed for Marcus and me and there was nothing we could do to stop it.

Chapter
20

I LEFT MARCUS IN THE hallway and walked into my first class of the day. The room smelled like dry erase markers and floor cleaner and was already full of students, who looked at me curiously. The desks were arranged in a U shape, facing the teacher's desk. Most of the seats were already taken; without looking at anyone directly, I found an empty seat and rushed to sit down, throwing my backpack on the floor. My phone buzzed and I picked it up. One new message, it said. I opened the message to see it was from Cal.

Sorry, didn't c you before . L8 for class. See u @ lunch. T2UL.

I smiled and wrote back, *Cool. Can't w8 to c u.*

After pushing send, I threw the phone back in the front pocket of my bag.

"I was starting to think you weren't going to make it," someone said from across the room. I immediately looked up. Sitting directly across from me, on the other side of the U, was Alex, and he was smiling widely at me.

"Hey, I didn't know we had any classes together." I hadn't made a real effort to speak to Alex ever since the afternoon in my house. I had said hello a couple of times, and he had tried to flirt with me on a few occasions. He wasn't happy that I had forgiven Cal so quickly. He had been sulking ever since.

"Me either." He picked up a pen on his desk and started scribbling on a piece of paper. The conversation was over.

Finally, the teacher walked in the room, and she wrote her name on the dry erase board. "Hello, class, my name is Ms. Epling, and I will be your political science teacher this semester," she said in a strong, clear voice. She was a tall, slender woman with tortoise shell glasses and deep red hair, which she had pulled up in a clip.

She handed a stack of papers to each student sitting near her desk and instructed them to pass the papers along. It was a syllabus for the class and I quickly started scanning the curriculum.

"This class will be focused on in-class discussions and group work."

Ugh, I always hated group work—even more knowing there was a possibility that I would have to work with Alex. I didn't want to be constantly hit on or given the cold shoulder while trying to work on a project.

"Homework will consist of group meetings and preparing for presentations for the class. The final assignment will be a mock U.N. Conference where you will be assigned different countries to represent at the conference and a paper that will be graded as your class final."

I looked at the material, familiar with most of it from classes I had taken at my school in Lexington. I wasn't afraid of speaking in front of the class, but it wasn't my favorite thing to do.

The class went by painfully slowly, as the teacher went into great detail about the syllabus, explaining each and every bullet on the paper. I looked at the clock every few minutes, wishing it would go by faster. I avoided looking straight ahead, afraid I would meet Alex's gaze. Finally, the bell rang, and I jumped from my desk and headed for the door—but I wasn't fast enough, because Alex ended up by my side.

"What class do you have next?"

We walked out into the noisy hallway. Students were scurrying to their lockers, chatting with friends, and running to their next class.

"Calculus II." I pulled out the slip of paper with my locker number and combination again.

"I have History and then Spanish IV."

As I looked through my locker, he stopped and waited for me, leaning against someone else's locker. He didn't say anything, just looked at me.

"We have Spanish together. Why do you need to take Spanish, aren't you fluent?" I asked. I thought I had heard him speaking Spanish on the phone at my initiation. It sounded to me like he had no trouble speaking the language.

"Yeah, but I need the classes for college. It's an easy A," he said with a smile, and for the first time since the awkward conversation at my house, he looked like the normal Alex I'd first met.

"I might need some help in that class. I don't know why they stuck me in the advanced class." I slammed my locker shut and zipped my books for the next two classes into my backpack.

"I can help you if you need it. It's not a problem. You can come over to my house and study if you want," he said with a wink.

Yeah, old Alex is back.

"Maybe I'll take you up on that," I said, trying not to hurt his feelings by saying no.

"Awesome. See you in *español, chica.*" He smiled and strolled confidently down the hallway. Maybe I should have said no after all.

The bell rang and I felt my heart jump at the loud noise. Loud noises still bothered me, and so did someone sneaking up behind me. I didn't know if that was something permanent or if it would fade eventually.

I jogged down the hall, up the stairwell, and into Calculus II. I looked around the room and Charlotte started waving at me wildly from the back of the class. I was excited to see her and we handed notes back and forth while Mr. Perry, our teacher, droned on about how exciting calculus could be. I wasn't convinced.

Spanish sucked, since not only was Alex in the class, but his sister was, too. It was going to be a *long* semester. She had said a curt hello to me, but nothing else. I could feel her eyes on me, and occasionally when I turned around, it was to see her looking at me with a smug expression on her face.

The bell chimed and I couldn't wait to get out of there. Alex walked with me to the cafeteria, chatting about something, but I wasn't listening. I was too busy looking around at all the unfamiliar people who kept staring at me. All I wanted to do was find some corner to hide in.

We finally entered the cafeteria, which looked more like a cathedral than a high school cafeteria. The same dark wood paneling from the hall lined the walls, and there were several stained glass windows that let limited light into the already-dark room. Iron chandeliers helped dispel the dark feeling of the room. Circular tables with chairs were arranged neatly on the wood floor. Actually, it reminded me a lot of Hogwarts from *Harry Potter.* I wished I could've had a magic wand to make all these people quit staring at me.

Alex placed his backpack on one of the tables near the windows. I threw my backpack next to his and got in line. We both ended up with a salad and slice of pepperoni pizza. As we sat down with our trays, Charlotte and Sara sat down at our table.

"Hey, Casper, Alex. How's the first day going?" asked Charlotte, as she opened a bottle of water and set it next to her tray.

"It's not been too bad. Spanish is going to be a pain," I said, picking up the pizza slice and taking a bite.

"How'd you end up in advanced Spanish?" Charlotte picked up her fork and took a bite of salad.

I shrugged my shoulders. "No clue."

"At least you have Alex to help you," piped in Sara, who I could barely hear over the noise in the room.

"Yeah, she's lucky to have me," Alex said with a wink. I looked away so I wouldn't roll my eyes at him.

"Oh, Jacob, come sit with us!" shouted Charlotte over my head. I turned to look at a tall, lanky guy waving back at her. He was cute, with light blond hair, light green eyes, and tan skin. I had never seen him before, so I knew he wasn't a member of Kythera, which was a surprise. I hadn't met anyone who hadn't been involved with Kythera all summer.

"Hey," he said, as he took a seat next to Sara, who was turning bright red and smiling.

"Hey, Jacob," she said meekly, tucking her brown hair behind her ear. Jacob looked at her and smiled, then turned his attention to me.

"Hi, I'm Jacob Walker," he said, as he sat his book bag on the empty chair beside him.

"I'm Casper Whitley. Nice to meet you."

"Hey, guys," said Cal, as he sat down next to me. I gave him a quick smile, happy to finally see his face. Marcus completed the table at the end next Charlotte.

"I'm thinking about playing lacrosse," blurted Marcus. He took a giant bite of pizza.

"*You* play lacrosse? Why wouldn't you play football?" asked Cal, as he opened a bottle of water.

"I dunno. I want to try something different." He shrugged his broad shoulders and finished off the pizza.

"Well, I think you would be awesome at it," Charlotte chimed in. She had a syrupy sweet smile on her pouty lips as she stared at Marcus.

"What about you, Casper?" asked Sara.

I took a bite of salad and set the fork aside, chewing as I mulled over her question. "I hadn't really thought about it. I spend all my free time at the Hunt Club or doing other stuff."

"You mean hanging out with Cal," Charlotte interjected, finally tearing her eyes away from Marcus. Out of the corner of my eye, it looked like Alex was fake gagging.

"Well, don't count on that for much longer," Alex added, his voice full of sarcasm. The whole table went quiet. "He's going to be too busy kissing up to Daddy to spend time with you," Alex said, as he picked at his leftover pizza crust.

Cal looked in his direction, but didn't respond.

"What about you, Jacob? You interested in

any sports?" asked Sara, trying to deflect some of the tension that was building in the room.

"Not really. I'm not that athletic. Maybe drama or art clubs," he said, shrugging his shoulders. Sara smiled.

"So, where you from, Jacob?" asked Cal out of the blue.

"Detroit." Jacob looked around anxiously at everyone. He was pretty shy and hadn't said much to the group, except the occasional whisper to Sara.

I nudged Cal, and gave him a look. "Sorry, Jacob, Cal's lost his manners. Jacob, this is Cal Roman."

Cal nodded at him, then looked down at his phone, uninterested. "Why did you move to Charleston?" Cal asked absently, still staring at the bright white screen of his iPhone.

"My parents relocated for their jobs."

"What do they do?" A *beep* sounded from Cal's phone, and he started typing furiously.

Jacob paused and looked down at his half-slice of pizza. "Dad manages a manufacturing plant, and Mom's a physical therapist."

Cal didn't respond or look up at him. I couldn't help but stare at him. He could be a jerk, but he never ignored people.

Before I could say anything, the bell rang, and everyone in the cafeteria started picking up their trays and walked to drop them off at the counter. Our little table dispersed, and Jacob disappeared in a flash.

"I hope Cal didn't scare him off. Sara's got a

crush on him," commented Charlotte, as she passed by me to put up her tray.

"Yeah, me, too. I've never seen him act that way," I said, staring at where he had been sitting moments ago.

"Boys," Charlotte said loudly.

"Where did he go?" Sara responded, as she looked around the room for Jacob.

"Come on, let's get to cooking class. I'm sure we'll see him again . . . don't worry," Charlotte said, wrapping an arm around Sara's shoulders. She waved to me and they strolled out the cafeteria doors. I looked around for Alex, but he was already gone.

"Hey I'll see ya in P.E.," called Marcus from across the cafeteria. I nodded and looked back at Cal, who was still staring at his phone.

"Hey, what are you doing?" I leaned over his shoulder, but couldn't see who he was texting.

"Finding out some information about Jacob," he said absently.

"Why?"

"Got to know what he's up to." He shrugged his shoulders, but didn't turn around to look at me.

"You think he's a spy or something?" I laughed at the thought, but Cal didn't answer. "You're kidding right? He's a nice guy who doesn't look like he could harm a fly."

"Those are the ones you have to look out for." Cal finally turned toward me, putting his phone in his pocket. The cafeteria was almost empty as everyone else hurried to their next class.

"This is insane," I said aloud.

"Welcome to our world." Cal put out his arms and gave me a hug. I wrapped my arms around him and enveloped his warmth.

"Get to class," said a gruff voice. I looked behind me to see the football coach staring at us, his arms crossed and his bushy gray eyebrows in a furrow.

"Yes, sir," Cal responded, taking my hand, picking up our trays, and heading for the door. He dropped off our trays and we entered the hallway.

"You want to go to the movies or something tonight?" Cal asked, his shoulder brushing against mine.

"Sure, a movie sounds good."

"Pick you up around seven?"

"Sure."

He gave me a quick kiss on the forehead before turning to go up the stairwell.

I swiveled around and headed for the gym, which was on the total opposite side of the building. I looked at the clock on the wall and I was officially five minutes late. I had never been late for class before. I was a goody two shoes, who always did her homework and didn't skip class. *Great,* now the P.E. teacher was going to think I was a troublemaker.

Then it hit me. No, it wouldn't matter if I was a few minutes late. I would just flash the tattoo on my ankle and I'd be all right. Being a member of Kythera did have its perks.

Chapter

21

T HE LAST CLASS OF THE day couldn't come soon enough. The first day of school was always tough, even when I had known everyone in the school. All the information, books, and the inevitable first day homework made me depressed.

"You will need to read the first act of Shakespeare's *A Midsummer Night's Dream* tonight, and be prepared for discussion tomorrow," droned Mrs. O'Conner, my Renaissance Literature teacher. There was a collective sigh in the room.

"Hey, do you have the book already?" whispered Jacob from the seat behind me. I nodded in response. "I didn't get it yet, I think I missed it on the list of books. Can I borrow it from you after you read the first chapter? I'll give it back to you, or I can read it at your house real quick."

"Yeah, sure. I'm planning on reading it as soon as I get home so I can go out with Cal. Come over around six-thirty and you can sit in the library or wherever and read it," I responded, craning my head over my shoulder.

"Thanks, where do you live?" I could smell his cinnamon gum as he tried to whisper. He looked up at the teacher to see if she was paying any attention.

"South Battery, right in front of White Point Gardens. A black Audi will be parked on the street in front of the house." I turned back my attention to Mrs. O'Conner, who had begun writing on the dry erase board as she spoke about which authors we would be studying this semester.

"Thanks, I'll be there at six-thirty."

I nodded in acknowledgement and started taking notes.

Jacob seemed like a pretty nice guy, and I couldn't figure out why Cal would suspect him of anything. What could he be worried about enough to have Jacob checked out? Were members of Kythera *that* paranoid—or did they have every right to be?

The bell finally rang and I felt a sense of freedom take over my body. I pulled my notebook and things together in record time and headed for the door. I waved at Jacob as I left the room and raced to my locker. I put my books up and slammed the door shut before practically running down the hall.

As I turned toward the exit, I knocked someone hard on the shoulder. Books clattered to the floor and I scrambled to help them without even looking at them.

"Sorry, I'm such a klutz," I said, as I picked up an algebra book.

"I don't need your help, bitch," said a familiar smooth and sexy voice. I looked up to see Veronica staring at me, her eyes smoldering with anger. Not a great way to end the day.

"I've already used that word, can't you think of one on your own?" I handed her the algebra book and she practically ripped it from my hands.

"I don't think there's a better word to describe you," she sneered.

"Is it really going to be like this all year?" I asked, rolling my eyes and placing a hand on my hip.

"Yeah, unless you decide to go back to your stupid horse farm in hick town." She raised a jet-black eyebrow. I felt the blood rushing to my face.

I breathed out deeply. "You are so lame and not worth my time. You need to move on. I'm not going to play this game with you the entire school year."

She shrugged her shoulders. "You might as well get used to it, because I'll never give up. Cal will be back with me in no time."

She breezed past me, brushing up against my arm and pushing me into the nearby lockers. I wanted to run after her and rip out her pretty, shiny hair, but I decided to take the high road and ignore her. She wasn't worth the effort or getting into trouble. She wasn't even that great at arguing or trying to start something. Hick town? That one just made me laugh.

~ * * * ~

I looked at my cell phone, which was sitting on the vanity in my bathroom. It was six twenty-five, and Jacob would be walking in at any moment. I was still in my school uniform, and I hadn't taken a shower or gotten dressed for my date with Cal.

The doorbell echoed through the hall like a giant church bell. I rushed out of the bathroom and looked in my closet. I pulled out a pair of jeans and a T-shirt. I didn't bother with makeup or hair, I just ran down the stairs.

Jacob was standing in the foyer, looking up at the chandelier. His mouth was open wide and he looked like he was in his own little world.

"Hey, Jacob," I said, as I descended down the last step. My sandals made loud noises as they touched the wood floor.

He pulled his gaze from the chandelier and looked at me. "Wow, your house is amazing."

"Thanks." I walked to the middle of the foyer and motioned for him to follow. We walked into the kitchen. The chef was busy stirring vegetables in a pan; the smells of cream and garlic filled my nose.

"You have a chef, too!?" Jacob exclaimed. I nodded. "We don't have anything like this," he whispered, and I wasn't sure if he was talking to me or not.

"Where do you live?" I asked, stepping into the library and grabbing the book off the desk in the corner.

"I live near downtown on Spring Street. It's a nice house, but I think our house would fit in your kitchen," he said with a laugh. "My parents make good money, but nothing like yours or anyone else at St. Mary's." He looked at the leather loveseat and rubbed his hand against the back of it.

"Yeah, but money isn't everything," I said, but I wasn't convinced of what I was saying anymore. Not after what I had joined to save it.

I held the book out to him. "Here it is. You can read it in here or any other room downstairs. I would just stay out of the kitchen. This time of day, there's a chance you'll see fireworks between my mother and the chef. Plus, she'll ask you twenty questions. If I were you, I would just sit in here."

He took the book from my hand, and opened the front cover. "Thanks, this is really nice of you. I'm a fast reader, so it shouldn't take me long."

I leaned against the door frame. "You're welcome, and I'll come back down before I leave for the movies."

"What movie are you going to see?" Jacob rounded the loveseat and plopped down in the corner.

"I don't remember the title, but some action superhero movie," I said, looking at the back of Jacob's blond head.

"Cool. See you later." He flipped a page and began reading as I stepped out of the room.

At seven o'clock, the doorbell rang again, and this time I was ready to go. I had taken a shower and put on a nice pair of dark blue jeans and a white, cap-sleeved top. I walked down the steps to the front door and my face immediately lit up.

"Ready to go?" Cal asked, a dazzling grin on his face. He was dressed in dark jeans, a tucked-in red polo, and brown loafers. It was about as casual as Cal got.

"Yeah, let me just go check on Jacob."

"Wait, why is Jacob here?" He caught my arm before I could turn toward the kitchen.

"He's borrowing one of my books for a class. He hadn't bought a copy yet, and we have to read some tonight for class tomorrow. I told him he could come over and read it this afternoon."

"Why would you volunteer to do that? Couldn't he go buy the book after school?" He was visibly annoyed with me. His eyebrows were furrowed and he swept his hand through his dark hair.

"I didn't exactly volunteer—he asked me. I didn't think it was a big deal." I crossed my arms and looked at him, equally annoyed with the way he was acting.

"You just need to be more careful . . . that's all. You're a member now, and there's people looking to get rid of us." He looked at me and I just stared back.

I looked at the round table in the middle of the room that stood between us. I hadn't noticed it before, but the crystal horse figurine had been replaced with a vase full of fresh purple orchids.

I knew he was telling the truth, but I couldn't believe it. I didn't want to believe it.

"You mean I have a target on my ankle," I said sarcastically, walking out of the room and pushing the kitchen door open with more force than was necessary. As I approached the library, Jacob got up from the leather loveseat, book in hand.

"Thanks for letting me borrow this. I'll go ahead and leave."

He held the book out to me and I took it from him. "Sure, no problem." I swiveled around and strolled back through the kitchen with Jacob behind me. As I opened the door, I could see Cal pacing impatiently in the foyer.

"Hey, Cal," Jacob called out as we approached him.

Cal smirked. "Hey."

"Casper was letting me borrow a book." Jacob stopped at the door and waited for Cal to open it.

"That's what she told me," Cal said, his voice less than cheery. He opened the door and gestured for me to walk out first, then Jacob. Cal closed the door behind us firmly.

"Have fun at the movies," Jacob called, as he

got into his electric blue Ford Fusion.

I waved and smiled at him. Cal threw his chin up at him and opened the door of his Mercedes.

"You didn't have to be such a pain, you know," I said, as I settled into the passenger seat.

He took a deep breath. "I know I shouldn't be that way, but he just gives me a funny feeling. You ever get that about somebody? A feeling you shouldn't trust them?"

Yeah, plenty of people gave me that feeling. I had that feeling more often than not in Charleston. "Yes. But Sara likes him and everybody else didn't have a problem being nice to him."

"He just gives me an uneasy feeling. I'll quit, but don't expect me to be his best friend or anything." Cal put the car in reverse and entered the busy street.

We didn't talk much on the way to the theater, but he did reach over and take my hand. The tingly feeling I always got when we touched surged through my body. I felt a smile form on my face as I stared out the window.

We pulled up to a little theater on James Island. The parking lot wasn't packed, and a few couples, hand in hand, strolled to the ticket counter. The bright neon lights of the theater were the only things that illuminated the otherwise dark parking lot.

Cal parked the car and we walked to the ticket counter. He purchased two tickets for some action movie that I didn't even pay attention to the title of, and in the lobby, he bought some popcorn. He grabbed my hand as we walked into the dark theater. It was nice to finally do something normal. I felt like a normal teenager again. Hanging out with my boyfriend at the movies, wondering what he was thinking about me. Maybe my life could be normal.

The thought sparked hope in my heart. Maybe Kythera would just be in the background of my life and I could pursue whatever I wanted. But that thought was followed by the same feeling Cal had about Jacob. That feeling that I knew deep down it wasn't the truth.

Chapter

22

*T*HAT WAS GREAT. BUT NEXT time, I'm picking the movie. Too much blood and guts for me," I said, as we walked through the quiet lobby of the movie theater.

It was eleven and the place was almost completely deserted. A thin girl with black hair was cleaning out the popcorn machine, while a guy in a maroon uniform ran a vacuum over the carpeted floors.

"Too much blood and guts? I thought there wasn't enough. Next time, I'll let you pick the movie, but it's going to cost you." He pushed open the glass doors and motioned for me to go out.

"What's it gonna cost me?" I lifted an eyebrow

and smiled.

Cal grabbed me and pulled me against his chest. My heart went out of control and I felt breathless. "A kiss."

I laughed, wrapping my arms around him. "Is that it?"

He looked at me, astonished. "Hey, I don't go around giving kisses for free. My kisses are valuable because I'm such a good kisser."

"You are so full of it," I said, breathing out heavily.

"But that's why you like me." He pressed his lips against mine, sending fireworks up and down my spine. The kiss ended too quickly for me, but he hugged me tightly.

A few seconds went by and I tried to pull away, feeling claustrophobic standing so close for so long. But he wouldn't let me go.

"Okay, I think this is long enough of a hug, don't you?"

Cal didn't respond. He stood motionlessly, not letting his grip on me loosen. In fact, it seemed to tighten.

"Casper, I need you to do something for me." His voice was calm and controlled. All the playfulness had disappeared. Dread instantly filled my veins.

"What?" I whispered, confused by his sudden seriousness.

"I need you to run."

"*What?*"

"I need you to run as fast as you can from here."

"Why? I mean, I'm not leaving you here. What's wrong?" I asked frantically.

"Just do it. I don't have time to explain right now. *Just go.*"

"But—"

Before I could say anything else, he had forcefully turned me around. I got a glimpse of two guys who were standing at the edge of the sidewalk, looking our way, before Cal gave me a push in the other direction. I didn't want to run, but as he pushed me forward, my legs began moving beneath me without my conscious decision to start going.

I pushed faster, afraid to look back. I could hear heavy footsteps behind me, and the feelings from the night of Fourth of July came rushing back.

Not this again.

My heart felt like it was about to explode. I ran through the parking lot and made it to the four-lane highway. I made a quick turn to the left and followed alongside the quiet road. A couple cars passed by. Their bright lights made me squint, and I held my breath as they kicked up dust on the side of the road. I took a quick look back and saw that one of the men had followed me, but he was pretty far back. I looked forward again and saw a semi-truck coming down the lane closest to me. Without thinking, I crossed the two lanes of oncoming traffic only a hundred feet in front of the truck driver, who blew his horn at me.

As I reached the median, I stumbled and fell

hard to the ground, but I got up in record time and crossed the remaining two empty lanes. I ran along the edge of the road, passing several closed businesses. I looked for any signs of life, but there were none. There were several honking horns from vehicles, and I knew the man had followed me across the road. My legs were burning and my lungs felt like they were going to explode out of my chest. I didn't know how much further I could go without stopping.

The road was quiet, and all I could hear was the crunching of my feet. The road had grown dark and the businesses had given way to thick trees. I didn't know where I was going, or when I could stop running. I glanced back again—the man had picked up the pace and had gained some ground on me.

I needed Wendy right now. She could have outrun this man in no time, with her big, strong legs and graceful, thoroughbred strides. Tears wet my cheeks at the thought of her. I didn't dare try to wipe them, as I searched for some sort of light from a house in the woods or anything at this point.

Finally, a sidewalk appeared and I felt like I was getting somewhere. Maybe a neighborhood was just up ahead, with people outside or on their front porches. It was all that kept me going. My sight was beginning to blur and my breathing was uneven. My body screamed for me to stop, but my mind wouldn't let me.

I took another quick glance behind me and as I turned my head around, I tripped on the uneven sidewalk and fell forward onto the concrete. My hands and forearms scraped the ground hard. My skin burned and I felt tears creeping up in my eyes. I paused for a second to catch my breath before I got up. I looked at the ground, the broken fragments of concrete and road debris. How did this happen? Would I always be on the run now? Was the money really worth it? I knew saving my family and the horses were, but I had my doubts about the money. But it was too late to change the decision I had made.

Or was it?

I glanced up to see a light shining from the stained glass windows of a church. It was only a few feet to the steps. I got up and ran up the steps and opened the heavy wooden doors. The slam of the doors shutting echoed through the cavernous space. Instantly, a man dressed in robes looked my way. He was standing near the front of the room, cleaning up a tray of bread.

"Can I help you young lady?"

I stood motionless, breathing heavily wishing he could help me. "No, I don't think so. I just . . . I needed . . ." My words became jumbled as the exhaustion from running so far set in. Where was Cal? I started to worry about what had happened to him. I was paralyzed, unable to speak or move.

The man, who I assumed was a priest, walked down the aisle to the back of the church, where I was standing. He was smiling as he put his hands behind his back and studied me for a moment.

"Are you lost?" His eyes were blue-green and filled with concern.

"Kind of . . ." I said.

I didn't know if he was referring to me being physically lost or something more. My parents weren't particularly religious or spiritual. We were part of the crowd who went to the Methodist Church on Christmas and Easter, mainly so my parents could be seen and heard. I believed in God, but I didn't know how he really fit into my life.

"Well, maybe I can help you then. Do you need me to call a cab or someone to come get you?"

"No, I mean . . . yeah. But my boyfriend . . ." I pointed to the heavy oak doors, unable to finish the sentence.

Should I tell him that someone was chasing me? That my boyfriend could be lying dead in the parking lot? Tears formed in the corner of my eyes and I looked away, hoping he wouldn't notice.

Suddenly, a buzzing sound came from my jean pocket. It was my cell phone! I hadn't realized I had it. I answered quickly, and prayed it was Cal.

"Casper, where are you?" Cal said frantically.

"I'm at a church up the road from the movies. It's on the right."

"Good. I'll be there to get you." He hung up the phone and I stared at the blank screen. I breathed out a sigh of relief, knowing that Cal was still alive.

"Are you okay? Here, sit down." The priest gestured to the back pew. I took a step toward the seat, but could barely walk. My legs were numb and tingly, and my right ankle seared with pain. I winced as I tried to walk. The priest gave me his arm and helped me to the pew.

"You look hurt, I should call the hospital." He looked at me, his eyes filled with pity, as he took a step back from me.

"No, thank you. I think I just twisted my ankle." I pulled up my jeans and looked at my ankle. It was swollen to twice its normal size—and so was the Kythera tattoo.

"Oh," said the priest. I immediately put down my pants, hoping he hadn't noticed the tattoo. "So, someone is coming to get you?" The priest sat down in the pew across from me. He swung his legs out so that he could face me.

"Yes, he should be here any minute. Sorry for bothering you. I'm sure you have somewhere to be or . . ." I looked at the clock on my cell phone. It was almost eleven-thirty. I thought about calling my parents, but they were probably still at the country club, drinking with friends. "You might want to go to sleep."

"It's no trouble. What brings you to Charleston?"

I looked at him curiously. "How did you know I'm not from here?"

He smiled softly. "Your accent. You have a bit of a Southern drawl, but not a Charleston one."

"Huh, I guess I never thought about it. I'm

from Lexington, Kentucky. My parents moved here for business." *Or, rather, they moved here to use me to keep their business,* I thought—but didn't say it out loud.

Suddenly, the heavy wooden doors of the church swung open and Cal walked through. I immediately stood up, my ankle throbbing in protest. I walked slowly toward him.

He furrowed his eyebrows. "You're hurt." I didn't speak, just threw my arms around him and felt instant relief.

"I'm fine," I finally said, breathing out heavily.

"Let's go," he said, pulling away and taking my hand in his. I looked back at the priest, realizing I didn't even get his name.

"Thank you," I said and he nodded.

"I'll pray you find your way," he said with a small smile.

I felt awkward, but comforted at the same time. I needed prayer, possibly just to stay alive. My world had become so complicated and mixed up. I believed in God, but didn't really take him into account when I made decisions. But after seeing the priest and the look in his eyes, I couldn't help but wonder what God thought about all of this. Would he applaud my decision to save my family's legacy or look down with disappointment?

All of a sudden, the answer to that question mattered to me.

Chapter

23

AL PULLED UP TO HIS house. The heavy iron gates rolled open and he sped up the driveway, screeching to a halt at the front porch. We hadn't spoken a word since leaving the church. I was too shaken up to ask questions about the men or what had happened to them. Had they met the same fate as the intruders who attacked me on Fourth of July? I wasn't sure I wanted to know.

Cal opened the door and got out. He ran to open the door for me. He gave me his hand to help me get out. My ankle was continuing to swell and looked like a tennis ball. I limped out of the car and put my arm around his shoulders as he helped me up the steps. The front porch hurricane lights flickered with flames, and all the front windows were alive with bright yellow light.

Before we reached the front doors, they swung open, and we were greeted by the Romans' butler, who stepped outside to help me into the front living room. Several people were standing in the room. They stared at me as the butler guided me down onto one of the sofas. Cal sat down next to me, his hand on my knee.

I looked up to see Alex and Marcus, both standing with their arms crossed against their chests. Xander sat casually in a chair, picking at the threads of his jeans. Several other members of Kythera stood around, including my dad, but he didn't come over to me or even look at me. Tyson Roman stood near the fireplace, talking on his cell phone.

"What did you do with the car?" he said as he paced the floor. "So no one will find it?" Tyson ran his free hand through his hair, just like Cal often did.

"Damn it, we have to figure out who these people are," he said in a harsh tone, and put the phone in his pocket. Tyson stared at Cal and me.

"How the hell did this happen?" he asked Cal, pointing his finger at him.

Cal shrugged his shoulders. "I have no idea."

The sound of shoes clicked across the marble floors in the foyer. A few seconds later, a man in a police uniform walked in. I immediately noticed his long face and extra wide chin.

He tipped his hat to Tyson. "We couldn't find

anything in the parking lot . . . nothing but the car. We got rid of the bodies."

I felt myself jolt. *Did he just say he got rid of the bodies?*

"Well, that's not good enough, Sheriff. You're up for re-election this year. You better get on this problem—and fast," said Tyson.

The sheriff simply nodded and walked out of the room, the noise of his shiny black shoes echoing in the otherwise quiet room.

"There's got to be something we're missing." Tyson looked up at the Kythera painting above the mantle, his back toward the crowd.

"I think it's someone our age," Cal blurted out.

Tyson laughed as he slowly turned around. "You think some kid is capable of all this?"

"No, but I think they could be giving information to whoever is."

Tyson was silent for a minute, his lips set in a hard line.

"I think it's logical. The attacks are happening to Casper and Cal, not us, Tyson," added Fernando Alamilla, Alex's dad. Alex was a carbon copy of his father, except Alex wasn't as tall, and his dad always looked so serious.

Tyson paced a moment more, then stopped. "All right, I'll contact the headmaster and see what we can do about this."

Everyone got up and started moving toward the door. I sat motionlessly on the couch, staring at the Kythera painting above the mantle. "You ready to go home, Casper?" asked my dad, who I hadn't even realized had moved next to me.

I looked up at him. His eyes were pink and puffy, as though he had been crying. I looked at Cal and he nodded in agreement. Cal got up from the couch and threw my arm around his shoulders and walked with me to the car. He gave me a hug before lowering me into the passenger seat of the black Jaguar.

I was too numb to talk during the short ride home. Had this night really happened or was I dreaming? I kept hoping it was a nightmare and I would wake up any second, but it never seemed to happen.

We pulled out of the driveway and onto the deserted street. I looked at the clock. It was one a.m. I groaned and slumped down in my seat. School was not going to be fun tomorrow. I would need to drink some serious caffeine just to stay awake during class.

"This is my fault," Dad said, breaking through my thoughts about school. I didn't say anything. I just looked at our house as we turned onto our street.

This wasn't *totally* his fault. Cal *had* played a part in all of this—but, unlike Cal, my parents had never tried to figure out a way out of this thing, except for that split-second before Mother found out we would lose our money. They had no desire to get out, and they didn't care what it had done to our lives, so long as they got to keep the money.

"I wish there was something I could do," he muttered, as he pulled the car into our driveway.

I felt adrenaline pumping through my veins and heat rising to my face.

"There *is* something you can do. You can find a way out of this," I said angrily. I had never really argued with my dad, or even raised my voice to him. I could handle a screaming match with Mother, but not Dad. It just felt *wrong*.

"And lose everything? Including the farm?" He turned the engine off and looked over at me.

"Figure out how to keep the farm. That's all we need." I looked down at the floorboard of the car and at the mat emblazoned with the Jaguar symbol.

"I can't get the farm back—I signed that lease, and if we don't keep our end of the bargain, they get the farm no matter what we do. I didn't have a lot when I was growing up. We didn't make it big with the horses until I was in my teens. And your mother has no clue what it is to have nothing. She'll leave me." His voice was quiet and nervous.

"She loves you, and she wouldn't leave you. The only reason she is afraid to lose the money is that she feels all she knows how to do is throw parties. If you let her know she can do so much more, she'll be okay. And so what if we don't have as much money? You made it once, you can do it again. Having no money would be better than being chased by masked men who want to kill you . . . especially for me." I turned to face Dad. He was looking at the center console and tapping his fingers against the leather. He shook his head after a minute.

"I can't do that. Everything is going to be fine once Tyson finds who's responsible for hurting you. Once they're gone, things will be fine, and we can live and be a part of Kythera without problems."

My jaw dropped. "You're in denial." I unbuckled my seat belt and put my hand on the door. All I wanted to do was get out, but I couldn't. I needed to hear him say I was wrong.

"Casper, it's going to get better from here. All that stuff is behind us. Cal's right . . . it's someone your age that's been hanging out with members," he said with a smile.

"But we just started school. That doesn't explain what happened this summer."

"School just started, but do you know every person that all the members have been hanging out with?"

I thought for a minute. No, I didn't, because most of my time had been spent with Cal or Charlotte. I had spent some time with Marcus, but I had no clue who he was hanging out with the rest of the time. And everyone else, I only saw at the meetings.

"I guess not." I rubbed my hands over the seat belt.

"So, see, Cal's probably right. Once we find them, all of this will stop." Dad put his hands on the steering wheel and gripped it tightly.

I unbuckled my seat belt and let the hard metal hit the door with a thud. "It will never stop. They want what Kythera has, even if that means we're all dead." I opened the car door and slammed it shut before he could say anything.

I stared up at the house that had become my prison. I felt like one of the many ghosts I was sure roamed the halls. I was trapped, unable to move forward or determine where I could go.

Sirens roared in the background as I started up the stairs. Turning toward the sound, I noticed that there was a police car parked in the front of Mrs. Hamilton's, its blue lights flashing in the darkness. Two more patrol cars came down the street, closely followed by a speeding ambulance; they all parked in front of her house.

Strange, I thought as I hobbled toward the scene, my ankle still pulsing with pain.

The policemen and the paramedics rushed into the house. A group of police officers began to put up yellow tape around Mrs. Hamilton's front yard. I approached one of the officers and tapped him on the shoulder.

"What's going on?"

He turned around and I took a couple of steps back. He was the policeman who had been at Romans' house earlier. "This is a crime scene, miss. Could you please step back?"

I stared at him, unable to say anything. He turned back around without another word.

Dad came up behind me, putting his hands on my shoulders. "Casper, let's get in the house and let the cops do their job."

I didn't move as the paramedics came back out and talked to the cops. A neighbor from down the street walked over to us.

"What's going on?" she asked.

"We don't know, something happened at Mrs. Hamilton's house," said Dad.

Another van arrived, the word "coroner" in big block letters on the side. They rushed in with a gurney.

"Oh, no," gasped the neighbor.

The air felt strangely chilly, and I hugged my arms against my chest. Minutes later, the gurney was wheeled out, a sealed black body bag on top. I covered my mouth with my hand in horror.

No, she can't be dead.

A second gurney was brought out with the same black bag and put into the coroner's van.

"I thought Mrs. Hamilton lived alone?" I said out loud. I knew she wasn't married, and there were never any cars in her driveway besides her own.

"She has a daughter, who was supposed to be visiting this week. She hadn't seen her in years. She doesn't come to Charleston very often, ever since she quit her job at the newspaper," said the woman.

I turned to look at her. "What's her daughter's name?"

"Kelly Winters."

"I'm sorry, what did you say her daughter's name is?"

"Kelly Winters. She was so excited about Kelly's visit. They'd had a falling out over something, nobody really knows." She shook her head and wiped a tear from her eye.

"Come on, sweetheart, let's get inside." I let my dad guide me toward the house, but I couldn't help but continue to glance at Mrs. Hamilton's house.

My ankle still hurting, I hobbled up the front steps, and into the house. I ignored my mother, who was standing in the hallway.

"Casper, why are you walking funny? And what's going on outside?"

I didn't respond. I slowly walked down the hall to the kitchen. I couldn't deal with her right now. I opened the freezer and pulled out a bag of frozen peas. I also grabbed a dish towel. I turned and went up the servants' stairs just as Mother walked into the kitchen.

"Casper?" she called, but I said nothing and she didn't follow me.

Once I was in my room, I went to the bed, wrapped the peas in the dish towel, and put the package carefully on my swollen ankle.

Could this really be happening? Who would want to kill Mrs. Hamilton?

I was struck by a memory of the conversation I'd had with Alex in our house right after coming home from the hospital. He had said, "She needs to stay out of other people's business." Could Kythera have wanted her dead? She had been telling me things they hadn't seemed to want me to know, and her daughter had been writing articles about them that they wanted to hide. *Was I the reason Mrs. Hamilton and her daughter were dead?*

I tossed and turned all night, thinking about the man who had been chasing me, the man who had held a knife to my throat, and the body bags being wheeled out of Mrs. Hamilton's house. I sat straight up in the bed, gasping for air. I looked around the dark room, and it took a few seconds for me to realize where I was.

God, please help me.

I remembered the priest and his words. I threw the covers off the bed and slowly got on my knees next to the bed, the bag of mushy peas falling to the floor. I had never before prayed, but it seemed like the only thing I could do. I didn't even know how to begin, but I sat there for a few moments, praying over and over again for God to help me and tell me what I needed to do.

~ * * * ~

I picked up the can of Coke from my tray and took a long gulp. Everyone at the lunch table was chatting away, but it all sounded like a buzzing in my head. I looked over at Cal, who looked pretty tired, too, as he picked at his salad. He wasn't paying attention to the conversations around him, either.

"Hey, Casper, you have last period with Jacob right?" Charlotte asked. I looked up at her. She was unscrewing the cap on a bottle of water.

"Huh? Oh, yeah, I do. Why?" I looked down at my tray of food that I had barely touched.

"Sara has a big crush on him. You think you could find out if he likes her?"

Sara punched Charlotte in the shoulder. "Don't tell her to do that! That's so juvenile. Casper, don't listen to her. She's a moron."

I just looked at her.

"You've been crushing on him all summer, ever since you met him at that coffee shop you always read at downtown, and you haven't had the guts to ask him out," Charlotte said, pointing at Sara with her fork.

"I'm *not* asking him out. If he likes me, he'll ask me out." Sara looked down at her plate of food and stuck her fork in a piece of broccoli.

"Why don't you have Marcus find out? They've been hanging out after school," chimed in Alex, who was sitting next to me.

"No! We're not asking anyone. Charlotte, if you don't stop, I'll never tell you another secret!" Sara's face was turning bright pink and her lips were pursed. After a second, she got up from the table and took her tray to sit the table with Veronica.

Veronica looked over at our table and turned her gaze on me. I was too tired to care, or even stare back. I looked down at my food and picked up my fork. I searched the plate for something to nibble on, but I wasn't the least bit hungry. I put the fork back down and took another sip of the Coke.

"It's okay, she'll be back. She always gets mad at me, but we always make up later." Charlotte got up from the table and sauntered over to Sara, who turned her away.

The bell rang, and, feeling like I was moving in slow motion, I got up from the table with my tray and backpack.

"Here, let me take it," Cal said, and scooped

the tray out of my hands.

"Thanks." I smiled weakly at him.

"No problem, I'll see you after school. Don't worry about walking to the car in the parking lot. I'll come to the front and pick you up."

I nodded at him.

He smiled and walked to put our trays up. I walked out of the cafeteria and toward the gym. I wasn't limping as much, but it was still pretty obvious that my ankle was hurting. I made it to the gym and the teacher took one look at my ankle and told me to sit on the bleachers.

Marcus came over to me and gave me a look full of pity. "Rough night, huh?"

"You could say that." I put my backpack behind me on the bleaches and leaned back.

"Dad told me what happened. I can't believe it. It sounds like something out of a spy movie or a mob movie."

"Welcome to Kythera, right?"

"Yeah, I guess so." The teacher blew his whistle and told all the students to assemble in the middle of the gym. "I'll see you later, Casper. Hope you feel better."

"Thanks."

Marcus waved at me as he ran to the middle of the court and joined the rest of the students. Within seconds, I had fallen asleep, and did not wake up until the bell rang.

In the last class of the day, I tried to focus on the board, where Mrs. O'Conner was scribbling our homework assignment, but it was almost impossible to keep my eyes open. I looked up anxiously at the clock. The time was ticking by so slowly. I was fighting the urge to slump over my desk from exhaustion.

"Hey, Casper, you look like you had a rough night," whispered Jacob. I jolted at his voice.

"Um, what? Yeah . . . I didn't get much sleep." I leaned my head to the right, glimpsing him out of the corners of my eyes. There was a look of concern across his face.

"Must have been some movie," he said with a laugh.

"Yeah, you could say that."

Finally, the bell rang and I jumped up from my seat. I stuck my notebook in my backpack and sprinted for the door as fast as my ankle would let me. I was in the hallway in two seconds flat, zooming toward my locker.

"You need a ride home or anything?" Jacob asked, leaning against a locker near mine.

"No, I'm fine, thanks. Cal's taking me home." I rummaged through the loose notebook paper and folders in my locker, looking for my political science textbook. I hadn't really been able to focus in class today, but I knew we had some kind of homework. I would just have to ask Alex about it later.

"Okay, cool. See you tomorrow." Jacob strutted down the hall and out of view.

I gathered the rest of my things, slammed the metal door shut, and walked toward the parking lot. I walked down the concrete steps of the school, barely noticing the groups of people hanging out, chatting about homecoming and what they were going to wear, or the group of kids playing soccer on the front lawn. I was absorbed in my own thoughts as I stood on the sidewalk, waiting for Cal to pull up. I looked around, confused, and then pulled my cell phone from my bag.

"Hey, Casper, Cal had to leave. He told me to give you a ride home," said Charlotte, who had pulled in front of me. I snapped my phone shut and got into her BMW. We weaved through the parking lot, and toward the highway.

"You look terrible. What going on with you? Since Mr. Perry made me move to the front of the class, I didn't get to ask you and I had to spend most of my lunch begging Sara not to be mad at me," asked Charlotte, as she studied her reflection in the rearview mirror.

"You don't know?" I looked at her, shocked.

"No, silly. That's why I'm asking."

"Cal and I went to the movies last night . . ." I took a deep breath.

"Sounds like fun. I'm glad you two are together. I hope he never gets back with Veronica. She's my friend, but she's a—"

"Charlotte, we were attacked by two men," I blurted out.

Charlotte slammed on the brakes, but kept going when she realized there were cars behind her.

"What? Why? Who?" Her voice went up an octave, and she nearly knocked her pair of Gucci sunglasses off with her hand.

"We don't know, but it has something to do

with Kythera. How could you not know about this?"

"I hung out with Sara and Jacob last night, and my parents are out of town, so I'm out of the loop." Charlotte turned her blinker on and turned onto my street.

"They don't tell you when there's a meeting?"

"Not all the time. Not unless it involves me. And I don't exactly answer my phone all the time—or my emails. I might have been invited or told to show up, but I have a bad habit of ignoring those things," she said, shrugging her shoulders.

I shut off the vent that was sending frigid air toward me, and crossed my arms over my chest for warmth. "They think it's a student at school that's telling whoever it is where we are going to be and what we are doing."

Charlotte pulled into my driveway and looked at me, the shock written all over her face. "Why would they think that? It's not like we go around talking about Kythera and what's going on with it to everyone."

"All they need to know is that we're members and we make that pretty obvious." I pulled my foot up into the seat and pointed to my tattoo. "And if that wasn't bad enough, every car is marked with the symbol, too."

"It's never been an issue before. Actually, it's been a benefit till now. People who know see it and they do whatever we want. Why does someone want to hurt us?" she asked.

"Because we have money and power. Isn't

that what most wars are about?" I raised an eyebrow at her. She could be so dense sometimes.

She let out a heavy breath. "I guess you're right."

I pushed the car door open. "I'll see you later."

She waved at me and I shut the door. She reversed her car down the driveway and turned onto the street. Her black BMW disappeared in record time.

As I turned to walk up the steps, my cell phone buzzed in my backpack. I pulled it off my shoulder and retrieved my phone. I had one new text message. I opened the message from Cal.

U need to come over NOW was all that it said.

It was a weird message from Cal, so I turned back to the driveway and walked toward the garage. I had the keys to the Audi in my backpack. I got into the car and made the quick drive to his house. I pushed the code to the gate into the keypad and waited impatiently for the gates to open. What was so urgent? I was afraid to ask.

The heavy gates squeaked open and I pulled up in front of the house. There were several cars I recognized, including Alex's Porsche and Xander's Lexus. But one car stood out from the crowd of black. Jacob's electric blue Ford Fusion was in the middle of the pack of luxury cars.

As I crunched across the driveway, another car pulled up and skidded to a stop in the gravel. I turned around to see Marcus jump out and practically run to the front door. I shouted a hello and smiled, but he ignored me. My heart dropped, and a feeling of dread crept into my body. I figured by now I would be used to the feeling—but I wasn't.

Although I really wanted to know what was going on, I was paralyzed in the driveway. I looked up at the soft, gray sky above the Roman's mansion. The sun was obscured from view and several white seagulls dotted the sky. What I would give to be able to fly away.

Chapter
24

I FINALLY WILLED MYSELF TO move up onto the porch and into the house. The foyer was empty, but I could hear muffled voices coming from one of the rooms at the end of the hall. I pushed open the door of the library and looked at the group of guys standing around in a circle, angry expressions on all of their faces. They were all looking at one thing, but I was unable to see over their shoulders. I pushed through Xander and Marcus. My mouth gaped open as I stared at Jacob in the middle of the circle.

"So you can't tell us anything?" barked Cal. Jacob, whose face was blood-red, shook his head. He looked terrified, like a cornered animal.

"I don't know who they are. They just paid me to tell them what was going. They didn't give me their names or anything. I swear." Jacob's eyes were wide, and there were beads of sweat on his forehead.

"Do you realize what those people have been trying to do to us?" Cal asked. He moved forward, his face inches from Jacob's. "They attacked Casper at her home, almost killing her, and then they tried to attack us again at the movies. They broke into Xander's car last night, and they ran Veronica off the road last weekend. Is that what you want to be a part of?"

I'd had no idea anything had happened to any of the others. I didn't like Xander or Veronica, but I still felt some sympathy for them.

Jacob straightened his shoulders and his jaw became tight. "No, but they are no better than you. I'm sorry they tried to hurt Casper, but the rest of you were asking for it with your stupid club."

Xander lunged forward, his shoulder grazing mine, but Marcus held him back. "This idiot isn't going to tell us anything. We should just get rid of him," called Xander.

I froze in horror at the suggestion. Were they really talking about this? This had to be rehearsal for some play at school . . . it couldn't be real.

"I'm not going to do that, Xander. I'm not going to stoop to that level," Cal said, moving away from Jacob.

"But I will," said another booming voice.

Everyone turned to see Tyson Roman standing in the doorway. He moved into the room and everyone moved out of his way. He stood in front of Jacob, his imposing figure looking down at him.

"Son, you might want to tell us who's been paying you if you value your life." Tyson pulled a handgun from the inside pocket of his black suit jacket. I couldn't breathe or move.

"No!" I shouted. For the first time, everyone looked at me. They had been so concentrated on Jacob and Cal, I was sure they hadn't even known I was there. "You can't do this. This is insane!"

"She's right, Dad. What are you doing?" Cal pleaded, all the strength in his face slipping away. He stared at the gun as he edged away.

"If he won't give us their names, we can't let him walk out and continue to give them information." Tyson didn't take his gaze off Jacob, who was on the verge of tears.

"I would tell you if I knew. They just called me on my cell phone and said they would pay me money and pay for my tuition to St. Mary's if I told them things about all of you. They told me where to find Sara at the coffee shop and what questions to ask. My family could use the money, so I went for it. Not everyone is like you with your butlers, maids, and chauffeurs."

At the mention of Sara's name, I felt a sense of sadness. So Jacob didn't really like her at all? He was just using her to get information. Had he really needed to borrow my book, or had it just been a way to get into my house? He'd known I was going to the movies with Cal, and he'd even left when we did. Had he followed us, or had someone else been waiting for us after Jacob gave them a call?

My anger burned, but I still didn't agree with Tyson's answer to the problem.

"Please, don't do this," I begged, looking up at Tyson. He didn't even acknowledge me.

Cal moved across the room and stood in front of me. He put his hand out for me to grab it. "Dad, please don't do this."

"Fine. Everyone can leave, but I need to have a little chat with Jacob."

Without hesitation, everyone started shuffling out of the room. I breathed a sigh of relief as we walked into the foyer. Everyone went out the front door, but Cal and I lingered in the hallway. He pulled me into a bear hug.

"That was intense," he said, as he held me. I could feel his body shaking, his nerves on edge.

"I know. I can't believe that happened. I can't believe any of this has happened." I choked back tears as I lay my head on his shoulder.

"I'm so sorry I brought you into this. It was dumb—but I'm not sorry I met you." He pulled back to look at me, brushing my hair from my face. "I love you and I'm going to get us out of this one way or another. I promise," he said, and I nodded my head in agreement.

I wasn't sorry that I had met Cal, but the rest of my life had been ripped to shreds. I didn't know what I wanted anymore—except for him. I knew we would find a way out. I knew I couldn't count on my parents to help anymore, but I knew I could count on Cal and on me. I was stubborn, and determined to get back what I had lost.

Hand in hand, we walked to the front door. As Cal opened the door, the sharp sound of a gun pierced the air. Instantly, we both turned and ran back down the hall. Cal reached the door before I did, as I tried my best to ignore the pain in my ankle. As I reached the door, my heart pounded and ached, because I knew without a doubt what had happened, without even looking.

Cal forced the door open. I rushed in after him and I ran right into his shoulder, the air leaving my lungs. As I stared at Jacob's limp body on the ground, I couldn't speak. I tried to regain my breath.

"How could you do this!?" Cal screamed. Tyson looked up from the floor and slowly put the gun back in his jacket pocket.

"It had to be done. It sends a strong message to the people he was helping that we aren't going to keep taking this."

I ran past Cal and knelt down by Jacob. Blood was already pooling around his head, leaving a bright red stain on the Romans' expensive rug. I felt sick as the smell of copper filled my nose. I couldn't bring myself to touch his body or to feel for his pulse. I knew he was dead.

Tears rushed into my eyes, blurring my vision. I looked up in an effort to keep the tears from falling across my cheeks. How could he do this? Jacob was my age. This made Tyson Roman no better than the men who'd attacked me on the Fourth of July and at the movies.

The feelings of fear from that night crept into my mind, and I realized it must've been how Jacob felt moments before the trigger was pulled. I couldn't keep the tears at bay any longer and I let them fall to the floor, mixing with Jacob's blood on the rug.

"This is insane," Cal murmured. I wiped the tears on my face, took a deep breath and stood up. I turned to look at Mr. Roman, my gaze steady and my heart thumping in my chest.

"I'm out. I don't want to be a part of this."

Tyson looked at me and laughed, tilting his head to the ceiling. "That's out of the question. Once you're in, that's it."

"No, it isn't. You let Callie go. You can let Casper," Cal chimed in.

Tyson's jaw tightened and he stared at his son. "That was your one favor. You don't get any more," he said, his voice hard and angry.

"I didn't ask to leave. I'm telling you I am," I said, my own voice sounding harsh.

"You think your parents will like this? You think they will go along with it? You're just a kid, you can't make that kind of decision." Tyson readjusted his bright blue tie.

"No, they won't agree at first. But I think they will come around, especially when I tell them what just happened." I took a few steps back, toward Cal.

"You think your father didn't already know

what would happen today? He knew what would happen to Jacob if he didn't give us what we wanted, and he agreed to it."

I stared at Tyson. I knew what he was saying was true, but I had to believe deep down that my parents would understand. That they could forgive me for letting them down and realize that the money wasn't worth selling our souls.

Without speaking, I whirled around and opened the library door and walked out. I picked up the pace to the front door, forcing them open. Cal was not far behind me, but I didn't stop to say anything to him. I needed to get out of there.

"Casper! Cal! Come back here. You can't do this! I promise . . . you'll regret it!" called Tyson, but I just kept moving. I reached my car and got in, pushing the key into the ignition. As I put the car in drive, Cal jumped in front of the car, causing me to jump.

"Wait!" he yelled, and ran over to the passenger side and got in. "I'm going wherever you go."

I smiled at him and nodded. I pushed the accelerator and sped out of the driveway, gravel flying up behind the car.

"Where are we going, by the way?" Cal asked, leaning against the center console

"It's a surprise."

Cal laughed. "I guess I deserve that one."

I really didn't know where we were going. I just knew I needed to get out. I couldn't take it anymore. I wanted, more than anything, to return to Kentucky and the horses, but I knew that was out of the question. They would find us in hours. I thought about Montana, like Cal had suggested before. The open space, the ranches, and the horses all sounded like my idea of an escape.

I needed to be somewhere where I felt free and alive. I needed to see Wendy and feel her strength under me as I flew across some beautiful field. But that wasn't an option right now. They knew I would go there.

I would be back for her and my parents. I just needed time to figure out what to do next. Cal held out his hand for mine. I grasped it tightly with my free hand. The city of Charleston flew by in a blur of colors as I headed for the interstate.

My cell phone buzzed in my pocket. I released Cal's hand and pulled it out with one hand, keeping the other on the steering wheel. We came to a stoplight, and I opened the phone. *One new text message,* read the screen. I opened the message.

You can run, but you can't hide for long.

I didn't recognize the number, but I knew there were only two possibilities. The message had to be from either the people looking to destroy Kythera or from Kythera itself—because we had just become targets of both.

The End

About the Author

KAT H. CLAYTON IS ORIGINALLY from Kentucky and attended Eastern Kentucky University. She now resides in South Georgia with her husband, Michael Tyler, Frank, the cat and Lil, the dog. For more information on Kat H. Clayton please visit:

www.kathclayton.com